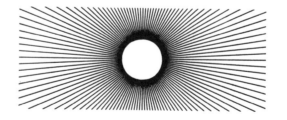

Pottersfield Press

THOMAS H. RADDALL

Footsteps
On Old Floors

True tales of mystery on land and sea

Pottersfield Press

Canadian Cataloguing in Publication Data

Raddall, Thomas H., 1903-
   Footsteps on old floors

ISBN 0-919001-47-5

1. Adventure and adventurers.   I. Title.

G525.R33   1987   910.4'53   C87-094266-2

Copyright © 1988, Thomas H. Raddall
Cover Illustration: *The Herbert Fuller* by Are Gjesdal
ISBN 0-919001-47-5
Published with the Assistance of The Canada Council.

Pottersfield Press
RR 2, Porters Lake
Nova Scotia B0J 2S0 Canada

Footsteps On Old Floors was first published in the United States by
Doubleday and Company in 1968.

CONTENTS

Author's Note

These stories are true, and each of them touches on the Nova Scotia scene in which I live. I came on them in the course of other work, and because each had some mystery to be fathomed I put them aside for times when I had leisure to seek the clues. Hence, this book is the result of literary detective work pursued over many years. Like the small nuggets that appear in a gold miner's pan after much delving and sifting, the tales are pure metal in themselves and I have added nothing.

The encounter of H.M.S. *Blonde* and the *Duc de Choiseul*, with its revelation of the hitherto secret alliance between France and the young United States, I first discovered in the diary of Col. Simeon Perkins, who saw the fight and interviewed the British and French officers. The sequel, the wreck of the *Blonde*, came to me when I visited Seal Island, a grim place with a history of shipwrecks and death. There I saw Brig Rock and the little pond where the British castaways threw their weapons, and looking southward I could see the white spouts of seas breaking on Blonde Rock. There, too, I heard the story as it had been handed down in the families of fishermen from Cape Sable, and in the family reminiscences of Mrs. Winifred Hamilton, the owner and chief inhabitant of Seal Island, whose ancestors established the first lifesaving station there in the early years of the nineteenth century. The rest of the story came from the Public Record Office, London, and from the National Maritime Museum, Greenwich, whose collection includes the journals of

Capt. John Milligen and Capt. Edward Thornborough, as well as a picture of H.M.S. *Blonde*.

The macabre story of the barkentine *Herbert Fuller* I found in Halifax and Boston newspapers of the time, and in the excellent marine collection and library of the Mariner's Museum, Newport News, Virginia.

My interest in the romantic figure of "Grey Owl" began long ago when I found that he had lived with Micmac Indians in Nova Scotia, and enlisted in a Nova Scotian regiment in World War I. I am most grateful to Mr. Lovat Dickson, who permitted me to quote from his own reminiscences; to the Macmillan Company of Canada Ltd., which permitted me to quote from the books of "Grey Owl"; to W. E. Macfarlane, James Mackinnon and Albert Chandler, who served in the army with "Grey Owl" and told me what they knew; to W. B. M. Clarke, District Forester, North Bay, Ontario: to S. F. Kun, Superintendent, Prince Albert National Park; to the Public Archives of Canada.

In the case of the *Mary Celeste* I had help from Mr. Frederick Hill, retired curator of the Mariner's Museum, Newport News; from the present staff of that Museum; from various people at Spencer's Island and along the Parrsborough shore, including Mr. Lester Dewis, grandson of the shipbuilder, and from an anonymous old gentleman who lent me a hand at pulling up sunken tombstones in a search for the grave of Capt. Robert McLellan.

The story of Jim Charles and his gold mine was still a popular mystery in western Nova Scotia when I first visited Kejimkujik as a young man. In the course of years I picked up details among the white and Indian inhabitants; but it was not until the Reverend Clayton Munro came to me with the inside story, a secret for eighty years, that I learned the final truth.

Sadie Davenport came into my view when Judge M. B. Archibald, of the Nova Scotia Supreme Court, related her story as his most interesting case. Archibald died before I had a chance to gather details, but I had valuable help from Mr. Roy A. Laurence, Q.C., who was one of the counsel in the case and who lent me complete copies of the court documents.

As T. B. Macaulay said of Catherine Sedley in his History of England: "So much is history stranger than fiction; and so true is it that nature has caprices which art dares not imitate."

T. H. R.
LIVERPOOL, N.S.

Adventures of H.M.S. *Blonde*

H_{er} name sounds like something out of Gilbert
and Sullivan, but there actually was a ship in His Majesty's
Navy named *Blonde*, and in the course of her affairs she put a
mark on history. Naturally, with a name like that, and a large
and shapely female in daring *décolletage* for her figurehead, she
she was not of British design. She was French, and in the early
days of the year 1760, when she was a smart new frigate, she
was one of a squadron under Admiral Thurot lying in the port
of Dunkirk. Things had been going badly in the war with Britain.
With their command of the sea the British had made successful
expeditions against the French forces in India and the West
Indies. In Canada they had captured Louisburg and Quebec,
and in the coming spring their armies marching up from the
American colonies were bound to take Montreal, and with it
all that remained of French Canada. The French empire was all
but gone. At home the remnants of the French fleet were pinned
in their ports, and not safe even there, for the British fleet and
troops had attacked forts and burnt ships at Aix, St. Malo,
Cherbourg, Le Hàvre and Quiberon Bay.

In February 1760, Admiral Thurot embarked six hundred

soldiers and slipped away into the North Sea for a counterraid. Taking advantage of the thick weather and long winter nights, he worked his way north along the coasts of Denmark and Norway, rounded the tip of Scotland, passed the Hebrides and slipped into the north channel of the Irish Sea. Here he was in a position to play cat-among-the-pigeons with the busy sea trade of Glasgow and Liverpool, and in a place where the British would least expect it. First, however, he decided to land his troops and plunder the small Irish port of Carrickfergus on Belfast Lough. This was done, but unfortunately for the Admiral, his soldiers lingered too long on the job; it was several days before he got them aboard again, and by that time the British were alert. When Thurot sailed down the north channel toward Liverpool he was intercepted by three British frigates, and in a fight off the Isle of Man his ships were defeated and captured and the Admiral himself was killed. Thus the *Blonde* came into British hands.

No one knew better than the British that French warships, especially their frigates and corvettes, were admirably designed and built, and they made a point of taking captured ones into His Majesty's service and retaining the French names. Hence, H.M.S. *Blonde*. The war ended in 1763 with the Peace of Paris, in which France, in effect, abandoned her whole empire in North America, not to mention other matters. And as things turned out within another twenty years, in quite another Treaty of Paris, Britain was to give up all her American colonies except the ones she had taken from the French. This amazing topsyturvydom involved another war, in which H.M.S. *Blonde* was to have her interesting little part.

Soon after the beginning of the American Revolution, the Continental Congress realized that they had to have a lot of help in their war against Great Britain, and there was one obvious nation to approach. France was the old and inveterate enemy of the British, still smarting from the defeats and especially the surrenders of the last war. Here was her chance to turn the tables in a revenge both neat and sweet.

In March 1776, the Congress sent Silas Deane to Paris. His negotiations with the French Government were secret, of course, and he found a cautious interest. The French were happy to see Britannia and her American offspring in a noisy family brawl, but they doubted the Americans' ability to win an outright war and they had no intention of getting involved in one themselves. In November 1776, the Congress sent Benjamin Franklin and Arthur Lee to join Deane in pressing their cause at Paris. The wise and wily Franklin was top man, and he made his headquarters in a small chateau on the bank of the Seine at Passy, which then was some distance outside Paris, a discreet base of operations. He found sympathy for the Americans in high places. On the face of it, of course, the notion of rebellion against a king could hardly appeal to the French monarchy; but the French king was Louis XVI, not yet twenty-two years old, and very much in the hands of his advisers. And so it came about that early in 1777 the French Government gave Franklin a credit of two million livres, with a promise of more to come. To turn this into arms and supplies, and to get the munitions to America, the French Government called on Pierre Caron de Beaumarchais, the head of their secret service.

He was a man of parts. Born plain Pierre Caron, the son of a watchmaker, he became watchmaker to the King. When he married the widow of a court official he assumed the name Beaumarchais, and later he confirmed it by the purchase of a patent of nobility as secretary to His Majesty. He was a gambler and his speculations got him into trouble, but he soon got out of these scrapes and made himself useful in the secret service of the government. As a hobby he amused himself by writing plays. One of his comedies, *The Barber of Seville*, was staged in Paris in 1775. In 1778 he finished another comedy, *The Marriage of Figaro*, but some of the court circle around Louis XVI saw under its wit a deliberate mockery of the aristocracy, and Beaumarchais was unable to stage it until 1784. In after years Mozart and Rossini made these comedies the themes of famous operas.

With his own secret contempt for the aristocracy, who naturally looked upon him as an upstart, Beaumarchais was an immediate enthusiast in the American cause. He set about his new task with energy and skill. His first step was to create a fictitious shipping firm under the title Rodrique Hortalez et Compagnie, with offices in various French ports. He then supplied the firm with ships. Some were ordinary merchantmen, some were naval craft flying false colors or no colors at all. On paper their cargoes were consigned to ports in the West Indies. Actually, they went to ports in the United States, and it was part of the secret agreement that the Americans should repay the French by loading the ships with return cargoes of tobacco and other produce.

So the game began. Before long a British secret agent in France discovered what was going on. He was Paul Wentworth, an American by birth, a cosmopolitan by taste and choice, and for many years a successful speculator in London, Paris, Amsterdam and other centers of trade and finance. He was a native of New Hampshire, a kinsman and lifelong friend of John Wentworth, the royalist governor of that colony, and his London home was the refuge of John Wentworth and his family during the greater part of the American war.

During 1777, Paul Wentworth gave the British Government several warnings of the activities of Hortalez et Compagnie, pointed out that the French Government was behind them, and even predicted a Franco-American alliance in the war against Great Britain. He made these reports to Sir William Eden in London. Eden passed them to the prime minister, Lord North, who passed them on to King George. However, that dull monarch refused to believe that his fellow dullard across the Channel would permit French aid to rebellious British subjects in America. Indeed, he declared that Paul Wentworth was trying to create a panic in the London stock exchange and make a profit for himself.

Meanwhile Hortalez et Compagnie went on carrying military supplies of all kinds to America. In all, Beaumarchais provided forty ships for these voyages. The North Atlantic is a rough ocean and a wide one, and how many of these wooden windjammers completed their voyages we do not know. As tobacco was specified as a chief item for the return cargoes, most of them must have gone to ports in the southern states. The region around New York and Philadelphia had to be avoided because of the British land and sea forces there. Nevertheless, the Americans were able to equip and supply a large army in the North, and in the autumn of 1777 they won a complete victory over Gentleman Johnnie Burgoyne's expedition at Saratoga. This changed the whole face of the war.

During the following winter Franklin and his companions in Paris used Saratoga as their talisman, a clear proof that the Americans could not only hold out, but eventually win, their war against the British. They convinced the French Government, and as the winter cold deepened in the early months of 1778 the French made their plans to enter the war. Whatever further aid they gave to the Americans across the sea, it was clear that they would have to fight a British fleet at home. Therefore they proceeded carefully. On March 13, the French ambassador in London informed the British Government that his country had signed a treaty of friendship and commerce with the United States. Nothing was said about war. Indeed, the French note protested a peaceful attitude to Britain.

Meanwhile, in their winter quarters at Valley Forge the American troops were desperate for fresh equipment and supplies. General Washington was having a hard job merely to hold them together, let alone make any preparations for the spring campaign of '78. Word of their plight had reached the American agents in Paris, who prodded Beaumarchais.

About the middle of March 1778, while London was considering the note from Paris, a vessel slipped out of Nantes for a voyage across the Atlantic. She was a frigate of the French Navy, the *Duc de Choiseul*, of 24 guns, 105 officers and men, under a commander named Heraud. She had a valuable cargo on board. It consisted of army supplies, including brass cannon, together

13

with muskets, ammunition, clothing and other equipment suffi-cient for 5000 men. There were other stores, such as salt, which was hard to obtain, especially in the northern states, and ingots, or "pigs," of tin, necessary for the making of army kettles, can-teens and spoons.

Captain Heraud had been provided with one of the new American flags, the stars and stripes, to hoist for recognition at the proper time. Also, he had some mysterious passengers. Col. Simeon Perkins, the Nova Scotian diarist who interviewed some of them later on, described them as "gentlemen of distinction." One who spoke English gave Perkins their names, which may have been true or false. Thus, one was "Jetteau" or "Jet d'eau," an obvious witticism, and so was "Baudier" or "Baudet." At this time a considerable number of French and other Continental officers were sailing to join the American forces, following the example of Lafayette, Steuben and Kosciusko. Undoubtedly the gentlemen of distinction who had taken passage in the *Duc de Choiseul* were volunteers of this kind.

As the *Duc de Choiseul* made her way across the sea in the boisterous winds of March and April, another frigate of French build, this one in British hands, lay in the port of Halifax, Nova Scotia. She was His Majesty's Ship *Blonde* and her commander was Capt. John Milligen, R.N. During the cold months of January, February, and most of March she was at the naval dockyard for careening and a general refit.

Milligen was a zealous and capable officer, and when he sailed from Halifax on March 27 he set about his ordered task, a careful patrol of the southwestern coast of Nova Scotia, which had been harried by American privateers almost from the outset of the war. He looked into Port Mouton, an almost uninhabited bay a few miles west of Liverpool and a favorite rendezvous for Yankee raiders. He did the same at Port Roseway and other notorious lurking places about Cape Negro and Cape Sable. He spent many days cruising off Cape Sable, the first landfall of Yankee priva-

14

teers heading eastward out of Boston and Salem, and then turned back along the Nova Scotia coast.

On April 24, 1778, H.M.S. *Blonde* was drawing abreast of Port Roseway but well to seaward when her lookout spotted a ship under full canvas coming down from the north. The hour was half past four in the morning. Captain Milligen hoisted the British recognition signal and got no answer, although by 5 A.M. the sun was up and the light was good. He fired a gun for attention and showed his British ensign plainly, but still there was no answer. The stranger was a frigate of French build and rig, but so of course was H.M.S. *Blonde,* and no doubt the stranger was puzzled by these incomprehensible signals. She held on her course, coming down toward *Blonde,* and the suspicious Milligen fired four more shots. Suddenly now the stranger hoisted the French flag and a man-o'-war pendant. At the same time she changed course sharply and dashed away toward the Nova Scotia coast. Milligen followed with every bit of canvas he could get aloft, and the chase went on for more than four hours. By eight o'clock in the morning the stranger was plainly heading straight in toward the port of Liverpool. Here was a puzzle. Two frigates of French build, one flying French colors, the other British, and the French one steering with speed and apparent confidence right into a British harbor! France and Britain were not at war, of course, but why was the Frenchman acting in this peculiar fashion when all he had to do in reply to Milligen's challenge was to show his own colors and keep on his original course?

At 9 A.M. the Frenchman passed Coffin Island and entered the outer reach of Liverpool harbor. Half an hour later, still heading up toward the inner harbor and the town, he struck a reef called Neal's Ledge, near the village of Herring Cove. The harbor slopes were covered with dark-green woods of spruce and fir, with a few huts of fishermen here and there along the shore. The wooden cottages and shipyard of Herring Cove were mostly out of sight along that inlet from the harbor. For that matter, so was the town of Liverpool except for its seaward end, a scatter of wooden cottages on a point of land a mile and a half away. On appearance it might have been any of fifty narrow bays and harbors along this rugged coast, most of them thinly settled and many not inhabited at all.

Up to this point Captain Milligen, although puzzled at the Frenchman's behavior, was mainly concerned "to make her pay respect to our colors." In other words, he was determined that the French ship must dip her flag in salute, as any ship, naval or merchant, was supposed to do when she met one of His Majesty's ships in British waters. Seeing the Frenchman hard aground, Milligen anchored the *Blonde* and again fired a gun. His crew were at their quarters, ready for action, and they had hoisted the port-lids and run out their guns. The *Duc de Choiseul* —for this ship it was, with her interesting cargo and passengers —did the same, and now in answer to the British shot she belched a ragged broadside at the *Blonde*. Milligen returned it promptly and much more accurately, and so the fight began. Captain Heraud must have known his case was hopeless, for the *Blonde* could maneuver and he could not. He was not merely a sitting duck, he was a duck securely fastened to the ledge, and the Englishman with his cool professional skill was bound to take a position where his own broadside could fire with full effect while the Frenchman's could do the least. Nevertheless, Heraud continued to fight, even though most of his crew fled belowdeck. After more than an hour a British shot carried away the Frenchman's ensign staff. At the same time Captain Milligen saw a Frenchman at the halyard of the man-o'-war pennant, as if to haul it down. The *Blonde* ceased fire at once.

But Heraud had no intention of surrender. Most of his crew were below, in a drunken state, for they had got at the generous stock of Nantes wine and brandy there; but he and his officers gathered enough hands to man a few guns and start firing again. Consequently, the *Blonde* resumed her methodical broadsides, and in a short time the Frenchman's cannon were silent. Heraud and his few faithful hands now attempted to lower a boat. It was important that his passengers, those "gentlemen of distinction," should escape capture, even if it meant hiding like animals in the forest. But a shot from the *Blonde* destroyed the boat as soon as it touched water. By this time the French crew were not only drunk and mutinous, but they were looting the cabins of the officers and passengers. At eleven o'clock in the morning Captain Milligen sent an officer and a boat's crew to board the silent wreck of the *Duc de Choiseul*. There was no resistance now. Captain Heraud and his officers and passengers were now concerned chiefly with their own crew.

Captain Milligen, finding the French sailors "very drunk and insolent," decided not to take them aboard the *Blonde*. Instead, he sent his boats to take them up the harbor to the town of Liverpool, where he turned them over to the colonel of militia.

Col. Simeon Perkins was a merchant and shipowner. He was also the chief magistrate, town clerk, and member of the provincial Assembly for the County of Queens. He was also a copious diarist, and his record covering nearly forty-six years in a small Nova Scotia town remains one of the most interesting colonial documents in Canada. His record of the affair of the *Blonde* and *Duc de Choiseul* begins thus: "Fryday, April 24th. This morning a ship came into the Harbour and run ashore the easterly side of the harbour, a little below Thomas Harrington's. Soon appeared another ship and fired upon her. The first soon returned the fire, but not very brisk, for some time. The last ship keeping up a constant fire for about 2 hours. The first ship had French colours and fired under them. They cut away their ensign staff but could not get down their pennant, as it was fowl, which was unfortunate as the firing began again, and several were killed or drowned getting ashore, etc. I cannot learn exactly the number of killed or wounded. She proves to be a French ship from Nantz, loaded with salt, cannon, Arms and ammunition, Dry Goods, etc, a valuable prize. I go on board the King's ship and find her to be the Blonde, Captain Milligan. The Captain treated me and the other gentlemen that went on board with great politeness, and desired assistance. The Prize is full of water, and I fear will not

17

be got off. Captain Milligan has sent the French prisoners on shore, to the number of near one hundred, or full that number. They are distressed for provision and apply to me. I send my people to find lodging for a number of them, 2 or 3 in a house."

For all his imposing titles, Colonel Perkins was no autocratic Pooh-Bah. His various duties had been thrust on him by his fellow townsmen and the provincial government. He was a busy, worried, and rather meek little man from Connecticut, who had moved to Nova Scotia in 1762 and set up a trading business in the raw town of Liverpool, settled only two or three years before. In the spring of 1778 the town was a thin straggle of wooden homes, stores and fish sheds along the west bank of the Mersey River. The main part was fully a mile from the river entrance. At the actual mouth of the river was a much smaller cluster of dwellings on Fish Point, later called Fort Point, but undefended in April '78. This cluster included the house and store of Colonel Perkins, well inside the shelter of the point. On the point itself stood Dexter's Tavern, a modest little public house that catered mainly to sailors and fishermen.

Altogether the town had about 700 people, a mixture of loggers, ship carpenters, seamen and fishermen and their families. The outbreak of the American Revolution had placed them in a bad position. Nearly all of them were settlers from New England. Most were from the region of Cape Cod in Massachusetts, and of these a great many were direct descendants of the Pilgrim Fathers. Naturally, during these troublesome times in America their sympathies were largely with their brethren in New England; indeed, some were ardent partisans of the rebel cause against the King, communicating with Yankee privateers on the Nova Scotia coast and giving food and shelter to escaped American prisoners on the run from Halifax. On the other hand, there were many like Simeon Perkins who deplored the whole quarrel and hoped to keep out of it. At a time when roughly two out of every three white inhabitants of Nova Scotia were of Yankee

18

birth or descent, the English governor at Halifax was deeply suspicious of their loyalty. Queens County then included the whole southwestern end of the province, with Liverpool as the county seat, and the Governor had taken the precaution of removing the two cannon on Fish Point—the settlers' only means of defense against armed ships. At the same time New England privateers, following the example of Capt. John Paul Jones, had begun to raid the small and lonely coastal towns of the Nova Scotia Yankees on the excuse that "them as aint fer us is agin us." Thus, Perkins and other neutral minds were caught in the pinch of British and American hostilities, and they did not know which way to turn.

April was always a hard time in fishing settlements like Liverpool. The months of winter had exhausted their stock of food, except salt fish, and they could get nothing from their small gardens until the summer's end. Formerly they had been able to get through the lean months of spring by trading fish and lumber in New England for cornmeal etc., but the war had put a stop to that. When the captain of H.M.S. *Blonde* sent more than a hundred Frenchmen to be housed and fed in the town, Perkins explained the lack of food, and Milligen sent salt meat and biscuit salvaged from the *Duc de Choiseul*. Still, the prisoners were a problem. Captain Milligen had found them "very drunk and insolent." Even the French officers complained that their own men had robbed them of much clothing and so forth.

Most of them soon sobered down, and on the following Sunday Perkins noted that "some of the French gentlemen and many of the seamen" attended the church service in the meetinghouse. It must have been an odd spectacle—these strangers, undoubtedly Catholics, and most of them unable to understand a word of English, standing through the long grim service of the Congregational Church of that time, and listening to the interminable sermon by the Rev. Israel Cheever.

The supply of food from the wreck was not enough for the

hungry French crew, and much of the salt beef turned out to be bad. Perkins had divided them into messes of ten men, and each mess got fifteen pounds of beef and three pounds of ship biscuit. To this he added several bushels of turnips from his own cellar, a precious gift at the end of a long winter season. The Frenchmen were not grateful. Perkins soon had trouble keeping track of them. Some, if not all, of the French officers, including those mysterious "gentlemen of distinction," were billeted at an inn kept by the widow Ford in the heart of the town. On Sunday, May 3, Lieutenant Griffith of the *Blonde* came up to town with a boat to take the French officers aboard. Several had vanished, leaving their clothes and baggage at the Ford inn, and Griffith ordered Mistress Ford to hold these things until further notice. Soon after he had gone back to his ship, two of the "gentlemen of distinction" turned up at the inn, paid their bill, and demanded their property. Mrs. Ford refused, and there was a frightful row. The French gentlemen swore that they would have their clothes or die fighting for them. The widow, alarmed, gave in. The gentlemen took their things and departed. Where? The diary of Simeon Perkins does not say. Posterity can only speculate.

In 1778 there was no road linking the towns and villages scattered along the southwest coast of Nova Scotia. Only a footpath led from Liverpool to Port Medway on the east and Port Mouton on the west. Both of those places were sparsely inhabited, and their wooded islands gave shelter and hiding place for American privateers. The French gentlemen had no intention of being taken to Halifax as prisoners in H.M.S. *Blonde* if they could help it—and in Liverpool there were American sympathizers quite ready to point out the paths to a rendezvous with a privateer. Apparently, some of the Frenchmen tried it, lost heart in the gloomy forest, and returned to the town. They gave up too easily. A pair of Yankee privateers had a rendezvous at Port Mouton, as we shall see later on.

On May 12, Captain Milligen sent an armed party ashore to round up the prisoners and bring them aboard. Perkins and his militiamen lent a hand, and there was no trouble. Milligen told

Colonel Perkins that he was sailing to Halifax for repairs, and that he would be back again. Meanwhile he gave Perkins full charge of salvaging cargo from the wreck and promised him a substantial payment for all he recovered. And away he went the next day. The distance from Liverpool to Halifax in a straight sea line was only seventy miles, but the *Blonde* had ill winds and she did not moor at the Halifax dockyard until May 15. The dockyard people examined her masts and bowsprit, which had been damaged in the fight. The mast repairs did not take long, but the bowsprit was condemned and replaced, and all in all the *Blonde* was held at Halifax for ten days. Meanwhile some odd things had been happening at Liverpool.

With Perkins in charge, the salvage work on the *Duc de Choiseul* went on well for nearly a week. The weather held calm, and quantities of muskets and clothing were hooked up out of the hold and sent to the town to be dried and cleaned. But when Perkins took his boat down the harbor to the wreck on May 19, he found it swarming with townsmen and fishermen busy with pillage. When he remonstrated, they had news for him. Two American privateers were on the way to claim what was left of the cargo, so why not have a free-for-all while the chance remained? Colonel Perkins took out his written authority from Captain Milligen and read it aloud, like a magistrate reading the Riot Act. He did not need to point out that the *Blonde* was coming back, and that with any kind of fair wind she could reach Liverpool in six hours. The looters grumbled, but they left, taking with them the firearms and other matters they had fished up from the hold.

As things turned out, these fellows knew exactly what they were talking about. It was common in this strange civil war in America for Yankee privateersmen to hide in Port Mouton and send a few Cape Codders over the footpath to call on uncles and cousins and friends in Liverpool, and incidentally to discover what ships were about to sail or were expected, and what their

21

cargoes were. They looked and spoke and dressed exactly like the men of Liverpool, and although they usually came at night and left before daylight, there were some who spent days in the town, fed and housed by congenial sympathizers. Colonel Perkins, distant a mile from the town in his house and store, could only hear rumors and ponder how much truth was in them.

The truth in this case was that the American privateers *Washington* and *Lizard* were lying behind the islands in Port Mouton, barely ten miles to the west. They were well aware of the wreck and what it contained, and they also knew that H.M.S. *Blonde* had gone to Halifax. Indeed, they were about to sail around Western Head into Liverpool harbor, where they would lay claim to all the cargo of the *Duc de Choiseul* as property of the United States.

This leads to another interesting speculation. Was it all prearranged? Was the French frigate intended to rendezvous with the two Americans in the well-hidden shelter of Port Mouton, and to transfer her cargo to them here on the Nova Scotia coast where the British would not have the least suspicion? If not, why did Captain Heraud steer straight for the coast when *Blonde* challenged him? And why did he steer so confidently into Liverpool harbor? French naval captains were highly competent navigators, and the French Admiralty had charts of the whole coast from Newfoundland to Florida. It is fantastic to suppose that Heraud mistook Liverpool for some part of the New England coast, more than 300 miles to the west. But it was easy to mistake the Liverpool entrance for that of Port Mouton, just around the corner. Even in modern times navigators have mistaken one for the other.

However, let us return to the definite, as recorded carefully in Colonel Perkins' diary. Soon after he had chased away the unauthorized "salvagers" from the town, Perkins observed the pair of Yankee privateers entering the main harbor channel between Western Head and Coffin Island. He and his men retired to the town at once, and Perkins called together the militia officers, all of whom were merchants like himself, born in New England. Should they offer resistance to the Americans?

The men of Liverpool had not a single cannon. They had one or two "swivel-guns" about the caliber of a large musket, useful in shooting wild geese but hardly the thing to damage or even impress a lot of tough Yankee privateersmen armed with cannon. Although they now had available the French muskets fished out of the wreck, the official firearms of the Liverpool militia consisted of fifty-seven old army muskets sent down from the garrison stores at Halifax a few weeks before. The decision, therefore, was to offer no resistance to the Americans "if they were civil." The word "civil," in the sense of neighborly politeness, was much employed between roving Yankee privateers and the people of the Nova Scotia coast. One of the Yankee ships was even named *Civil Usage.* The attitude of the privateers was that they wanted to use the Nova Scotian creeks and harbors to get firewood and fresh water, and to seize any ship of British ownership except the fishing and trading vessels of the local inhabitants. Any attempt of the inhabitants to get cannon or troops for their own defense would be reckoned "uncivil," exposing their own ships to capture and their homes to attack.

So the merchants of Liverpool decided to be "civil." Rebel sympathizers in the town passed the word quickly to the privateers, who sailed boldly up the outer harbor and anchored off the wreck. Toward noon on May 19, Capt. William Preston of the *Washington* sent a boat up to the town with a polite request that Colonel Perkins come on board for a talk. Perkins went and was "very handsomely treated" by the Captain. Preston said that the privateers' errand was to take into American possession all the arms, clothing and other material from the wreck, and he promised that no damage would be done to the people and property of Liverpool. More than that, he promised that Perkins and his men should have payment for all the goods they had salvaged. Perkins, a very unmilitary figure in his plain coat and waistcoat, breeches and wool stockings, could only agree on behalf of the townsmen.

In the afternoon, therefore, a strong party of American officers and men came up to the town in boats to collect the salvaged stuff. Seeing their approach, some distrustful townsmen fled up the river, taking with them muskets and clothing they had salvaged. However, Simeon Perkins showed the Americans a considerable quantity of arms and materials, enough to fill their own boats and several others which they "borrowed" from the town wharves. They took the stuff off to their ships, and in the evening Perkins again went aboard the *Washington* for a chat with the Captain. Again, all was politeness, but there was no mention of the salvage money. Indeed, while Perkins sat in the *Washington's* cabin under the whimsical eye of Captain Preston, boats filled with armed men from the *Washington* and *Lizard* were pulling over the river bar in the gathering darkness for a looting raid on the town itself. As Perkins penned it ruefully in his diary, the Americans "ravaged and pillaged a number of houses and stores. Broke open my store and robbed me of a number of things, which I represented to the Captain, but had no redress or scarcely an answer. They got under way and went down the harbour."

However, the Americans had not finished with Perkins and his people. Far from it, they simply went around Western Head to their hidden anchorage behind the islands in Port Mouton and lay there all the next day. This was to give the men of Liverpool a chance to salvage more stuff from the *Duc de Choiseul*, which then could be seized in the same manner. And sure enough, as Perkins and his crew were at work on the wreck on the morning of May 21, they saw the *Washington* and *Lizard* slipping into the outer harbor again. As Perkins wrote afterwards:

"I came directly home with all hands and mustered to arms as soon as possible." This was a matter of some difficulty. The town proper lay a mile upriver from the little straggle of houses at Fish Point, where Perkins had his wharf and store, and the men employed at the sawmills were another three miles upriver at the Falls, the fishermen were scattered in their boats, and the carpenters at the various shipyards.

The *Washington* and *Lizard* came up to Fish Point before any

24

of the militia could gather there. They anchored just outside the river bar and sent a boat full of armed men over the bar and into the river mouth. There they found a Bermuda vessel which had just arrived that morning. The Americans swarmed aboard, cast off her moorings and hoisted her sails. The wind was very light, and to speed matters they placed some of their men in the boat to tow. By that time Colonel Perkins had mustered about twenty men at the little wooden tavern on Fish Point. "I ordered Joseph Freeman with ten men down to the shore, to hale the sloop and order the boat to leave her, which Mr. Freeman did, but they continued to tow her out. One of our swivels was then fired upon them, on which the Privateers discharged a broadside from each schooner, of cannon, swivels and small arms. Our party returned the fire and stood their ground, sheltering behind rocks, etc. The Privateers continued a brisk fire for three quarters of an hour upon the town, and as they went out fired upon the people at Herring Cove. I paraded our men on the Point, and marched down towards Peirce's in order to show the Privateers that we had a good number of men under arms, and dismissed for ¾ of an hour. Mustered again in the afternoon and went to work upon a breastwork on the Point, and made some progress, so that we got some swivels mounted. Sent a party to the Western Head to watch the motions of the Privateers."

For the next two days Perkins and his men labored on their crude little defense work at the Point, and the Colonel sent a fast sloop to take word of these affairs to Halifax. On May 25, he saw the familiar sails of H.M.S. *Blonde* turning the corner of Coffin Island and heading up the harbor. The American lookouts a few miles to the west saw the unmistakable topsails of a man-o'-war, and the privateers lost no time in slipping out of Port Mouton and away to the westward.

Captain Milligen sent a boat for Colonel Perkins and they inspected the wreck together. The Captain and some of his officers returned the visit the same day, calling at Perkins' house and walking through the town with him. There was a good deal of discussion about the visit of the Yankee privateers, and Milligen took a sour view of the way in which Perkins' people had handed over the salvaged goods, especially the muskets. Perkins protested that his people were quite powerless in the face of ships and cannon, but the American origin and sympathy of many Liverpool folk were well known in Halifax, and Milligen suspected collusion.

On the next day Perkins went to the wreck in Captain Milligen's boat and watched while the seamen recovered some "pigs" of tin. Meanwhile Milligen's officers had obtained and paid salvage money for ten chests of French arms that had been hidden from the Americans in their raid on the town. On the whole, Captain Milligen seems to have decided that Perkins had done his best in the circumstances. He was certainly pleased with the Colonel's final stand in actual fight with the Americans, and at Perkins' request he furnished him a jack for elevating cannon, a barrel of gunpowder, a supply of "match" for firing the swivel guns, and fifty flints for muskets. Perhaps he saw this affair in the light of what it really was, the small but significant turning point in the hitherto neutral attitude of most of the "Nova Scotia Yankees." The marauding of the New England privateers, as George Washington himself foresaw, was forcing the Nova Scotians to take a stand against them, and that meant a stand on the side of the King.

Milligen sailed off to hunt for Yankee privateers on their home coast, in the vicinity of Cape Cod, Boston and Salem, and did not return to Liverpool until June 20, 1778. The outer harbor was exposed to southeast gales, and in her position on Neal's Ledge the *Duc de Choiseul* must have gone to pieces by that time. Captain Milligen sent a boat for Perkins, and was displeased to find that no more of the goods, especially the muskets, had been recovered from the wreck. There remained in the town some goods and muskets, hidden by various people at the time of the American raid. Perkins had located them, and on June 23 he dined aboard the *Blonde* and delivered forty-one French muskets. In lieu of salvage money for these, Milligen gave Perkins leave to sell the remaining goods. And that was the end of the matter.

Among the other discoveries on board the *Duc de Choiseul,* such as the new American flag in her signal locker, was a letter being conveyed by the gentleman of distinction who called himself "Mr. Baudier" or "Baudet." It was from Silas Deane in Paris, and was addressed to Gouverneur Morris, the financial expert of the Continental Congress. All of which was convincing proof of what Paul Wentworth had been telling London for the past year. When the tale of the *Duc de Choiseul* reached London, however, no proof was needed. The King and his ministers had put aside their illusions at last and they knew that war with France was inevitable. In July came the first clash of British and French fleets in the Channel.

Simeon Perkins made no further mention of H.M.S. *Blonde* in his diary for almost four years. We know that she was cruising the Bay of Fundy in search of Yankee privateers in July 1778, and that in November she was in Halifax, where Captain Milligen attended a court martial aboard H.M.S. *Savage.* About the end of 1778, Milligen was transferred to the command of H.M.S. *Scarborough,* which had been on the North American station for several years and was now ordered home for a refit. He arrived in England in March 1779, and there he vanishes from our history.

As for the *Duc de Choiseul,* her position on the reef was utterly exposed to a heavy sea from the southeast, and she must have disintegrated in the first hard blow from that quarter, probably some time before Captain Milligen's last call at Liverpool in July 1778. The sea water on this part of the Nova Scotia coast is very cold until August, and naked seamen diving into the black depths of the hold could not have recovered the entire cargo. This applies also to her own twenty-four cannon. In order to tip the French frigate off the reef, the British sailors evidently trundled the guns on one side to the other, the common prac-

tice in careening a ship. She fell over on her side, killing or
drowning three of the British seamen, and remained aground in
somewhat deeper water. Milligen's carpenters then cut holes in
the upper side, and through these his seamen salvaged cargo for
eighteen days. By that time they had got all that could be removed with any ease. The rest lay submerged in dark and icy
water. Milligen engaged three Liverpool schooners to carry the
salvaged stuff to Halifax on May 5, 1778. The stuff included a lot
of wine and spirits, and on the same day Milligen noted in his
log: "Punished Jno. McCarty & Peter Ryley, seamen, & Wm.
Lloyd, marine, with one dozen each, for Drunkenness and Riot."

The Frenchman's own cannon, and some, if not all, of the brass
field guns intended for Washington's army, must have gone to
the bottom of Liverpool harbor, where they remain, covered
now with several feet of muck dredged from the Brooklyn docks.

After General Cornwallis surrendered his army to the French
and Americans at Yorktown in the autumn of 1781, there was
little fighting on land. On the sea, however, a swarm of American
privateers continued to attack British shipping in the North
Atlantic and to harass the Nova Scotia coast, where H.M.S.
Blonde remained in service until the war's end. She cruised much
of the time in the wide mouth of the Bay of Fundy, and in May
1782 she was off Salem, Massachusetts, a notable home of Yankee
privateers. Her commander now was Capt. Edward Thornborough, a capable and energetic officer, like Milligen before him.

On May 6, 1782, the *Blonde* met the American ship *Lyon*,
Captain Tuck, coming out of Salem harbor. She was formerly
the British merchantman *George*, captured by the Salem privateer *Ranger*, and now sent forth in a double role. She had a cargo
of spars consigned to Spain, which had joined France and the
United States in the war against Britain. She also had a letter of
marque, twenty cannon, and a crew of sixty-five, for action
against British shipping along the way. Unfortunately for all these
arrangements Captain Tuck, probably deceived by the French

28

look of the *Blonde*, held on his course until it was too late to turn
back. He made no attempt to fight when he saw the British naval
ensign and the guns at the frigate's open ports. Captain Thornborough took the Yankee crew aboard his ship, put a prize crew
aboard the *Lyon*, and sent her off to Halifax. Soon afterwards
he headed for Nova Scotia himself. It was the time of year when
warm airs over a cold sea breed fog, and in the mouth of the Bay
of Fundy the fog makes a deadly hazard of the ragged chain of
reefs and islands that lie off the western tip of Nova Scotia. The
outermost island, and the most dangerous, was Seal Island, small
and low, surrounded by uncharted reefs, and beset by strong
currents that shifted with the ebb and flow of the tremendous
Fundy tides. It was covered with stunted spruce trees, its only
inhabitants were seals and sea birds, and its shores were littered
with the wreckage of ships.

On May 10, 1782, H.M.S. *Blonde* struck a reef three miles off
the south tip of Seal Island—a reef known to seamen to this day
as Blonde Rock. Thornborough and his crew just had time to
launch their boats, snatch up cutlasses and muskets, and embark
with their Yankee prisoners before the ship sank. The sea was
rough as they headed for the island, and all their boats were
smashed in the surf on its east side, but they scrambled ashore.
By a miracle, only one man perished, but the prospect was a
dismal one. The British crew had clung to their weapons, but
they had little or no provisions, no blankets, and no shelter
except what they could make from the wreckage on the shore.
Captain Thornborough's men, although reduced by crews sent off
with prizes, still numbered over one hundred, and there were
sixty-five American prisoners. All were marooned on this bleak
little island eighteen dangerous miles from Cape Sable, in a spot
that was carefully avoided by all shipping. There was no hope of
rescue or escape from a lingering and wretched death. Yet rescue
came, and in a most unexpected form.

Some days after the wreck of the *Blonde*, two armed schooners
appeared off the east side of Seal Island and anchored in the
mouth of the shallow bay where the castaways had landed. At

the crest of the stony beach was a big flat-topped rock, and behind the beach lay a small pond with a spring trickling into it—
one of the few places on the island where fresh water could be
found. In later times a tremendous sea carried a brig over the
reefs and left it smashed at the beachhead by the rock, and
fishermen from Cape Sable called it Brig Rock and the brackish
pool behind it Brig Rock Pond.

The two visitors were American privateers: the Salem sloop
Lively, Capt. Daniel Adams, and the Boston schooner *Scammell*,
Capt. Noah Stoddard. Noah Stoddard was the greedy and ruth-
less man who afterwards led a privateering expedition to sack
the defenseless town of Lunenburg, N.S. Daniel Adams was another sort of man entirely.

Evidently, Adams and Stoddard were familiar with the passage
past the reefs of Seal Island, and probably they were in the habit
of calling at this remote spot for firewood and fresh water, and
to prowl the shore for any valuable flotsam or jetsam cast up from
wrecks. Now, to their mutual astonishment, the landing party
from the *Lively* found the farther shore of the pond swarming
with armed British sailors and American prisoners. Then came a
quaint conversation, shouted across the width of pond. Everybody had a problem. The Yankee privateersmen wanted fuel and
water. The British officers and men wanted to set foot on the
Nova Scotia mainland, preferably near a fishing village where
they could get some sort of passage to Halifax. The men of the
Lyon wanted to get home to Salem.

Captain Adams conducted the Yankee side of the parley,
standing with some of his men on Brig Rock, where they could
make a quick retreat to their boat. Captain Thornborough and his
seamen and prisoners clustered on the edge of the woods by the
pond, where they had thrown together some rude shelters of
wreck timber. Captain Stoddard remained aboard the *Scammell*,
aloof and suspicious, and he had no part in the deal that followed.

Adams made the terms. First, the American prisoners were to
be set free to join their countrymen aboard the *Lively* and

Scammell. Next, the British officers and men were to walk in single file around the pond toward the beach, each man tossing his weapon or weapons into the water under the watchful American eyes. Adams would then embark them in the *Lively* and set them ashore near the village of Yarmouth, thirty miles away. Captain Thornborough agreed to all this, and so the thing was done.

Unfortunately for Daniel Adams, this simple deal, which saved so many men from a miserable death, got him into trouble at home. Salem folk were rabid haters of the British and of "Tory" Americans, and Captain Adams' humanity to a British crew gave him a "Tory" smell which nothing could remove. His Salem owners fired him from his command and passed the word about to make sure he got no other. At last, like many other Americans, whether guilty or merely suspected of "Tory" sentiments, he had to leave his home and flee to Nova Scotia.

When Captain Thornborough reached the little town of Yarmouth he chartered a shallop to take him and his crew to Halifax. These shallops were sloop-rigged fishing craft, open except for a small cuddy at the stern. The distance to Halifax was more than 175 miles. With more than a hundred men crammed into it, the shallop was both unsafe and uncomfortable; but it was the only thing available at the time, and by now the men of the *Blonde* were used to the combination of danger and "hard lying."

They set out in the shallop, and after rounding Cape Sable they had a lucky meeting with H.M.S. *Observer.* She was a small brigantine, armed and manned by the Royal Navy for patrolling the Nova Scotia coast, and commanded by Lieutenant Crymes. Captain Thornborough and about sixty of his officers and men transferred to the *Observer,* which then headed for Halifax, leaving the shallop to make its way along the coast with the rest.

Thornborough and his men were not yet at the end of their adventures. One more was in store; indeed, it lay waiting for them a few miles off Halifax, where a bold Yankee privateer was cruising for prey under the very nose of the Halifax admiral. He

31

was Capt. David Ropes of Salem, and his ship was the well-named *Saucy Jack*, of fourteen guns and sixty men. When Ropes saw the British brigantine, he ran down and attacked her with confidence. Perhaps he knew the *Observer* and the number of her guns and crew—that is, her ordinary crew, which was less than his own. Ropes had been marauding along the Nova Scotia coast in various Salem privateers for the past three years; he had been captured twice and had spent some time in Halifax as a prisoner.

What Ropes did not suspect was the presence of sixty-odd passengers in the *Observer*, all veteran seamen and marines, skilled in the slam-bang warfare of their time. Captain Ropes fell wounded by the first British broadside, but Lieutenant William Gray and his equally tough and experienced Salemites worked furiously at their guns and carried on the fight for more than an hour. Then the *Observer* managed to get alongside, a rush of British boarders carried the *Saucy Jack's* deck, and that was that. Captain Ropes died of his wound just as his ship arrived in Halifax harbor as a prize.

So Thornborough and his men of the *Blonde* had a final satisfaction to top off their long and adventurous career on this rugged coast in time of war. Peace came soon after. Thornborough remained in the Royal Navy, and we find a final mention of him during the Napoleonic Wars, when he had attained the rank of Vice Admiral. His name appears in a pathetic document still preserved in the Public Record Office, London. This is what it says:

To the Honorable the Lords Commissioners of the Admiralty,
The Petition of Sarah Adams humbly sheweth,
That in the month of May 1782 His Majesty's
Frigate Le Blonde commanded by the then Captain, now Vice
Admiral Edward Thornbrough, [sic] was cast away on the Seal
Islands, on the coast of Nova Scotia, a desolate spot at a considerable distance from the main land, where the company of the

32

said *Frigate must inevitably have perished had they not received speedy relief.*

That Daniel Adams, the Husband of your petitioner, at that time commanded an armed sloop called the Lively, in the service of the United States of America, then at war with Great Britain, but seeing the distress of the said company, the said Daniel Adams did take on board and land them in safety at a place called Cape Resue on the main land of Nova Scotia, and did also furnish them with provisions.

That when the said Daniel Adams returned to Boston, to which place he belonged, his employers, in resentment of his conduct, removed him from their service.

That unable to procure employment in his own country, by reason of his services so performed, the said Daniel Adams removed with your petitioner and the rest of his family to Halifax in the Province of Nova Scotia, where he was appointed a King's Pilot with the pay of five shillings a day and the customary allowances. He died on the 12th November 1801, leaving his family unprovided.

That deprived of every other support than her own industry, with a family of five young children, your petitioner has struggled very hard for a living ever since her husband's death, but now advanced in years she is no longer able to procure a living. Your petitioner begs leave to refer your Lordships to the said Vice Admiral Thornbrough [sic] for the truth of these particulars which regard his relief, and to such characters in Halifax whom your Lordships may select, in support of the subsequent circumstances and of her irreproachable character, and your Lordships having done therein agreeably to your pleasures, your petitioner most humbly prays,

That your Lordships will take the premises into consideration and grant her such relief as your Lordships may deem her case to merit.

Sarah Adams

Halifax, Nova Scotia, November 29, 1808.

In the left margin of this document one may decipher a penciled "ask relief"; a large but illegible scrawl written over the original ink at the head of it, and finally a stamped date "6 Aug 1811." One can only hope that poor Sarah got the relief she asked for in 1808, twenty-six years after Daniel Adams rescued the crew of the *Blonde* from the barren shore of Seal Island.

The Murders
Aboard the *Herbert Fuller*

The affair began, appropriately, in the Mystic River. It was the summer of 1896, a famous presidential election year in the United States, with William Jennings Bryan, the Democratic candidate, arguing up and down the country for silver instead of gold currency—"You shall not crucify mankind upon a cross of gold"—while the Republicans held to the gold standard and chanted for "Bill McKinley and the McKinley Bill." The American newspapers were full of the campaign, and so was the chatter in American drawing rooms, kitchens, barrooms, barber shops and grocery stores. Yet in their practical way the American people went on with their work, whatever it happened to be, and early in July 1896 a sailing ship named *Herbert Fuller* was completing loading a cargo of timber in the port of Boston, Massachusetts.

She lay at Mystic Wharf, where the tidal part of the Mystic River bends south to join the Charles River at the head of Boston harbor. She was a fairly new ship, built in 1890 at the little port of Harrington, Maine, fifty miles from the Canadian border. She measured 158 feet long, 36 feet in the beam, and had a gross measure of 780 tons. Aloft she was rigged as a barkentine; which is to say she had three masts, and her sails were "square-rigged" on the foremast and "fore-and-aft rigged" on the main and mizzen masts. She had a black hull, but her trim was painted white, and so were the cabin houses which rose above the deck fore and aft.

Her seamen's quarters were in the fore house, which stood between the foremast and the bow. It contained also the galley, where all the cooking was done, and the cook's bed-place.

The officers' quarters were at the other end of the ship in the after house, which was partly above and partly below deck level. This cabin, or house, stood between the mizzenmast and the stern. Above deck level a number of small square windows gave daylight to its various compartments. It had two entrances, each with a short flight of steps from the deck down to the cabin floor, and in ship language these doors and steps were "companionways" or "companions." The forward companion, or front entrance, of this cabin opened on deck beside the mizzenmast. The after companion, or back entrance, opened on the stern beside the steering wheel. Thus, at sea the helmsman stood close by the back door to the cabin, with his head and shoulders above the cabin's flat roof, giving him a clear view on all sides except directly ahead of the ship. The view ahead was blocked by the square bulk of the fore house and the ship's boat lashed on its top. For that reason one man of each watch was posted on the fore house to act as lookout there. In that position also he could glance back over the deck and see the officer of the watch at his station beside the mizzenmast, and he could see the head and shoulders of the man at the wheel.

Capt. Charles J. Nash of the *Herbert Fuller* was from Harrington, Maine, where the ship was built, and he owned one third of her. His age was forty-two and he stood five feet ten, with a strong figure and a fair complexion. He was a capable commander who left his officers and men no doubt about his authority, but he tempered his discipline with a sense of humor, and a Nova Scotia captain who knew him well said he was "as jolly a skipper as ever paced a deck." His wife Laura, thirty-seven, had been sailing with Charlie Nash ever since she was a bride in her twenties, but they had no children. She was a shapely and pleasant brunette, quite at home on the ocean or in any port in the world, a typical North American seawife of the time.

As the loading drew near its finish, Captain Nash hunted up a new crew for his voyage to South America, and, as usual, he had to take what he could get along the Boston waterfront. Steamships were shoving old-fashioned windships out of the charter market, and the only way a windjammer could compete was to keep her crew small, work them hard, and pay them little. Consequently, few native Americans would sail before the mast in a windjammer, and a captain had to pick up all sorts of men without asking much in the way of credentials. Those to be had in this casual way were often the outcasts of the ports, the drunks, the escaping criminals, the absconding debtors, the fleeing seducers, the dullards and loonies. The best to be found were stolid and frugal European seamen who found the American dollar more useful than any money to be got at home.

With such human odds and ends, underpaid and overworked, hardly a week passed without some case of individual violence or general disturbance aboard North American windjammers on the high seas. It is revealing nowadays to find such reports continually in the shipping columns of old Canadian and American newspapers, and to realize that owners and masters ran these risks deliberately, as they risked winds and weather, because they had to, because there was no other way to stay in business.

For his chief mate Captain Nash accepted an alert, swarthy man who professed a long experience in windjammers, seemed to know a mate's job very well, and said he came from Nova Scotia. This was enough for Nash. The Nova Scotians—"Bluenoses" in sea slang—were good seamen; and Bluenose mates especially were famous for their ability to handle hard-case crews.

In truth, however, the new first mate of the *Herbert Fuller* was not a Nova Scotian at all. He was a native of St. Kitts in the West Indies, with a mixture of white and Negro blood. He was a seaman of experience right enough, but not all of his experience would have served him as good reference. Like Nash, he was about five feet ten but more heavily built, a quick, powerful man with a dark face, a large mustache, and bold, black eyes that could outstare anyone.

His name was Tom Bram. In the grand manner of West Indian mulattoes, he chose to sign himself with a longer one, Thomas Mead Chandler Bram, or, alternatively, Thomas Mead Chambers Bram. He had gone to sea as a youth and was now thirty-three. Somewhere along the way, with his sharp intelligence, he had learned the arithmetic necessary for a navigator, and although his spelling and syntax were not those of a grammar school, he wrote a remarkably fine copybook hand. In speech he was fluent and at times grandiloquent, for he had religious moods that came strongly and frequently. In New York, where he had a wife, he attended open-air meetings of the Salvation Army, and he liked to step forth and give aloud his religious testimony.

Bram was a born actor. In the world of the theater he might have played a very convincing Othello, for he was highly conscious of his abilities and sensitive and jealous where his dark skin was concerned. In fact, Tom Bram was a man of various parts. Aside from his experience at sea, he had spent some years ashore, working as a cook in restaurants in New York, Chicago and Boston. He claimed to be a Freemason. He was dapper in dress ashore, and a photograph taken in the 1890s shows him in a tall derby hat, a well-cut jacket, a high starched gates-ajar collar, and a neatly tied cravat.

He was a drinker of the fitful kind. Ordinarily he took a glass or two during the day, or in a night watch at sea; but there were frequent spells when he gulped neat liquor too much at a time, in not enough time, so that eventually his stomach revolted and made him sick. The retchings were followed by maudlin postludes in which he wept and babbled nonsense. His religious spells acted on him in somewhat the same way. He was apt to weep, to have what he called "a good cry," with tears dripping down his face, in the course of his preaching and prayers. Captain

Nash knew nothing of this, nor of other phases of Tom Bram's history, when the first mate signed the ship's articles with his precise and beautiful handwriting.

For his second mate the Captain signed a big blunt Finn named August Blamberg, who sometimes was called "Blom" for short. He was strongly built like the Captain and first mate. On the face of it, if any trouble arose with the sailors on the voyage, the afterguard were well able to take care of it.

The after house held a fifth person, not so robust as the officers or even Laura Nash—a passenger named Lester Hawthorne Monks. He was twenty, of a well-known Boston family, a student of science at Harvard University. He suffered from a bronchial ailment, and his doctor had recommended a long summer voyage to the tropics. He had in his baggage a revolving pistol and a box of cartridges, and after the ship put to sea he slept with the revolver, quite empty, under his pillow, as a child sleeps with a new toy. Presumably, he had heard tales of mutiny and derring-do at sea, and in this highly romantic but impractical way prepared himself for adventure. Much more practical was his habit of locking his door at night, like any landsman in a strange boardinghouse. No one else in the after house of the barkentine locked theirs, not even Mrs. Nash.

The ship's cook acted as steward to the officers, and he preferred to call himself by that more dignified title. It meant that in addition to cooking meals for all hands, he waited on the officers' table aft, and every morning tidied their cabins and made up their berths. He was a Negro named Jonathan Spencer, an excitable but intelligent man. Later on he was to show himself a man of courage, too, with more strength of character than all the rest of the forward crew put together.

There were five seamen forward: Francis ("Frank") Loheac, a Frenchman; Henry Flinn, of New Jersey; Oscar Anderson and Folke Wiessner, Swedes; and last, but very important in the course of events, a man who signed the articles as "Charles Brown" and gave his home country as Holland. In reality, he, too, was a Swede, and his name was Justus Leopold Westerberg.

For twenty-five years he had been sailing all over the world. He was a man of middle height with a small mustache and a caricature of a beard, an absurd round tuft on the point of his chin.

"Charles Brown" always carried out his duties in a seamanlike manner, but he talked to himself a good deal when alone, and seemed a bit muddled in the brain. About five years before, in a seamen's boardinghouse in Rotterdam, he had fired a pistol at someone under the delusion that he was a robber after his money. He remembered nothing of it until several days later, when he came to his senses in a mental hospital. Apparently no one was hurt, for although the Rotterdam police made a routine report of the affair, they laid no charge. In a busy port like Rotterdam the brawls of drunken seamen were a commonplace. After two weeks' treatment and observation in the hospital, Westerberg went free. After that he changed his name to "Charles Brown" and called himself a Dutchman. Most of the time he was diffident and withdrawn, but there were times when he told tales of his adventures, including the one in Rotterdam. However, most of his yarns were so fanciful and so mixed up that nobody believed a word he said. He was that not uncommon figure in human life, the man of much real adventure who cannot tell of it without adding patches of wild fantasy, and who, whatever his real name, winds up as a Munchausen.

As Tom Bram watched the Boston stevedores swing aboard the last planks of the deck cargo, he could turn his head and look over the rooftops to the tall monument on Bunker Hill, a mile away. Not so visible, but only a short walk from the monument, stood the Massachusetts State Prison.

In the hot evenings after the stevedores had quit work, Bram liked to saunter as far as Tom Walsh's barroom at the foot of Hanover Street. After a drink or two there, he would walk back to the corner of Monument Street and Bunker Hill Street and sit on the steps of Morris Shindler's little shoemaking shop, where he could watch the people passing and chat with any who cared to stop. In this way he came to know Shindler and also Officer Sheehan, the policeman on the beat, who stopped now and then to sit on the steps of the shop and rest his feet.

The next time Sheehan saw Tom Bram, the mate of the *Herbert Fuller* was locked up in the police station on Hanover Street, along with the steward and five sailors of the ship. Since leaving Mystic Wharf they had traveled nearly two thousand miles, and they had come back with a mystic problem for the police. One of them was a foul and bloody murderer. But which?

The loading of the barkentine was finished in the first days of July 1896. To secure the deck cargo from shifting in a sea, the crew fastened long cleated "lashing planks" over it from side to side. Tom Bram watched over this with care; it was one of the first mate's responsibilities, and with that done he could prepare himself for the voyage with a supply of comforts and necessities. The chief necessity was a supply of whiskey amounting to two gallons, which he kept in his cabin in a stoneware jar. It was not an excessive amount for a voyage that would take two months or so from Boston to Buenos Aires and then up the River Plate to Rosario—enough for, say, two stiff drinks a day. A supply like this was a common practice on long voyages for an officer who liked a nip now and then, and Bram did not attempt to hide the jar. The Steward, Jonathan Spencer, could see it every time he tidied the first mate's room in the course of his daily round.

Like the romantic passenger, Tom Bram had a revolver in his baggage, but it was an old thing he had picked up in Mexico. Most of the lead bullets he had got with it were battered and nicked, and did not fit the chambers properly. Also, the hammer spring was so weak that even with a good cartridge in the chamber it was apt to fail when he pulled the trigger. It might scare a mutinous seaman facing its muzzle, but in a real showdown it would be worthless.

The old gun of Bram's, and the efficient one that Lester Monks tucked empty under his pillow at night, were the only firearms on board. Charlie Nash had never met a crew that he and his mates could not keep in order, and for the present voyage he had mates Bram and Blamberg, a pair of burly partners in the discipline of the ship.

On July 3, 1896, a tug drew the *Herbert Fuller* away from the Mystic Wharf, and her crew missed the Fourth of July parade and speeches at Bunker Hill. As it turned out, they might have stayed and seen it all, for after passing through the inner harbor Captain Nash decided to anchor and await a fair wind. That did not come until July 8, when at last he was able to sail out past Nantasket Beach with its summer bathers and stretch his canvas into the Atlantic. His destination was the port of Rosario, 250 miles up the River Plate from Buenos Aires. In order to work his way around the distant shoulder of Brazil he first had to lay a course far out into the ocean toward the west coast of Africa, where the trade winds would be a help and not a hindrance.

In the hot summer nights Captain Nash chose to sleep on a light canvas cot in the chartroom aft, close to the stern companionway and the steering wheel. So Laura Nash slept alone in the wide berth of the Captain's cabin, which was at the fore end of the house on the starboard side, and separated by thin wooden partitions from the rooms of Lester Monks and second mate Blamberg. Tom Bram's room was on the port side of the house, beside the fore companionway. His door and the second mate's door opened opposite each other on the narrow alleyway there. Bram's was the only sleeping berth actually on the port side of the house. The rest of that side was occupied by the steward's pantry, a storeroom, and the lavatory. Thus, Tom Bram slept in a sort of isolation from all the others in the after house. The cabin of the first mate happened to be there. But what Bram thought of that, with his touchy attitude about his Negro blood, nobody ever knew.

At meals they sat together at the table in the main cabin, and through the open doors of the starboard rooms Tom Bram could see the beds and where the pillows were. Indeed, he had every opportunity to make himself familiar with every detail of the after house, including one item that hung on the partition between storeroom and lavatory. This was an ax, kept there for an important purpose. If the ship happened to be "hove down" by a violent squall or a hurricane—that is, thrown on her side with her masts and yards in the water—there was only one way to get the hull upright and save the ship and crew. It was to cut away quickly the rigging on the windward side, so that the masts would break off and so free the hull.

For that reason the ax was kept razor-sharp.

In the light westerly winds of summer the *Herbert Fuller* sailed along comfortably day after day, and by the evening of July 13 she was about 700 miles away from Boston, a speck in the North Atlantic, with a vast distance still to go to the River Plate. The weather was getting hotter as the latitude shrank, and for the sake of a draft of air through the after house the companion doors were hooked open day and night.

Second mate Blamberg had the watch from 8 P.M. to midnight of July 13. At the end of it he ordered the lookout to sound eight bells, and went below to wake Tom Bram, who had the watch from midnight until 4 A.M. Then he turned in to his little room, just across the alley from Bram's, and went to sleep in his bunk.

Less than three feet away, on the other side of the partition, lay Mrs. Nash.

Tom Bram's watch consisted of himself, a helmsman, and a lookout forward. The helmsman was Justus Westerberg, alias "Charles Brown." The lookout on the fore house was the Frenchman, Loheac. The mate took his usual post at the mizzenmast, beside the open door to the fore companionway. The wind was "on the quarter" (blowing to one side from behind) and the barkentine was going along at about eight knots, a fair rate of speed for a small ship of her class. On deck there were the usual sounds of a ship under sail in a good wind, the creak of spars and canvas under strain, an occasional rattle of rigging blocks, the swish of water as the ship parted the waves and shouldered them aside. Below in the cabin there were the usual creaks and groans of the ship's timbers as the stresses on them shifted with every lift and fall and roll of the hull; and more faintly, but plain to the captain's ear whenever he wakened in the night, the slither of rope-and-tackle steering gear as the helmsman moved the wheel.

The night was dark, but from his post on the fore house Frank Loheac could see the figure of the mate by the mizzenmast. The fore companionway stood open as usual, making a small rectangle of light reflected from the lamp in the main cabin. Loheac could also see the man at the wheel, because the helmsman's face caught the glimmer of the binnacle lamp as he peered at the compass before him.

Mate Bram always took a couple of drinks in the course of a night watch, and during the first half of this one Loheac saw him going into the cabin more than once. At some time close to 2 A.M., when it would be Loheac's duty to sound two bells, Tom Bram came on deck from a rather prolonged stay below. This time he seemed in a great hurry, running up the steps and out upon the deck cargo as if the Devil were after him.

The passenger Monks had undressed, turned out his lamp, and gone to bed about 8 P.M. As usual, he locked his door and put the empty pistol under his pillow. His bronchitis had eased in the humid sea weather and he could breathe and sleep well. After several hours he came out of a deep slumber with an impression of hearing a scream from Mrs. Nash's room. He was not fully awake and it might have been something dreamed, but he had a feeling of something very wrong—and close by. Without moving from his berth he reached down for the box of cartridges and loaded the revolver. He put his ear to the partition between his own and Mrs. Nash's room, but he could hear nothing. However, there was a strange sound from the other side of his cabin, in the chartroom where the Captain slept. At first Monks thought the Captain was chuckling in his sleep, but then it seemed more like someone gurgling and gasping for breath.

Naked except for an undershirt, the student crept to his door, unlocked it, and drew it open. As usual at night, the only lamp remaining alight in the after house was the one that hung over the main-cabin table. It threw a faint light into the chartroom, enough for Monks to see that the canvas cot was overturned and the Captain lying on the floor. He called out, "Captain Nash!" but there was no reply except the horrible gurgling. He went to the man on the floor and put out a hand to shake him. One touch was enough. The Captain was lying in a thick outpour of blood, some of which came away on the student's hand. This was no dream. Monks crept away through the main cabin, past the table and the lamp hanging over it, and found Mrs. Nash's door open. He called her name but got no answer. Still holding the pistol ready, he entered the room. The lamplight did not reach much more than the doorway, and the sleeping berth was in deep shadow. He put out his free hand to the berth, touched the pillow, and again drew his fingers away sticky with blood.

Monks now made for the deck in haste to call the officer of the watch. He did not know the time, and as he ran toward the fore companionway he did not know which officer he would find on deck. In going along the alley to the companion steps he passed the open doors of Bram and the second mate, but their rooms were dark and he did not pause.

As he emerged on deck he saw Tom Bram standing on the planks of the deck cargo, a few steps away toward the port side. The mate was facing him and lifting high a piece of timber as if to strike a blow at him. Monks pointed his pistol at this menacing figure and called out, "It's me, Mister Monks! Come below, for God's sake!" Seeing the pistol, Bram dropped the piece of board. Monks was stammering about what he had heard and found below, and after some hesitation the first mate followed him down the companionway, past the dark doorways of his own room and the second mate's, and on into the main cabin. In the light of the

45

lamp Monks noticed now that the cabin clock showed nearly two o'clock. Tom Bram took down the lamp and followed Monks into the chartroom. They peered at the body on the floor. It was a hideous sight. The Captain's head was hacked out of all recognition, apparently by an ax. And there were no more gurgling sounds. He was dead.

Suddenly Bram went into a hysterical state, and Monks was so frightened and bewildered himself that this sudden change in the strong first mate seemed quite natural. The mate was babbling something about mutiny aboard, and that Second Mate Blamberg had gone forward to join the seamen. Monks now went into his own room to put on trousers and a shirt, and Tom Bram considerately left the cabin lamp there, saying that he was going to his cabin to get his revolver.

When Monks had dressed himself he left the lamp in his own room and once more ran up on deck to join the first mate. This time Tom Bram was staggering about, retching and weeping. He had lost all of his usual bold attitude. He dropped to his knees, clutching Monks about the legs, begging for his protection, and crying that he had been hard on the crew and they would kill him for it. Among other things he babbled that he was a Freemason and Captain Nash was a Freemason, and that he, Tom Bram, had a poor old mother.

Monks begged him to stop crying and get hold of himself. After a time Bram did so, but he still insisted that he had seen Blamberg go forward to rouse or join the seamen in mutiny. The obvious inference was that Blamberg had murdered the Captain as the first step in the mutiny. Monks believed him. After all, as officer of the watch Tom Bram must have seen anyone coming out of the cabin. Meanwhile the helmsman and lookout remained at their posts as if nothing had happened, and the ship ran on briskly with the strong warm wind on her quarter. Monks and Bram crouched together on the deck cargo near the mizzenmast, Bram covering the helmsman with his antique revolver, and Monks watching forward with his own pistol cocked.

Nearly three hours passed before daylight. Once Bram walked

46

aft to the wheel, where "Charles Brown" was steering in the normal fashion, and asked him a routine question about the course. The custom of the officer of the watch was to look at the compass himself, to make sure. Instead, Tom Bram moved aside and stooped to peer in a small window, the only window in the stern bulkhead of the cabin house. He arose and looked back to the wheel as if to make a rough measure of the distance. Then he walked away and resumed his vigil on the deck beside Monks. Their attitude was that of men alone and surrounded by mortal enemies, who might rush upon them at any moment. Back to back they waited for daylight, and at last it came.

Monks knew that Spencer the cook-steward had a high regard for Captain and Mrs. Nash. If August Blamberg had killed the Captain and then gone forward to arouse the men to mutiny, as Tom Bram suggested, Spencer was most unlikely to join them. So in the first light of morning Monks went forward with Bram and knocked on the galley door. When Spencer opened it they told him there was mutiny aboard and that the Captain had been murdered. Without hesitation the steward, unarmed, ran aft to the cabin to see for himself, leaving Bram and Monks on deck. Soon he emerged from the companionway shouting that not only Captain Nash but Second Mate Blamberg was dead, and that both apparently had been killed with an ax.

In the increasing daylight Spencer and Monks now saw a trail of blood drops leading from the forward doorway of the cabin and crossing the clean boards of the deck cargo toward the port side. Spencer followed it and found the ax, still bloody, tucked under one of the lashing planks. Bram was at his heels. Spencer drew the ax forth, exclaiming that here was the murderer's weapon, and at once Tom Bram plucked it out of his hands and threw it into the sea, crying that the mutineers might get hold of it and use it to kill the rest of them.

Unlike the bewildered Harvard student, Jonathan Spencer had a strong mind in this nightmare. It was clear to him that the murderer could not have gone into the cabin and out again without being seen either by the helmsman at the after door or by the First Mate at the forward door. At his demand they went to the wheel and confronted "Charles Brown." The helmsman, faced by three excited men, including Bram with a pistol pointed directly at him, stammered that he had neither seen nor heard anything unusual.

The steward then went forward, followed by Monks and Bram. The Frenchman, Loheac, was still at his post on the fore house. Like "Brown," confronted by these angry men and pistols, he declared that he had heard nothing and seen nothing about the deck. Now they plunged into the seamen's quarters and found the other three sailors asleep in their bunks. When they were roused they all seemed astonished at the news of murder aft. Jonathan Spencer now insisted on a thorough search of the after house, and he went there, followed by Monks and the seamen. Tom Bram stayed on deck, watching the helmsman.

In the full daylight through the cabin windows the searchers found three tableaux, each well worthy of Madame Tussaud's celebrated chamber of horrors. August Blamberg had been slaughtered as he lay asleep in his berth. One stroke of the ax had almost cut off his head, and the severed neck arteries had squirted blood high on the partition as well as the bedding. It was probably the first blow, neatly calculated, for he had made no outcry; otherwise, Laura Nash, lying on the other side of the partition, would have heard him and given the alarm. To make sure, or merely in the lust of killing, the murderer had chopped the second mate's face and skull several times.

His next victim lay in the chartroom, but here the first blow was not immediately fatal, for in some violent effort to arise, Captain Nash had upset the cot, and there was little or no blood on it. There was a great pool of it on the floor. The murderer had chopped Nash's head as he lay there. The Captain had put up both hands to defend his face, and the keen edge of the ax had cut through both wrists and almost severed them. The gurgling sounds Monks had heard must have been the Captain's dying gasps in a windpipe filled with blood.

Next to the chartroom was Monks's room, where the locked

door had saved him from the fate of the others. The murderer had passed on through the main cabin to get at Laura Nash. Up to this point there could have been no real outcry. The vicious chops of the ax and the gasps of two dying men had been overborne by the regular cracks and groans and thumps of a ship in motion. When the killer entered the cabin of Mrs. Nash the room was dark, but he knew where the pillows were and therefore how she lay. Again the first blow was not fatal, and this time the victim screamed loudly as she put up her hands to protect herself. A rain of ax strokes had fallen on her face and neck and shoulders. One hand was cut off completely, and the other hung by a flap of tendons and skin. She was hideously mangled, and tufts of her long brown hair were scattered over the bloody pillows.

In all three cabins the upward swings of the ax had flung blood drops on the ceiling, and in some of the swings the ax had scored the ceiling itself. Laura Nash was in her nightdress, and it was drawn up about her waist, probably in her own desperate struggles and agonies, although possibly the murderer had made an attempt to rape her.

The ships' emergency ax was missing from its cleats on the partition between lavatory and storeroom, and now of course it was at the bottom of the sea. Finally the searchers noticed something else. Although blood had dripped from the ax all the way up the forward companionway and across the deck cargo to the place where Spencer found it, there was not a single trace of blood in the after companionway nor around the wheel where "Charles Brown" stood at his post. Whoever he was, and however he entered the house, the killer had left by the "front door," and in doing so he had passed within a hand's touch of the mizzenmast, where Tom Bram supposedly stood at his watch.

Jonathan Spencer suspected at once that the murderer was either Tom Bram or "Charles Brown," and whichever was guilty, the other knew.

Tom Bram was now in full command of the ship, for the *Herbert Fuller* was in midocean and he was the only qualified navigator left alive. He called all hands together and made a

49

little speech, beginning with a cryptic, "The living should not suffer for the dead." He went on: "We had better all say that the murder occurred in this way. The Captain having come out of the chartroom, and going to his wife's apartment in the cabin, found the second mate in bed with her; and he then picked up the ax and immediately slaughtered her. The Captain then struck at the second mate and wounded him with the ax; but the second mate being a big, powerful man wrenched the ax from the Captain's hands and dealt him several blows on the head. Then both of them staggered away to their beds and died."

It was a neat Shakespearean solution, with all the actors falling dead in selected places on the stage. Tom Bram gazed from face to face with that black hypnotic stare of his, and nobody spoke except the steward. Spencer said bluntly, "I don't think that story of yours will do." However, the others all seemed ready to accept it. Bram was armed and Spencer was not, and Bram was certainly now the commander of the ship. The steward could only bide his time. When Bram ordered Monks to write a statement of the affair as he dictated it, the student obeyed. And when Bram ordered everyone to sign this statement, Spencer signed it with the rest.

The statement was in pencil, and written in such terms that it appeared to be Monks's own account. It related the events of the previous night as far as Monks knew them, and added "my" theory of the affair—which was of course Bram's own theory. At a further suggestion from Bram, Monks added: "The second mate offered Mr. Bram a drink at about 12 o'clock. This whiskey made Mr. Bram very sick while on deck with me, and he acted as if he had been drugged."

The first mate's entry in the ship's logbook ran as follows, with his free spelling and punctuation and syntax, and his fine handwriting with all the pen strokes slanting at exactly the same angle and all the loops exactly alike.

"This day comes in with mod breeze and smooth seas at or about 2 A.M. Tuesday there an alarm Made by passenger Mr. Munks that there was mutiny on board while none on deck at the time seen ore new nothing of what had been done but as it was my watch on deck myself an Mr. Munk went down in the cabin and found the Capt and his wife had been killed with an axe which whepon was thrown over bord by request of Mr. Munks and steward all hands was brought aft but none could account for it we concluded to put the vessel back to the nearest Port to make known the same."

Although Spencer and Monks knew nothing of navigation, Tom Bram now made them his assistants in the handling of the crew and the ship. Bram talked first of going to "French Cayenne," meaning the port of Cayenne in French Guiana, a vast distance to the south. Then he spoke of Bermuda, which was actually the nearest land; but the prevailing winds made that course difficult and there would be great danger among the Bermudian reefs. Finally, he announced that he would turn the ship about and steer back the way she had come, for Boston.

There was another pressing matter. The three victims had been killed in the early hours of July 14. With the present winds, at least eight more days would drag by before the New England coast came in sight. Long before that the bodies would turn putrid in the hot summer air. Bram was for dropping them overboard at once. But now the Negro steward spoke up manfully, insisting that they must be kept aboard as evidence for the police, and for decent burial ashore. He insisted, too, that nothing in the victims' rooms must be changed or cleaned until the police had seen them. Monks backed him in this, and Bram could only agree.

For the next four days all hands in the *Herbert Fuller* lived on deck. Neither Bram nor Monks would sleep in the bloody afterhouse, and the sailors were afraid to sleep in the fore house lest the mysterious killer catch them unconscious in their berths and try his hand again. In mingled fear and suspicion they all watched each other. But most of them watched "Charles Brown" and Tom Bram. The third man aft at the time of the murders, Lester Monks, was obviously innocent, for the bloody ax was already lying on the deck cargo when the passenger first emerged from the cabin.

On the day after the murders Jonathan Spencer led the sailors into the after house, and they carried the horrid bodies to the deck and covered them with canvas. "Charles Brown" took his part in this gruesome job, and Tom Bram watched it. He said to "Brown" with a note of challenge rather than question, "Do you have the heart to handle the bodies?" And the helmsman answered dourly, "I *must* have the heart to do it!" In lifting and carrying the carcasses like butchered beef from a Chicago slaughter-pit "Brown" got some smears of blood on his overalls, and in the presence of the crew he took them off and cast them overboard.

The steward went again into the after cabin, this time to tidy the rooms of its living tenants, the passenger and Bram; and in the first mate's room he made a discovery. The big whiskey jar now held no more than a pint. On deck Spencer asked Bram what had become of his liquor supply, and Bram said airily that the jar had upset just before sailing from Boston, and all but two quarts were spilled and lost. The steward made no comment. He had cleaned the room every morning except the day of the murders. A flood of alcohol like that must have left a powerful smell and a stain on the floor, yet he had noticed nothing.

On the day after the steward mentioned this remarkable dwindling of the whiskey in the jar, Tom Bram told Spencer that he had seen "Charles Brown" leave the helm shortly before two o'clock on the morning of the fourteenth, and he was certain that "Brown" was the killer. He did not say why he had not mentioned this before, nor why he had made no attempt to seize "Brown."

Jonathan Spencer was a man of action. Also, he had the confidence of the seamen, which Bram had not. At five o'clock in the morning of July 16, he and three sailors pounced on "Charles Brown" asleep in his bunk, fastened his wrists with a pair of handcuffs from the Captain's cabin, dragged him to the deck and tied him to the mainmast. When "Brown" asked why, the steward snapped, "Because you killed the Captain!" Tom Bram walked up to the man bound to the mast and sneered, "You thought you would be smart and put me in for it, but I'm too clever for you." Later on, when the prisoner was allowed to sleep in his bunk, still in handcuffs, Bram said to the others, "I'm afraid that man will beat his brains out and kill himself."

Meanwhile there remained the problem of the corpses on the deck. After four days, in spite of the canvas covering, the stench was bad and getting worse. On the afternoon of July 17, under Spencer's direction, the sailors carefully wrapped each body in a flannel blanket, and over that a piece of sailcloth. They took the boat off the fore house, launched it, and drew it aft. They placed the bundled bodies in the boat, lashed a tarpaulin over the boat itself to screen it from sun and spray, and fastened the boat's stem to the ship's stern with a length of rope.

And so the *Herbert Fuller* sailed on, towing the boat and its hideous cargo twenty-five feet behind the helmsman, day and night.

On the morning of Saturday, July 18, they sighted a long low island composed of sand, in dunes and beaches, with a lighthouse at each end. There was no doubt about its name. This was Sable Island, a dangerous sandbar in the North Atlantic about 175 miles from Halifax, known to seamen everywhere as "The Graveyard of the Atlantic." If Tom Bram had honestly laid the ship's course for Boston he was a very bad navigator, for he was something like 500 miles out in his reckoning. To reach Boston now he would have to steer away to the southwest. Instead, he shifted the course enough to pass the island safely and then held on toward the north. Obviously he had no intention of returning to Boston. But where was he going? That evening he put some scouring powder into a bucket of water, washed a pair of trousers, drawers and a shirt, and left them to soak in the bucket all night.

Jonathan Spencer now came to another decision. He had felt all along that either Bram or "Charles Brown" was the killer, and that the other knew. Now the steward had learned something definite. The prisoner "Brown" had confided to his fellow Swede, Oscar Anderson, that he had seen Tom Bram striking the Captain with something like an ax in the chartroom during the early hours of July 14.

From the moment of his seizure by the crew, "Charles Brown" had maintained stubbornly that he did not leave the wheel during his watch on the fatal night. He pointed out that a wind of considerable strength on the quarter gave the ship a natural tendency to "broach," that is, to turn her bow into the wind. If this were allowed to happen it would set all the canvas aloft flapping and roaring, bring the ship to a shuddering stop, and damage badly the masts and yards as well as the sails. Therefore, the helmsman had to meet every tendency of this sort with a shift of the rudder. He dared not leave the wheel untended for more than a few moments.

Then how had he seen the murder of the Captain? He said that by stooping low and leaning to starboard—but keeping a hand on one of the lower spokes of the wheel—he was able to peer through the little window of the chartroom. He had seen the Captain lying on the floor, and although the light was dim in the chartroom, he had seen Tom Bram standing over the Captain and striking him on the head with "something that had a long handle." Later he heard two wild screams from the direction of Mrs. Nash's room. After that he saw Bram run out of the fore companionway, stoop on the deck cargo, and arise with a piece of wood in his hands. The mate had then turned toward the fore companionway, as if watching for someone to come out, and he had raised the stick as if to strike that someone as soon as he appeared. When Mr. Monks came on deck with a revolver in his hand, Tom Bram had dropped the stick.

Spencer had a poor opinion of "Charles Brown." The man was weak in the head and a clumsy liar. But of the two he considered Tom Bram by far the more likely murderer. He summed up what he knew. Nearly eight quarts of Bram's whiskey gone in eleven days at most, and apparently in less than a week. Bram having "words" with the Captain. Bram having "words" with the second mate. Bram in a drunken frenzy on the night of the crime. Bram knowing every inch of the after house and the whereabouts of its occupants, while "Charles Brown" had never set foot in it until he went with the other sailors to carry out the bodies. Bram tossing the bloody ax overboard, and wishing to do the same with the three corpses. Bram declaring that he was setting a return course for Boston and actually sailing the ship far away to the northeast. And now with the ship's position plain to be seen, off Sable Island, Bram still holding on toward the north.

Spencer chose a time when the mate was below and told his suspicions to Lester Monks. They considered what they should do. Tom Bram alone could bring the ship out of the ocean spaces to some part of the mainland, and they dared not make a move until the coast was definitely in sight. Apparently Bram was heading the ship for the east tip of Nova Scotia, or perhaps he intended going on to Newfoundland. So they waited.

On Sunday, July 19, the watch sighted land extending east and west to the horizon—the mainland beyond any doubt. Tom Bram brought up the Captain's telescope and sat on the after house to inspect his landfall. Then he turned the glass to inspect a steamer passing along the coast. In this absorption he was quite unaware that Spencer and the hands on deck were stealing up behind him. Suddenly they pounced. After a wild struggle Tom Bram was handcuffed, dragged to the mooring bitts aft, and chained there like some dangerous animal.

Jonathan Spencer now took charge of the ship, heading straight in toward the unknown coast. Eventually he saw a fisherman in a small boat and hailed him. In a brief conversation he learned that the land was the mainland of Nova Scotia near Cape Canso. The fisherman told him also the best course to steer for Halifax, about 120 miles to the westward along the coast. After that the navigation of the *Herbert Fuller* was a matter of steering the given course, keeping the land in sight on the starboard hand, and watching carefully for the outlying reefs and islands.

Early on the morning of Tuesday, July 21, a pilot named William White boarded the *Herbert Fuller* six miles off Devil's Island, at the entrance to Halifax harbor. He had noticed that she was being handled cautiously, even uncertainly. When he drew alongside, someone on deck called down to him that there had been murder aboard, and that three dead bodies were in the boat towing astern. White brought the barkentine up the harbor, dropped anchor off the town, and hastened ashore to notify the police. News of this grim arrival spread quickly along the Halifax waterfront, and a large crowd gathered with the police on Market Wharf. There was something else on the wharf, a horse and wagon with three pine coffins in charge of John Snow & Sons, the chief undertakers of the town. Halifax newsmen were on the spot, of course, and the leading afternoon paper came forth with the headline:

A CARNIVAL OF MURDER ON THE HIGH SEAS

Under this title was a brief account of the murders at sea, and then:

No more gruesome sight can be imagined than that presented by the ship's boat as it came slowly along, in tow of the undertaker's men. It was seen to be a jolly-boat, covered over. Slowly it forged in to the slip and was moored alongside. One of Snow's men cut the fastenings and ripped off the canvas cover, and the bodies were seen, or rather the packages in which they were wrapped. The bodies were lifted out and put into coffins that were brought to the water's edge from Snow's wagon.

The bodies were taken first to John Snow & Sons' undertaking establishment. Later they were removed to the morgue. Last night crowds visited the place, drawn by a morbid curiosity, which was more shocking from the fact that a majority of these sightseers were women. Many of them fainted, and it was no more than they deserved.

The Halifax reporters did a thorough job on the story. Among other things, they dug out, as a matter of melancholy interest, the fact that Captain and Mrs. Nash had been in Halifax once before, in the barque *John F. Rottman* with a cargo of sugar from Brazil. That was in 1885, on what may have been their honeymoon voyage.

The Halifax police made sure that none of the witnesses disappeared. Not only Bram and "Charles Brown" but Jonathan Spencer and the other seamen were locked up in the police station. Lester Monks was allowed to sleep in the police office. He had telegraphed his family in Boston, and they were prompt to engage a Halifax lawyer to watch over their son's interests. News agencies had telegraphed the story to Boston and New York, and newsmen in New York lost no time in locating and interviewing Mrs. Thomas M. C. Bram.

The Halifax newsmen were allowed to interview the prisoners freely, and one reporter began his account with the chief suspect.

MATE BRAM'S STATEMENT

Bram says that most of the statements in the New York despatches are correct. He was surprised to hear his wife had applied for divorce, and says she had no grounds. Bram says he frequently attended services of the Salvation Army in New York but he was not a member of that body.

"God in Heaven knows I am innocent," exclaimed the first mate. "I may not be able to prove it here on earth; I may not be able to convince my fellow men that I am not guilty, but there is a Father above who knows I am speaking the truth, and some day I hope to find a place in his Heavenly tabernacle. There may be no earthly tabernacle for me, but I am secure in the love and protection of God Almighty, and in Him I place my hope of life eternal. Brown is the one who committed the crimes and he is shielding himself by accusing me. I could not kill a man or a woman. It is not in me. You need not say I have done this in a fit of insanity; it is impossible. I am wrongly accused, and if I suffer it is for the crime of another man. Brown is a crazy man. He is my enemy. He has it in for me because we did not get along together. He told me himself that he killed a man in Holland once, and escaped on the ground of insanity. He was always queer and I had to watch him constantly. He says he could not leave the wheel the night of the crime. He could leave it, and he did. I saw him leave the wheel a few minutes before two o'clock that morning. That day he swore he knew nothing about the murders, and four days after he had been put in irons he said he saw me do it. Why did he keep quiet all that time? I knew nothing about the killing until after Monks came on deck. When I saw him with a revolver in his hand I thought he was going to shoot me, and I picked up a piece of wood to defend myself. It was after that that I heard of what had been done below. So help me God, I didn't do it! Honest to God! If my heart was torn out, I would say I am innocent."

A New York dispatch, containing the interview with Bram's wife, revealed that he was a West Indian. A Halifax reporter quizzed him on this and Bram admitted it. He said he sometimes claimed to be a Nova Scotian because his mother had lived at Bridgewater, N.S., before her marriage to a Dutchman. To the next question he replied that she was not a native of Nova Scotia, but he refused to say where she was born.

All these statements, given to newsmen in Halifax immediately after the crew came ashore, when the affair was still hot, have an importance that was ignored in the subsequent trial in Boston, when all the testimony was given after careful reflection for months, after cautions by lawyers, and in the portentous surroundings of a courtroom.

Of his talk with the helmsman the Halifax reporter wrote:

BROWN'S POSITIVE STATEMENT

Brown, the man at the wheel, says shortly after 1 o'clock, while he was steering the ship, he heard a noise in the cabin, and he stretched himself out, and holding one hand on a spoke of the wheel, he looked in through a window and saw the captain on the floor. Brown said he stood up again to the wheel, but on hearing a thud he looked in through the window again. The captain's head was lying towards the window, and he states that he distinctly saw the mate appear with something in his hand, with a wooden handle. The mate raised it over his shoulder and struck the captain on the head. The first thought to come to his mind was to call out for help, but became afraid to move for fear that the mate would kill him. He saw only one blow struck. He saw the mate leave the chartroom and go in the direction of Mrs. Nash's room. Not more than a few seconds elapsed till he heard two frightful screams, and then all was silent. The mate then came on deck through the forward companionway. The lumber on the deck was in line with the top of the house, and he could plainly see the mate. The mate walked up and down for a moment, and then came towards Brown. The thought crossed his mind that the mate was going to kill him, and his eyes were strained looking at the mate's hands to see if he had anything in them, but he had not. The mate asked some questions as to how he was steering.

At this point there was a sudden interruption in the interview. Two cell doors away stood Jonathan Spencer, with his face to the bars, hearing every word. The steward shouted, "That man's an awful liar! You can't believe a word he says. He knows more about that murder than he wanted to tell at first, and he hasn't told all yet. It's all between himself and that mate Bram, if they would only tell. They could give the whole story, but they want to lie about it. He stands there telling a long story about himself that you can't believe. I wouldn't believe him, on my oath. Don't you listen to him. He's a liar. Why didn't he tell us at first what he saw? He's lying now and he's been lying all along."

"Brown" turned toward his own cell with a smile on his face, as though it were idle to pay attention to these accusations. "Me do it?" he exclaimed. "No! No!" slapping his broad chest. "I would not harm a cat, much less a human being. I never did anything of that sort intentionally. My hands are clean of these murders."

Here is the Halifax newsman's account of Frank Loheac, whose name he spelled as it was pronounced, *Loheese:*

THE LOOKOUT SPEAKS

Frank Loheese, the Frenchman who was on the lookout, saw the mate go down the forward companionway on more than one occasion on the night in question. The last time he went down he remained some time, and came running up the same way as fast as his legs could carry him. When Loheese heard the mate was in irons and securely fastened he made no hesitation in telling what he knew of the whole affair, to the steward and to Monks. He most emphatically states that Brown did not leave the wheel. If he did, he would most surely have seen him, as he was on the forecastle house.

Tom Bram and the others were questioned separately by Halifax Chief of Police O'Sullivan and Chief Detective Power. Meanwhile a police party had boarded the *Herbert Fuller* and examined the scene of the murders. They removed Bram's trunk, containing the shirt, trousers and drawers, still damp, which he had washed and soaked in a bucket on the night of the eighteenth. Examination showed that if these garments had been stained with blood, the stains were gone. The police also removed the ship's logbook, which Bram had kept in his neat writing until the crew put him in irons on the nineteenth. It was seen at once that Bram had tampered with the log—his handwriting was unmistakable—and entries and dates had been changed as far back as July 9, the day after the barkentine sailed out of Boston harbor. But if the handwriting was neat, the changes were crude. Two pages had been torn out altogether, and in rewriting these entries Bram had got the dates mixed up. On the still existing pages the dates of Friday the tenth and through Monday the thirteenth had been superimposed, without regard to the events that actually took place on those days. On more than one page there were two sets of entries written for the same date, as a clumsy or somewhat tipsy embezzler might attempt to keep two accounts, one for himself and one for the firm.

The police also removed the belongings of Captain Nash, Mrs. Nash, and August Blamberg, and sent them along to Boston with the logbook and other evidence, including Tom Bram's trunk. The Canadian authorities granted extradition quickly. To avoid a curious crowd, all the surviving people of the *Herbert Fuller* were spirited out of the police station at midnight on July 24, and placed on board the steamship *Halifax* for her regular run to Boston. A Halifax police constable went along on the voyage to keep an eye on them until the Boston police took charge.

When the steamer arrived at Boston on the morning of July 27, she was boarded by eager newsmen as well as the police, and according to one account:

The comparative social status of the different men held in connection with the tragedy was well illustrated when they arrived at the police station on Hanover Street this morning. Lester H. Monks breakfasted in Capt. Cain's private office with his counsel, Mr. Forbes of Halifax, his father Mr. F. S. Monks, and his uncle Dr. George Monks. He also entertained as visitors lawyer Alfred Hemonway and several other friends who called.

On the same floor but in the cell room, and confined in one of the barred cages of the station, sat Mate Bram. He too had breakfasted but he ate and drank with his wrists bound in steel bracelets. Two cells away from him, with an officer standing between the grated doors to prevent any conversation between the two men, was Brown the helmsman. Like Bram he was enjoying a cigar furnished by the police. The rest of the prisoners were in the tier of cells under those occupied by Bram and Brown.

When Police Officer Sheehan went through the cell corridor this morning the Mate accosted him. "Wonder if I could send for Morris?" he asked, referring to Morris Shindler the shoemaker. "I guess so," said the officer. "Or Tom Walsh," continued Bram, referring to a well known liquor dealer at the foot of Hanover Street. "I want to get a good lawyer and I want them to pick one out for me."

Thomas Bram was arraigned on three counts, the complaint charging him with the murder of Captain C. J. Nash, his wife Laura Nash, and the second mate August Blamburg [sic], with an axe, on the vessel on the high seas on July 14. He stated that he had no counsel but desired an attorney before he said any more in the case. He was informed that he was entitled to continuance for one day. Accordingly his case was continued till tomorrow at 10 o'clock. Charles Brown was arraigned on a like complaint. Brown also pleaded not guilty, and his case was continued till tomorrow at the same hour.

The preliminary hearings followed, and the result was that Tom Bram and "Charles Brown" were committed to appear before the Grand Jury in October.

Meanwhile the owners of the *Herbert Fuller* had engaged a tough and able Nova Scotia skipper named Tom McLaughlin to take their ship and cargo to Rosario. He picked up a crew in

Halifax and sailed on August 17, 1896. This time the barkentine had a peaceful voyage. She arrived at Buenos Aires on October 14, just before the trials were due to begin in Boston. By now the news of the *Fuller* affair was all over the world, and her arrival at Buenos Aires created a lot of excitement, especially among the North American skippers in port. Several of them visited the ship and talked to her new captain, and among them was Capt. C. V. Corning of Yarmouth, N.S., an old friend of McLaughlin.

In discussing the voyage McLaughlin said there were the usual rumors of "ghosts" aboard the ship, and the crew were none too happy. As for himself, he was neither superstitious nor concerned in any way. He had even slept on the same cot in the chartroom where Captain Nash was killed, and declared that it was the most comfortable bed in the ship and he had enjoyed sleeping on it.

During eight weeks of sailing the *Herbert Fuller* there had been many opportunities to test the statements of the former helmsman "Charles Brown." The Nova Scotian skipper and his men had proved that it was possible for the helmsman to keep one hand on a low spoke of the wheel and lean away far enough to peer into the chartroom. At night they found that the light in the chartroom, reflected from the lamp in the main cabin, was dim but enough to recognize a man lying on the floor and a man bending over him.

Most important of all, they had proved that under the conditions on the night of the crime—with a wind on the quarter pushing the ship along at eight knots—she had a constant tendency to "come up into the wind," which had to be offset with the rudder. It was utterly impossible for the helmsman to leave his post, even with the wheel lashed, for more than a couple of minutes, without the ship veering to windward and setting everything aloft in an uproar that would waken everyone on board. All the investigators, ashore and afloat, agreed that the three murders must have taken at least fifteen minutes, from the time the killer left the deck until he got back again.

McLaughlin's tests, made with the ship at sea, proved that

*whatever the helmsman knew about the crime, he could not have
been the murderer.*

Captain McLaughlin made these tests and experiments to satisfy his own curiosity, and he noted the results in the ship's
logbook. He was not asked about them until the ship returned
to the United States many weeks later, and even then he was
not asked to testify or make a deposition of any sort. By that time
the trial was over and the police considered the case closed.

On October 15, 1896, the Grand Jury was sworn in at Boston.
District Attorney Sherman Hoar had as his assistants J. H. Casey
and F. P. Cabot. The notorious affair of the *Herbert Fuller* had
attracted the interest of every lawyer in Boston, and Tom Bram
had no trouble in getting two able men to defend him: James E.
Cotter and Asa P. French. An equally able lawyer, Frank D. Al-
len, undertook the defense of "Charles Brown."

Ever since they returned to Boston late in July the two accused
men and the rest of the barkentine's crew had whiled away the
time in the prison on Charles Street. Tom Bram chatted daily
with the jailers, read the newspapers, and frequently reeled off
long religious declamations to his visitors. According to one Boston newsman he "sounded as though he were an evangelist rather
than a prisoner awaiting trial for his life." His fellow prisoner
"Charles Brown," on the other hand, had very little to say. He
too read the papers and seemed unconcerned about his fate, although by this time the District Attorney had been in touch with
the Rotterdam police, had got an account of the helmsman's
shooting affray there, and knew that his real name was Justus
Leopold Westerberg and his nationality Swedish. Both prisoners
could look out of their cells and watch the seamen who would
testify in their cases being marched to and from their daily exer-
cise in the prison yard. Lester Monks was not confined, of course,
and Jonathan Spencer had been released with due warning to
appear when summoned.

"Charles Brown" was the first to be taken before the Grand

Jury, and Monks, Spencer and the four seamen gave their testimony. The helmsman was charged as "Charles Brown alias Justus Leopold Westerberg," and the police report from Rotterdam was produced in court. The evidence took three days. After careful deliberation the Grand Jury found "No Bill," and "Brown" was absolved of the murder charge. However, he was to be a material witness in the case against Bram. Bail was set at $5000. No one offered to put up the money, and "Brown" was returned to jail.

Boston newsmen assumed that "Brown" had turned state's evidence with some sensational evidence not yet revealed. There was a general idea that "Brown" knew of the murderer's intentions and motives before the crime took place. Actually, he had merely repeated, in his stumbling way, what he had told the police and newsmen in Halifax. The evidence of the sailors, especially Loheac, the lookout man, was enough to release him from the murder charge. District Attorney Hoar was certain that Tom Bram was the guilty one, and he needed "Charles Brown's" testimony, for his was the only direct evidence. All the rest was circumstantial.

Late in October the Grand Jury made an indictment against Thomas Bram, mate of the barkentine *Herbert Fuller*, for murder on the high seas. The case came to trial on December 14, 1896, exactly five months after the murders.

Justices Colt and Webb were on the bench of the U. S. Circuit Court, and District Attorney Hoar confined his effort to the charge of murdering Captain Nash. Early on a cold Boston morning the corridors of the Federal Building filled with people eager to watch the trial, but owing to the small number of seats available, only those with important references got inside. Many were lawyers, who followed the trial with close attention from first to last.

After the court opened, Tom Bram was escorted to the iron-barred prisoner's box and locked inside. He was neatly dressed and looked well and cheerful. Choosing the jury was a long business. A hundred men had been summoned for duty and ninety-seven were rejected. More had to be summoned. The twelve finally chosen included a lumber merchant, two farmers, two commercial travelers, a leather merchant, a florist, a carpenter, a shoemaker, a sailmaker, and two citizens of no stated occupation.

The trial went on slowly and monotonously day after day, as trials do. There was a brief buzz when "Charles Brown" took the witness chair, but he added little to what the newspaper readers already knew. He mentioned a hot passage of words between the first and second mates a couple of days before the murders. Bram had said, "I want you to do what I tell you. Don't intend to run me!" And August Blamberg had snapped back, "I don't want you to run me, either!"

Mr. Hoar showed "Brown" the statement written by Lester Monks on the day of the murders, with Bram's own theory of the killings, which all of them signed. He said to "Brown" crisply, "You knew the statements were not true?"

"I knew they were all lies," he said.

"Then why did you sign?"

"Brown" answered that as far as he could see then, the ship was going on to Brazil in charge of Mate Bram, and during the voyage it would not be safe to say what he knew. He merely said to Oscar Anderson, "When we arrive in port everything will be all right."

Lawyer Cotter, defending Bram, had an absurdly easy task in cross-examining the weak-witted helmsman. It was no trouble at all to get "Charles Brown" to contradict himself on many points. For example, he had shot a man in Holland—and he had never shot a man anywhere. He had been confined to a mental asylum —and he had never been in such a place. At the ship's helm he always held the steering wheel with both hands—and he sometimes held it with one. From his post at the wheel he could see into the chartroom—yet he did not know the Captain slept there until the night of the murder. Finally Cotter made the usual insinuation that "Brown" had been promised his freedom if he spoke the right words against Tom Bram.

One of "Brown's" statements was new and he stuck to it. He had first noticed "trouble" in the chartroom about 1:30 A.M. If this was true the murderer must have been below nearly half an hour.

The trial crawled on, with a brief pause for Christmas. Late in December, Bram's lawyers sent him into the witness chair in his own defense. He stated that his name was Thomas Mead Chandler Bram, and that he was born at St. Catherine's Island, commonly known as St. Kitts, in the British West Indies. He told of his jobs ashore in New York, Chicago and Boston. Most of that time he managed restaurants for one Dennet, who had a chain in various cities. He related the events of the voyage, and especially the night of the murders, when he said he saw "Brown" leave the wheel before two o'clock. He described the ship and its cargo, and the sails that were set on the night of the murders, pointing frequently to a model barkentine on the table before him.

He explained how the rudder could be set with the wheel lashed, and said the sea and wind conditions on the night of July 13 were favorable to lashing the wheel. With the wheel lashed, the ship would only slightly change its course for the next ten or fifteen minutes.

He described the old revolver he had got in Mexico. He explained his store of whiskey, and how the jar upset and spilled all but two quarts before the ship left Mystic Wharf. He just had time enough to go ashore and buy another quart. He usually took a couple of drinks a day, no more. On the night of the murders he had gone to his room briefly to take a drink, "as customary," about one o'clock in the morning.

It was his custom to change and wash his clothes every Saturday. On the Saturday after the murders he had put his soiled trousers, drawers and shirt in a bucket of water and washed them with "Gold Dust." (This referred to a brand of washing and scouring powder, popular in the 1890s; its label bore a picture of two Negro children called The Gold Dust Twins.) There was no blood on his clothes. He left them to soak all night after washing, but that was his custom.

After he was grabbed and fastened by the crew, the steward Spencer had said to him, "We ought to get $500 each for salvage money. If you had brought the ship in, we would get nothing. Also the Captain's folks ought to pay us for bringing the bodies to port."

Tom Bram gave all this testimony in a firm, clear voice, with intelligence and dignity, looking straight into the eyes of the examining counsel. When he described the ship, the sails, the details of the after house, and so on, he was seamanlike and explicit. Altogether an admirable witness.

The District Attorney could not shake him a bit.

For the defense, lawyers Cotter and French relied mainly on one thing; that the only direct evidence against Bram was that of "Charles Brown," a man with a false name, a record of attempted homicide and of treatment in a lunatic asylum. To parry the District Attorney's circumstantial evidence, they provided similar evidence to show that Justus Westerberg, alias "Charles Brown," himself had ample opportunity to kill the three victims. In support of this, they brought in a succession of retired sea captains to declare that under the weather conditions described, in a barkentine like the *Herbert Fuller*, the helmsman could lash the wheel and leave it for as much as fifteen minutes without the ship changing her course very much.

In rebuttal, District Attorney Hoar fetched other mariners to refute this argument. The matter was vital, of course. With his one direct witness of such doubtful character, Hoar had to concentrate on this nautical point, which was the true key to the case.

Under date of January 1, 1897, a Boston newspaper reported:

THE BRAM MURDER TRIAL

Thomas Bram wore an anxious look as he came into court this morning. Although he maintained his sphinxlike stoicism there is no mistaking the fact that he is undergoing a severe mental strain. His eyes lighted up for a moment as the friendly faces of his counsel, Cotter and French, appeared at the door. With both hands clasped and one leg thrown carelessly over the other, the position in which Bram usually sits, with his head thrown against the rail of the dock, he rivetted his eyes on the District Attorney as he rose to make the final assault on the prisoner's life.

In the race for places in the courtroom the women seem to have come out ahead, fully four-fifths of the spectators being of the fair sex. District Attorney Hoar resumed his argument immediately after the judges had taken their seats. Hoar assailed Bram in the beginning, first calling attention to the plucky conduct of the negro Spencer, and saying that Bram showed none of that man's courage. Spencer was not a man to clasp the knees of people, he did not ask whether there were any Freemasons on board, nor did he make any signals of distress; he went to work and did just what Bram ought to have done; he went to see what was the matter on board, what had happened to those people, and how they had been killed. He did not know how many of the crew were aft. He only knew that Lester Monks and Charles Brown could be aft of him besides the dead bodies. That negro went right down there.

Mr. Hoar asked why Bram told Monks that the second mate was forward, when he knew that man was downstairs. And why did not Bram bring the lantern forward? Why did he leave it in Lester Monks's room? It was for the mighty good reason that if he brought it, Lester Monks's eye might have lighted on the dead body of the second mate.

Mr. Hoar went on to describe the movements of the captain and his wife on the eve of the murder. He dwelt at length on the charge that Monks had committed perjury, contrasting the passenger with Bram. He defended Monks and Brown from the impeachment brought against them by Mr. Cotter, and contended that their evidence was truthful and sufficient to warrant conviction of the prisoner.

He took up the alleged claim for salvage, and said the sailors had not claimed any. He went into the lashing of the wheel, and referred to "the antiquated captains of the defense," who had left the sea before he was born, and their testimony that the wheel could be lashed, etc. He claimed that the captain was the only man that would take the risk of lashing the wheel, and said that Brown could never have done it with Bram sitting in the lee.

The District Attorney spoke for upwards of half an hour, and closed with a fine bit of forensic eloquence: "In the new year beginning this day, many sailors will meet the god of storms and the demons of the deep. But if this cunning daring devil goes unpunished there is to be a new terror added to those which threaten the men who go down to the sea in ships."

The newspaper account goes on:

For nearly two hours the jury listened to a summing up of the law and the evidence by Justice Webb. The judge declined to say that the witness Charles Brown was not to be believed, but suggested a doubt had been cast, by physical impediments, on his statement that he saw the captain murdered—the measurements of the cabin window, the light, and his position at the wheel.

He referred to the contradictory statements of Brown regarding his Rotterdam experience, and left the jury to their own conclusions as to whether he was deliberately lying. If the jury found he was not telling the truth, it would destroy his evidence as far as direct proof of the crime went. However it would not make him incompetent to corroborate the evidence of other witnesses and add to its weight.

The medical experts' testimony, if believed, would lead the jury to say Brown was insane. Throwing out the testimony of Brown regarding his having seen the murder committed would still leave a large amount of circumstantial evidence on the part of the government. How far this tended to prove the guilt of the defendant it was for the jury to decide. The jury must be satisfied, not that someone else might have murdered Captain Nash, but that beyond a reasonable doubt Thomas Bram was the guilty man. If they were not satisfied on that point, they must find him not guilty.

On January 3, 1897, a Boston paper carried the verdict in this way:

Thomas Mead Bram was found guilty of murder in the U. S. Circuit Court yesterday afternoon. The twelve men who listened to the evidence and arguments for three weeks were out 26 hours and 25 minutes. The announcement of the verdict was attended by scenes of the wildest excitement ever seen in any courthouse in this part of the country for years. The verdict came as a surprise to almost everybody. The cry of "Guilty" was carried far and wide through the big building and out into the streets.

The story of the jury room was one of the most remarkable ever told, of the difficulties of twelve men with the life of a fellow man in their hands. While every man on the jury believed Bram was the murderer, some of their number were in doubt as to whether sufficient evidence was presented to prove his guilt. While 13 ballots were taken during those weary hours, which ran all the way from 5 to 7 and 11 to 1 for conviction, they never showed a belief in the innocence of Bram on the part of any member of the jury. There was however a disposition to give the man the benefit of all evidence favorable to him by having a disagreement.

Foreman Jack told the court that the jury had arrived at a verdict. The jury hardly looked at the prisoner. The clerk turned to Bram.

"Thomas Bram, will you look upon the foreman? Foreman, will you look upon the prisoner?"

There stood Bram, straight as an arrow, with his arm stretched high in air, his face pallid, his strong black eyes turned upon the foreman. He seemed cool, and his nerves had not forsaken him. The clerk turned to the foreman, who faced the prisoner but seemed unable to meet his glassy eyes.

"Mr. Foreman, what is your verdict . . . ?"

"Guilty," broke in the nervous foreman, and the clerk halted.

"Guilty or not guilty?" continued the clerk.

"Guilty."

Bram sat down. He grew black under the eyes. He clapped his hands before him and turned his eyes upwards to the stars on the ceiling of the courtroom, the attitude of a man searching out his God. He looked long and earnestly, and the eyes of all were upon him. Then those great black eyes became moist and blurred. Tears flowed, and he bowed his head. Women looked upon him and shed tears. The man of iron had weakened. He seemed to have lost control of himself. It was thought he would break down altogether. Again he turned his eyes upward. Again the tears came. He made a great effort to recover himself, and he succeeded.

The Boston *Transcript* summed up the case on January 4:

70

A JUST VERDICT

The people of the United States owe respect and honor to its jury in the Bram case, for the wise and courageous verdict of "Guilty."

All three of the victims seem to have been killed with the same axe, which was found on deck between the ordinary station of First Mate Bram and the regular station of the man at the wheel, Brown. The prisoner was supposed to have gone in and out through the forward door of the house; and the sailor Brown was claimed by the defense to have gone in and out of the after door.

The Government proved that the prisoner lived in that house, knew where the axe hung on its inside wall. The defense failed to show that Brown had ever been in the house or had even seen the axe or knew where it was. The Government also proved that blood dripped from the forward door, near where the prisoner was, to part of the deck where the axe was found; and that no blood was found near the after door, where Brown stood at the wheel.

This circumstantial evidence was corroborated by the direct testimony of Brown, that as he stood at the wheel he looked into the window only a few feet from him, and saw by the dim light of the lamp Bram strike with something like an axe handle at a man who lay where the captain was found, then go quickly forward, upon which a woman's shriek was heard, and soon Bram came up on deck.

This proof, conclusive if Brown was to be believed, rendered it imperative that the prisoner should try to shake the credit, not only of Brown, but of the other witnesses whose testimony was consistent with Brown's. But the attempt failed, and the prisoner's own testimony was utterly disbelieved.

The jury seemed to believe the following facts:—A young gentleman of 20 years, who happened to be a passenger, was aroused from a deep sleep by a woman's shriek from the cabin on one side of him, and by a horribly loud breathing from the cabin on the other side. He loaded his revolver, unlocked his door, rushed out, saw the captain on the floor, went to him, and found him nearly dead. He rushed to the captain's wife's cabin and in the dim light did not see her, but saw what he thought was blood on her bed, whereupon he rushed on deck to the First Mate, Bram.

Bram told him that there was a mutiny, and that the second

71

mate had gone forward with the men. The passenger took the First Mate down into his cabin with him, and kept him there while he hurriedly dressed, and then went on deck again with him. On deck the Mate staggered and vomited, and pleaded with the young man to protect him against the crew, for he said he had been hard on them and feared they would kill him.

At daylight they woke the steward, who found that the captain, his wife, and the second mate, were all dead, with their heads cut open by an axe. Then the First Mate pointed out [sic] a bloody axe lying on the deck and threw it overboard. When the crew awoke, and it was evident that there was no mutiny as the First Mate had claimed, he invented a theory that the captain killed his wife because of her relations with the second mate (of which there was absolutely no evidence in the case) and then fatally wounded the second mate, who wrested the axe from the captain, killed the captain, and then went on deck and dropped the axe, without being seen by the First Mate, and then returned to his cabin, crossed his feet, and died.

In the excitement of the moment, and under the influence of the First Mate, who had great gifts of persuasion, this theory was written out by the passenger and signed by him and all on board. But this theory being too absurd to sustain itself, and some scapegoat being desired, and the Mate thus far successful in keeping on good terms with the men, they arrested Brown. His manner after the murder had been gloomy. Brown said that they would find out who did it when they got ashore. It is significant that Brown helped to prepare the bodies respectfully, to be kept until they should reach home, but the First Mate proposed that they should be thrown overboard.

During the week before they reached Halifax, Brown's knowledge had its effect on the crew, and they arrested the First Mate. The First Mate, before his arrest, had begun a false logbook. To the writer present at the trial it was evident that Brown was telling the truth, and his testimony was corroborated by others of the crew. He was an outspoken sailor whose manner was in his favor. He admitted that he had told a shipmate that he had shot a man in Rotterdam and then got off by pleading insanity, but he testified that this was a sea yarn. Afterwards he admitted that he was unconscious for a fortnight and then found himself in a hospital in Rotterdam, where a doctor told him that he had shot at a man. He had since followed the sea for several years, being entirely recovered.

The counsel for the defense called medical experts, who swore that Brown was insane at the time of the murders, because of the Rotterdam incident, and because he talked to himself and gesticulated occasionally. The prosecution called medical experts who testified that in their opinion he had recovered. One of them doubted whether homicidal mania, so called, is a recognized disease.

The passenger, Mr. Monks, told what he saw and heard briefly and simply, and he sustained an extraordinary exasperating cross-examination with composure and good temper. The most striking part of the defense was the attempt to prove that Brown did the killing in a very brief attack of homicidal mania not discovered until this trial. The District Attorney made it clear that if Brown had done it, without knowing what he was about, he could not have escaped detection by the First Mate, who was on duty; and that if he was sane he would not have dared to leave the wheel, even lashed, to do so much in a house which he had never entered, with a weapon he had never seen, against persons whose respective places he did not know; and that in either case a Mate as acute and watchful as the prisoner was, and on deck where he swore he was watching, would have known something of what the man at the wheel was about.

The prisoner was ably defended by learned and experienced counsel, who rightly permitted him to go on the stand if he wished, for it was reasonable to expect that such an imperturbable and persuasive person would influence at least some of the jury. But the jury would not believe that so able a man would have known so much about what was done on deck, and so little about what he himself did and saw in the cabin. The distinctive traits of his testimony were a minutely detailed description of the deck, and a vague want of recollection about the cabin and the bodies.

On February 2, 1897, the *Herbert Fuller* arrived back in the United States from South America. She was visited in the port of New York by Tom Bram's counsel, together with Jonathan Spencer and a Boston shipwright. Spencer placed the Captain's cot in the position where it was found after the murder, showed exactly where his body lay, and joined in a test after dark with the lamp in the main cabin showing a dim light into the chartroom. He and the shipwright then made tests at the wheel. Both agreed that with both hands on the wheel they could see nothing. With one hand on the wheel, and leaning away from it, they could see the form of a person in the after cabin but could not identify him. They could see the lower end of the cot, and the feet and legs of a man standing there.

On the strength of this (and ignoring the tests made by Captain McLaughlin under actual sea conditions) the defense counsel applied for a new trial on grounds that Justus Westerberg alias "Charles Brown" had committed perjury. However, on February 12 the Boston judges decided that the alleged newly discovered evidence was merely cumulative. Tom Bram seemed to know himself that his lawyers' move was a forlorn hope. When he was ushered into the dock he did not face the court or look about the room as he did during the first trial. Instead, he sat down, placed his arm on the back of the seat, and stared at a spot high on the wall.

On March 9, 1897, the court sentenced Thomas Bram to death by hanging, with the execution set for June 17.

And now began a sequence, drawn out over years, which spared Bram from death, released him from prison, and at last whitewashed him of the crime. A new federal statute had been passed, enabling the jury in a capital case to find a new form of verdict, "Guilty, but without capital punishment." On the strength of this, Tom Bram's lawyers got a stay of execution, and then a new trial. The third trial took place in Boston in 1898, and the jury returned a verdict in the new form.

For the next eight years Tom Bram was confined in the Massachusetts State Prison, within easy sight of the Bunker Hill Monument and not far from the Mystic Wharf, where that momentous voyage of the *Herbert Fuller* had begun. He was a model prisoner, deeply religious, always preaching the golden rule to his fellow jailbirds. In November 1906, he asked for transfer to the warmer climate of Georgia, and he was removed to the federal prison at Atlanta. Here again he was the delight of the Warden and of various humanitarians, male and female, visiting the prison.

In 1913, after he had served seventeen years in Boston and Atlanta, these friends got him a parole, signed by President Taft. As he left the prison Bram declared to newsmen, "Brown accused me falsely. I do not know who committed the crime, but I hope to know some day. I know only that I did not do it. The aim of my life is to find the guilty man. I would be willing to suffer his punishment for him in order to clear my name. The first thing I am going to buy is a bunch of flowers, and I'm going to send them to Warden Moyer. He has been kind to me. Then I am going to get me a room and go into it by myself and have a good cry. I've got to have that cry before I can realize it's true. Then I want to pray a little. And after that I want work."

Tom Bram was now fifty years old and in vigorous health. Seventeen years of complete sobriety showed in their effect. He got work in Atlanta, and before long he was back at sea, sailing as a mate, working diligently and saving his money. He kept in touch with Warden Moyer and other friends, urging that freedom was not enough, and that the Government should now absolve him of the crime. The friends worked away, year after year, and in 1919 President Wilson signed a complete pardon of Thomas Mead Bram. This left a clear implication of guilt on the part of "Charles Brown." Under the United States Constitution nobody duly tried and acquitted of a crime can be "twice put in jeopardy of life or limb." But "Charles Brown" knew nothing of law —and he was still in the United States.

In a few more years Tom Bram was captain and chief owner of an old and somewhat leaky four-masted schooner named *Alvena,* carrying lumber to Florida from various ports in New England and the Canadian province of New Brunswick. In 1928, coast-guard vessels went to the aid of the *Alvena* in a storm off Cape Hatteras, and some newspapers noted that her captain, Tom Bram, was the man accused and convicted of the murders aboard the *Herbert Fuller.*

Bram made his home in Jacksonville, Florida, and registered

the *Alvena* there. In 1929 his name appeared in the newspapers again. The Federal Court in Boston was moving to a new building, and out of a musty vault in the old one came the famous trunk containing Tom Bram's clothes, including the trousers, drawers and shirt he had scoured in a bucket with Gold Dust.

In 1934 came another echo of the old crime. For many years the logbook of the *Herbert Fuller* was a souvenir in the possession of James Cotter, senior lawyer for the defense in the case. After his death it was sold to a Watertown antique dealer, who by chance had been a visitor in Halifax when the barkentine arrived there towing the bodies in the boat. The Boston *Herald*, in January 1934, ran a story on the old *cause célèbre*, with a description of the logbook and its faked entries and torn-out sheets.

Indeed, the horrid shadows from the cabin of the *Herbert Fuller* seemed to dog Tom Bram's footsteps for the rest of his life. Once, in Jacksonville, a couple of New England captains met him in the street and dragged up the story again. One of them shouted, "Now, Tom Bram, you know who killed those people. Why don't you admit it?" But Bram never admitted anything. In 1936 he sold the *Alvena* and withdrew to Atlanta, Georgia, where he set up business as a wholesale dealer in peanuts. He was still there in 1948, at the age of eighty-five, retired and alone. He died eventually in obscurity.

One day in 1919, the year in which Tom Bram received full pardon, his former defense counsel, Asa French, happened to be in Randolph, Maine. There in the street he met and recognized Justus Westerberg alias "Charles Brown," after all the years. But the man insisted to French that his name was "John Brown" and he did not know what French was talking about. He was then in his sixties, an inmate of the state poor farm at Randolph. Like Tom Bram he had kept his mouth shut on the *Fuller* murders. Still an enigma, he died in 1937 and was buried under the name of "John Brown" in the central cemetery at Randolph, a little over a hundred miles from Harrington, the birthplace of Captain Nash and of the *Herbert Fuller*.

The famous barkentine herself lived twenty-one years after the murders in her cabin. Part of that time she was commanded by Capt. E. L. Nash, a brother of Captain Charles. Superstition haunted her. Sailors whispered that on certain nights at sea several ghostly figures crept in and out of the after house, or engaged in a furious but silent chase about the after deck. Eventually new owners changed her name to *Margaret B. Rouss*, but she had no better luck with this than with her first one. On April 27, 1917, three weeks after the United States declared war on Germany, the old barkentine was on her way through the Mediterranean Sea toward Genoa. A German submarine surfaced and stopped her, ordered the crew into their boat, and sent a boarding party to scuttle the ship with explosives. Down she went, taking her ghosts with her. The crew reached shore safely at (of all places for lucky men) Monte Carlo.

What really happened aboard the *Herbert Fuller* that summer night in '96?

The answer lies in the character of Tom Bram. Under the rules of evidence, certain things that were known about him could not be admitted to the record. Other facts about him came to light later. Tom Bram had been in trouble in other ships before he ever saw the *Herbert Fuller*. In the ship *Twilight* he had stolen freight money belonging to its owners. He had done much the same in the ship *China* by selling a cargo of coconuts and disappearing with the money. In the barkentine *White Wings* he had conspired to kill the Captain and take over the ship, but a seaman denounced him and he was put ashore in Rio. In the schooner *Francis* he had conspired to mutiny and was thrown into jail at Kingston, Jamaica, where the Canadian skipper described him as "a bad, dangerous, man."

One of his fellow inmates of the Boston jail, Charles Avery of Natick, Massachusetts, afterwards revealed that Bram had talked to him about the murders. Bram said that Captain Nash intended to "break" him back to second mate and promote August Blamberg over his head; that he, Bram, was jealous of the friendship between young Monks and the Captain's wife; and that he, Tom Bram, had more brains and ability than any of these people.

Jonathan Spencer told how, one day at sea, he paused beside Bram and saw the first mate staring hard at Mrs. Nash and young Monks. They were on deck and chatting about Monks's studies. Bram had sneered, in an aside to Spencer, that Mrs. Nash was "just putting on airs—she was nothing but a factory girl before her marriage."

To Tom Bram, always conscious of his mulatto blood, always watchful for any slight or insult, all these people in the after house seemed to "put on airs." His troubles in other ships, and probably ashore in his role as cook in various restaurants, had given him a fixed attitude about the tint of his skin. He felt himself a man of superior abilities who was held back or slighted by people like Charles and Laura Nash. Aboard the *Herbert Fuller* he had driven the sailors hard to prove to the Captain how good a man he was, and he had tried to drive Second Mate Blamberg, but with no success. Captain Nash must have doubted the ability of the self-styled "Nova Scotian" mate as soon as the ship got to sea, for he consulted Blamberg's opinions rather than Bram's. Undoubtedly, in the chat about the meal table the Captain, his wife, the student, and the second mate must have shown a common interest from which in some way Tom Bram felt excluded.

With such matters to brood on, there was the whiskey in the jar for courage and reassurance. The faked entries in the logbook show that something began to develop on the day after sailing from Boston, and it must have been that Captain Nash reproved Bram for drinking on duty, surly behavior and incompetence— *and ordered him to write this reprimand in the log.* Keeping the log was the first mate's responsibility, but the book was subject to daily inspection by the Captain, and Bram would not dare to tamper with it while the Captain was alive.

Charles Nash was a sensible man, and a sensible captain does not bawl out one of his officers in the presence of his crew. Although the steward and "Charles Brown" noticed the Captain having what they called "words" with Bram, they did not know what those words were. In the slang of the time, "having words" with anyone meant a verbal quarrel of some sort. There must have been other, and probably harsher, exchanges in the privacy of the main cabin when the passenger and second mate were absent.

Such was the situation growing day by day in the after house, unknown to the passenger and the crew. By July 13, Tom Bram's temper was running out, and so was the Dutch courage in his jar. Something happened on that day to bring his fury to a peak. It may very well have been what the jailbird Avery said: that Captain Nash announced his intention of promoting August Blamberg over Tom Bram's head. When Bram went on watch at midnight he knew what he was going to do. For the next hour he nerved himself with strong drafts of whiskey, and each time he went below for a drink he looked about the main cabin to make sure that all his victims were asleep.

He would kill August Blamberg first, for he could not leave that powerful man alive beside his line of retreat through the fore companionway. Then the Captain, the student, and Mrs. Nash, in that order, leaving the woman for the last.

At some time between 1:30 and 2 A.M. he slipped below and took the ax from its cleats on the partition. Why the ax? Because it would be silent and sure, but more than that, the ax alone could satisfy his lust to shatter all those faces with their superior airs. There may have been a sexual aspect in his hatred of Laura Nash. He was a hot-blooded man and she was a comely woman. It irked him that she would chatter brightly to the weak bronchitic student but not to a strong burly fellow like himself. Also, she was her husband's natural confidant, and after the trouble be-

79

gan soon after sailing, she must have looked upon Bram with something of her husband's own contempt.

The first flaw in Bram's wild plan was the locked door to the student's room. With all three men dead in the after house, he might have raped Laura Nash to his heart's content before killing her. He could count on the helmsman's inability to leave the wheel, even if he suspected something wrong below. The only other man awake in the ship was the lookout Frank Loheac, posted on the fore house, out of sight and sound. But any attempt to force the student's door would have wakened him and probably Laura Nash as well. He had no choice but to slip past Monks's room and kill the woman where she lay. Under the savage but shrewd ax blows, the Captain and second mate had died almost without making a sound. There seemed no reason why he could not kill the woman just as silently. In this he failed. She screamed twice, terribly, before he finished chopping her to death.

Then came a desperate pause, listening at the partition of Monks's room, while Monks listened on the other side. Finally the sound of Monks opening his door into the chartroom, and the student calling "Captain Nash!" In that position Monks could not see the entrance to Mrs. Nash's room. For that matter, he could see little or nothing beyond the chartroom, where the skipper's body lay. It was easy for Tom Bram to slip across the main cabin and out by the fore companionway without being seen or heard. For all his size and muscular build, the first mate could move like a cat.

The reflection of light from the main cabin lamp outlined the doorway of the fore companion, and as he emerged Bram was visible for a moment to the helmsman, and to the lookout if he happened to glance aft—as he did. After that, Bram was a dark shape against the light boards of the deck cargo. He could be seen but not in detail—including the detail of an ax in his hand. He stepped toward the port side, intending to drop the ax overboard, but after two or three steps he heard the student running up the fore companionway. In Boston the first mate had watched the crew fasten the lashing planks to secure the deck cargo; it was part of his job, and he knew exactly where there was a space under one of those planks. The mate slid the ax under the plank, whirled about, and picked up a piece of wood as if to defend himself. He was play-acting now, and in his frenzied state he uttered the first lines that came into his head, trying to frighten Monks with a tale of mutiny led by the second mate.

It was a very bad lie. It would not hold for a minute after Blamberg's corpse was found. But there was the student with a revolver in his hand, and Tom Bram saw no course but to keep him bemused with one bogey tale after another. When he went below with Monks and took the cabin lamp to the bloody chart-room he had to risk the student seeing blood spots on his shirt and trousers. For there must have been some. The ax in his hands had thrown blood on the cabin ceiling at every upward swing, and some of that red rain must have touched him. However, Monks's own hands were bloody, and the frightful spectacle of the hacked corpse on the floor drew his whole attention. When Monks turned into his own cabin to put on some clothes, the obliging mate left the lamp with him and went to his own cabin "to get my revolver." While the student was putting on his clothes, the first mate was swiftly changing his own, and no doubt wiping his face and hands in case of blood spots there. He could not avoid close scrutiny by Monks and the others when morning came, and he had to prepare for that.

By leaving the lamp in Monks's room, he made sure of a concealing darkness in the alley, where the student must pass Blamberg's doorway at the foot of the fore companion. So Monks emerged on deck for the second time without seeing the second mate dead in his berth. And then, with the aftermath of the whiskey and that wild release of hate, Bram began to retch and weep and beg Monks to protect him from the crew, a maudlin spectacle. It was not until this wore off that he began to see a way out of the box he was in. That was to accuse the helmsman "Brown."

After that it was a case of two habitual liars accusing each other.

Bram was more glib and forceful than the feeble-witted Swede. Nevertheless, his lies were obvious; in fact, his whole behavior up to the moment of his arrest by Spencer and the crew was one long confession of guilt. His parole in 1913 meant simply that after seventeen years in prison he had paid his debt to society. But his pardon in 1919 made a mockery of justice.

One clue that was never followed up by the Boston authorities might have reflected some light on the murders aboard the *Herbert Fuller*. It was Tom Bram's statement to a Halifax newsman that he called himself a Nova Scotian because his mother had lived at Bridgewater, N.S., before her marriage to a "Dutchman."

In the last years of Queen Victoria, Bridgewater was a remote little sawmill town in western Nova Scotia, fifteen miles up the Lahave River from the coast. Ships loading lumber cargoes there had to be towed up and down the river by tugboat. The surrounding district had been settled in colonial times by German people —*Deutsche*—known locally as "Dutch."

Most of the timber from the Bridgewater mills went to the West Indies, and before sailing back to Nova Scotia most of the small windjammers engaged in this trade usually picked up a return cargo of sugar, molasses, rum and so on among the islands. In this process the island of St. Kitts was frequently a port of call. Yellow fever, the curse of white seamen in the Caribbean in those days, took a severe toll of sickness and death among the Nova Scotians in this trade, and when a man fell ill and went ashore to the hospital or the grave, it was customary to ship a West Indian seaman in his place. Evidently, Tom Bram was one who shipped in this manner. How else could he have known about the obscure little town up the Lahave River, and the presence of "Dutchmen" there?

Ships always had some delay at the Lahave mouth, waiting for the lone tug to arrive and tow them up, or awaiting a fair wind to put to sea on the way out. They anchored inside Kraut Point, close to the village of Riverport, and for seamen killing time it was an easy matter to row ashore for a stroll or a yarn with the "Dutchmen." Tom Bram was a man who liked to sit and yarn, and in passing the time in Riverport he was bound to hear the favorite local story. It concerned a brigantine called *Zero*, which was found abandoned off the Lahave mouth in 1865. Her crew had rowed ashore in a boat, saying that their captain had fallen overboard and drowned, and that the ship was leaking badly and sinking. A party of Lahave fishermen found her practically intact, brought her into the river mouth, and soon discovered that a clumsy attempt had been made to scuttle her by chopping holes in her sides. The *Zero's* crew had got away quickly from the scene, making their way along the coast by road and heading for the United States. A hue and cry rounded them up, and they were brought to trial at Halifax.

The trial revealed a case of mutiny, led by a masterful West Indian cook named Dowsey, with the collusion of the chief mate, Douglas. One morning between the hours of four and five, Dowsey had crept into the cabin where the Captain lay asleep, and smashed his skull with blows of an iron belaying pin. Then, with the aid of a seaman, he had dragged the unconscious but still breathing body to the deck and thrown it in the sea. The object of the plot was to take the ship to Mexico, sell it there, divide the money and disperse. However, the savage murder of the skipper frightened most of the crew, and they decided to scuttle the ship, row ashore, and make their way to the United States. All through the trial there was frequent mention of Dowsey's hypnotic black eyes and the combination of threats and glib persuasion that brought the crew under his power. And it was clear that, but for the fears of the seamen, Dowsey and his accomplice Douglas would have "got away with it."

The parallel of Tom Bram and the *Herbert Fuller* is impossible to miss.

For Bram there was no question of selling the ship and cargo. He could not afford the risk of awkward questions. Dowsey's attempt had been made just after the close of the American Civil War, when Confederate cruisers had set a pattern of captures and prizes and offhand sales all over the world. By 1896, however, nothing like that was possible. Apparently, Tom Bram's object was to scuttle or abandon the ship and its reeking boat in some lonely harbor toward the eastern tip of Nova Scotia. From there he could make his way by land or by some coasting vessel to Halifax, where he could change his name and sign on a foreign-going vessel that would take him far from any danger of arrest and punishment.

As things turned out, he was caught and imprisoned, but with the aid of his humanitarian friends and acquaintances he managed to save his neck and eventually get a complete pardon for his crimes.

The sequel of the *Zero* affair was very different. Dowsey was hanged, and Douglas died, a "lifer," in the Halifax penitentiary.

Grey Owl

He was the most romantic and the most successful impostor of his time. In figure he was tall and lean, with a jutting nose and a grey-blue gaze that could be bold and challenging, or shifty and furtive, or again as innocent as a child's. He was an obsessive liar, even in small matters where a lie had no purpose or advantage. He had a gift for his native English language, written or spoken, and with it he bamboozled hundreds of thousands of people, ranging from Canadian Army doctors to the King and Queen of England. And he got away with it to the very moment of his death.

The person who really started this career was of course his father, a wandering English ne'er-do-well named George Furmage Belaney. George's mother, Mrs. Julia Belaney, had a small income which supported her and her daughters Ada and Carrie in quiet comfort in the little English seaside town of Hastings: but it was not enough to support her spendthrift son George. In the early 1880s Mrs. Belaney wearied of the problem and of George. She bought him a one-way passage to America, and from that time he was on his own.

Nobody knows the course of George's wanderings in America, or what he did for a living, but one thing is certain. In the year 1887 he was in the sun-baked little town of Palatka, Florida, standing with a girl named Kitty Cox before a justice of the peace, and uttering the vows of marriage. She was only fourteen years old, a child of Florida's poor white "cracker" class, with little or no schooling. This ill-balanced union was recorded in the Palatka courthouse, where it came to light more than fifty years later.

In that same year, 1887, America's famous Col. William Cody ("Buffalo Bill") took his Wild West Show across the Atlantic for its first European tour. His troupe included genuine cowboys and plainsmen like himself, and he took along a few Apache Indians from New Mexico, where after a long war led by their chiefs Geronimo and Cochise, the tribe had just been subdued by United States troops. In that year, too, Britain celebrated with pomp and carnival the jubilee of Queen Victoria, fifty years on the throne. In the various kinds of entertainment offered to the British public, the show from the fabulous American West was new and fascinating—a smash success.

For the sake of seeing his old haunts again, George Belaney had got a job with the show as a roustabout, and he and Kitty traveled with the show to Europe. In June 1888, they turned up in Hastings. By that time Julia Belaney was dead, and her spinster daughters Ada and Carrie were living on their modest inheritance at 32 St. James Road. Naturally they invited George and his bride to stay with them awhile. During the next few weeks George entertained them with yarns of adventure in the Wild West, yarns undoubtedly borrowed from Buffalo Bill's troupe. Then he vanished, leaving Kitty nearly seven months pregnant in the care of his sisters. None of them ever saw or heard of George Belaney again.

On September 18, 1888, Kitty Cox Belaney gave birth to a boy in the little house on St. James Road. She was now fifteen. She cared little for the wandering scamp who had abandoned her, and nothing for his child. Three months after the boy's birth she vanished from Hastings as suddenly and utterly as George himself. She had no means of getting back to Florida even if she wished, which was doubtful. There were other men in England. Half a century later she was found still living there, according to herself a widow for the second time.

Ada and Carrie Belaney were too plain and shy ever to marry, and in a placid way they accepted the care of the child so callously dropped in their virgin laps. They named him Archibald Stansfield Belaney. As he passed from infancy to boyhood they told him that his father was in America, and related what they could remember of George Belaney's Wild West yarns.

Archie grew into a lanky teen-ager with dark hair, eyes grey in some lights but usually nearer to blue, a sallow face, and the nose of a Roman centurion—or a sachem of the Wild West. In his own world Hastings was just a dull hole on the Channel coast, sheltered by convenient hills, and for that reason a favorite watering place for Londoners in summer and the perennial home of many people like his aunts, living retired lives on little means. Hastings had prim public gardens and a promenade by the seashore called the Marine Parade, where in the season everybody strolled up and down. There were caves in the rolling hills behind the town where flint tools and weapons of a savage race had been found, and not far away was the famous hillside where the archers and horsemen of William the Conqueror had slain the English with sharp iron ones in 1066. These hills and dales offered a wandering ground for an imaginative youth, a "loner" by instinct, getting away from the boredom of school and the humdrum life of the town.

By the time he was fifteen, very tall for his age, his aunts faced the problem of their mother with George Belaney years before. Archie had got whatever education the town council school could give him, he was fast turning into a man, and Hastings had no industries whatever in which he could find a job or learn a trade. By nature he was moody and lazy, with spells of sudden wild energy. And he was a bland, instinctive liar like his father. The Belaney sisters knew little or nothing of the world, and when young Archie nagged them to pay his way to America they were ready to believe that he could make an easy, exciting living there just like his adventurous father. Archie passed his fifteenth birthday in September 1903. A few months later, in the spring of 1904, his aunts paid his passage across the Atlantic and gave him £5 for pocket money.

When they were asked about it many years later they had forgotten what passage they had bought for Archie. However, in their circumstances the Belaney sisters must have got the cheapest available, and in those days the shortest and cheapest passage to any point in North America was by small steamers of the Allan Line, running a service for frugal passengers and miscellaneous freight between Liverpool and Halifax, Nova Scotia. Most of the passengers were poor emigrants traveling at dirt-cheap rates in the steerage quarters, and probably that was the way Archie came across the sea.

Archie's life during his first two years in Canada is a matter for conjecture. According to one of the various yarns he spun afterwards, he worked a year as a clerk in a Toronto dry-goods store and then plunged into the northern woods heading for the silver strike at Cobalt. After his death a typed manuscript turned up in which Archie had written an account of a tenderfoot attracted to this silver boom and making his way there in the company of two white woodsmen named Hood and Campbell and a pair of Ojibwa Indians. On its face the tale seemed a bit of autobiography; but like so much that Archie said and wrote about himself, it probably was fiction larded with hearsay and some random experiences of his own. Silver was discovered at Cobalt in 1903, a year before Archie left England. The first positive date of his appearance in northern Ontario is 1906.

The dialogue in the story of "Hood" and "Campbell" and "the tenderfoot" is mostly slang, with a humorous twist of phrase suspiciously like that of American writer O. Henry, who flourished between 1903 and 1910, and whose tales were read and imitated everywhere in North America. Archie must have seen some of O. Henry's stories in magazines left in sporting camps and bush hotels by American anglers and hunters. The talk in his "tenderfoot" story has too much of the slick O. Henry style and vocabulary to be mere coincidence. In some part the tale may describe Archie's first journey in the north woods after passing through Toronto, but it offers no clue to the rest of the time between the early spring of 1904, when he sailed from England, and the summer of 1906, when he turned up at William Guppy's sporting camp at Lake Temiskaming. No one who knew Archie Belaney could believe that he spent a year or more selling corsets, stockings, "yard goods" and suchlike staples of the dry-goods trade in Toronto. Until his metamorphosis twenty-five years later in the fancy costume of "Grey Owl," Archie was slovenly in dress and habit, and he had neither the punctuality nor the temperament to hold down a job in a city store for even a week.

Where, then, did he spend those first two years?

It is now known that of the thirty-one years Archie actually lived in Canada he spent less than half with his self-styled "blood brothers" the Ojibwas, or even in Ojibwa country. The rest of that time he was among other Indians, including the Micmacs, whose habitat was the Atlantic littoral of Canada from the mouth of the St. Lawrence River to the southwest tip of Nova Scotia. In his stories, written or oral, he preferred to identify himself with his chosen "brothers" the Ojibwas of northern Ontario. He rarely mentioned the other Indian peoples of his acquaintance.

Yet it is known that he lived in the Micmac country in Gaspé and about Lake Temiscouata at the source of the St. John River. On one of his Canadian Army forms he wrote that his next of kin was John McVail (or McVaul, McVarn, or possibly McNeil—the handwriting is indistinct), whose address was clearly written as Westfield, New Brunswick, which is about fifteen miles from the mouth of the St. John. Also, he enlisted at Digby in Nova Scotia, and he mentioned to the doctor who examined him for army service that he was living in a Micmac camp at Bear River, ten miles away.

So Archie was familiar with the Micmacs through their whole

range. If he came to Halifax in 1904, as he must have done, he stepped ashore at the old Deep Water Terminal, where the Allan liners docked. From there it was just a short walk to the open-air "Green Market" of those days, held twice a week in a quadrangle of streets about the Halifax Post Office. Farmers from roundabout Halifax and Dartmouth came there to sell their produce, and among them squatted a group of Micmacs selling bunches of Mayflowers, baskets, toy bows and arrows, toy bark canoes, and the like. The Indian men wore the common clothing of white laborers, and their women wore cast-off dresses, shoes, hats and coats they had begged at the back doors of Dartmouth, where they lived.

The chances are that Archie made that short walk from the ship's side to mail a postcard to his aunts, announcing his safe arrival, and that he found the "Green Market" in session, with hucksters grouped about the Post Office doors. The Indians were unmistakable by the stuff they proffered for sale and by their long hair, plaited in twin pigtails. With £5 to prove that he was solvent, indeed rich to these people, it would not take him long to strike up an acquaintance, and at the day's end to board the ferry and cross over the harbor with them. They lived behind the little town of Dartmouth in a cluster of flimsy shacks and wigwams which were pitched by the shore of Banook Lake, the beginning of a canoe route to the interior.

As a tribe the Micmacs were a scattered people, living in small groups outside country towns, on the edge of the woods, where they could hunt and fish as they liked, and where they could earn cash as guides to sportsmen. Of old habit they were inclined to wander, and young Micmac men and women thought nothing of traveling for a year or two about Nova Scotia, Prince Edward Island, New Brunswick or the Gaspé peninsula, stopping here and there with small bands of their people. Hospitality was a right, extended to any wanderer, Indian or half-breed. All he had to say was the Micmac greeting, "Kway Needup!"

It seems most likely that in the first two years after he landed in Canada, a delighted and bemused young Archie Belaney was

90

drifting through the Micmac country from Halifax to the St. Lawrence, shacking up for the winter with some congenial family, and moving on again in the spring. After a time he may have heard of a rich silver strike in Ontario and turned his feet in that direction. Ignoring white folk, and passing out of the Micmac habitat in Gaspé, he would find hospitality among the Malecites on the shore of the St. Lawrence, then the Caughnawagas at Montreal, and finally the Iroquois and Ojibwas of Ontario.

If he was attracted by the Cobalt boom, there is no evidence whatever that he worked there. Indeed, Archie never really worked anywhere, except on compulsory fatigues in the army. Like his father, he had a strong distaste for work in the sense of a steady job, of labor to be done day after day, year after year. Archie was charmed with the Indians' way of life, in which women did all the work about the camp and the men enjoyed indolence, with occasional necessary spells of hunting and fishing, and trapping fur to get money for tobacco and ammunition and, whenever possible, firewater.

Archie was many miles short of Cobalt when he arrived at Temiskaming on the Ottawa River in 1906. He took a job there as a canoeman with Bill Guppy, and when Bill moved off to build a small hotel for sportsmen at Temagami, Archie went along with him. By this time the youth from Hastings was eighteen years old, stood over six feet, and was an adept trapper and canoeman. He had let his hair grow down to his shoulders, but he made no attempt to pass himself off as an Indian or even a half-breed. Much living outdoors had tanned his face and emphasized the lightness of his eyes, and he spoke with what any Canadian, regardless of fine distinctions, would have called a "Cockney" accent. He gave his name correctly as Archie Belaney. He told Guppy that he had spent some time in England, and had ventured into the north woods from Toronto.

The first winters at Temiskaming he spent in trapping, and sometimes he got paid for carrying mail by dog sled between Temiskaming and Temagami, a village about thirty miles north-

91

ward. He spent four years in this way, offering his services as a guide to Guppy's customers in the summer season. His winter journeys between Temiskaming and Temagami took him over the ice of Lake Temagami, passing Bear Island, where a band of Ojibwas lived. One of them was a young girl named Angele Uguna. Eventually she became his wife.

The accounts of their wedding vary. Many years afterwards Miss Maud Leopold, who had been a desk clerk in the Temagami Hotel in 1908, told it in this fashion. One summer day she heard a lot of shouting on the lake. She and others ran out to find the cause and saw Archie Belaney paddling madly in a canoe, with half a dozen Ojibwa canoes in hot pursuit. In one of the Ojibwa canoes sat Angele Uguna. A lone canoeman, however strong and skilled, cannot outrun a canoe paddled by two, even with a good start. Archie was overtaken near the hotel and forced ashore. Soon afterwards a local justice of the peace married Archie and Angele in his office, with the grim Ojibwas waiting outside.

According to Mrs. Arnold Leishman of Temagami, Archie and Angele were married by an American preacher who happened to be summering at Bear Island, and the ceremony took place in the wooden hut of the provincial forest rangers there. The date was 1908, and their first child was born in 1909.

Whatever the circumstances, this was Archie Belaney's first and only legal marriage. He was twenty and his bride was in her teens, and this was the only ceremony with authentic witnesses linking Archie in any way whatever with the Ojibwa people. His long subsequent tale of formal entry into the tribe as a "blood brother" was one of Archie's many fabrications, the root of his legend and the beginning of his repertoire.

A few years before Archibald Belaney was born, the rugged wilderness between the Great Lakes and Hudson Bay was threaded by the steel line of the Canadian Pacific Railway. Just before he landed in Canada the Ontario Government began to build the Temiskaming & Northern Ontario Line, thrusting up into the wilderness. Its object was to connect with the newly promoted National Transcontinental Railway, whose track lay far to the north of the C.P.R. Construction work on the T. & N.O. revealed the silver at Cobalt, and later gave access to other rich mineral finds in the north.

The presence of these railways, running through a landscape seamed with rivers flowing either to the Great Lakes or Hudson Bay, offered a marvelous new facility for prospectors, trappers and wanderers. They could travel by train for hundreds of miles, get off at any of the whistle-stop stations popping up like mushrooms by the railway lines, and explore virgin waterways and trapping grounds and mineral sites.

Archie did not stay very long at Bear Island in the role of husband and father. In 1910 he slipped away and took the T. & N.O. train south to its junction with the C.P.R. at North Bay. Thence he traveled northwestward by C.P.R. to the little bush hamlet of Biscotasing ("Bisco" to white bushmen), a supply base for trappers, hunters and prospectors.

In Archie's words: "It was not much of a town. It had no sidewalks and no roads, and consisted mainly of a Hudson Bay store, a sawmill, probably fifty houses scattered on a rocky hillside, and an Indian encampment in a sheltered bay of Biscotasing Lake. It was a rather noted little place, being within measurable distance of the headwaters of a number of turbulent rivers such as the Spanish, the White, the Mississauga and others . . . the gateway to a maze of water routes that stretch southward to lakes Huron and Superior, and northward to the Arctic Ocean. The fame of its canoemen was widely known."

South and west of Bisco stretched wild land in an enormous government reserve called the Mississagi Provincial Forest. It was a hunter's or an angler's dream. Therefore at Bisco Archie built or acquired a cabin, got a canoe from the local Indians, and set himself up as a trapper and hunting guide. One of his clients was a Toronto businessman named Frank Coryell, who in 1913 set out for a hunting trip in the region of the Mississagi Forest. He got off the train at Bisco, where the Hudson Bay agent provided him with tent, supplies, canoe and guide. The guide was Archie Belaney.

As Coryell wrote afterwards: "He was a prolific storyteller and entertainer—fighting Yaqui Indians in New Mexico, his father's violent death as a member of the Texas Rangers, etc. At that time he was frankly a white man, although he could talk to the Ojibwas in their language. We paddled down Ramsay Lake and up the Spanish River, the main idea being to get a moose or two. Archie failed to show even one. As a guide and cook he was just a good canoeman. He was a lousy cook. That winter Archie called on me at my place of business in Toronto and had lunch with us. Years later I went to the Book Fair in the King Edward Hotel in Toronto, a publishers' show, and saw "Grey Owl" stalking around in buckskins and braided pigtails. I thought him pretty theatrical but of course did not connect him with Archie Belaney."

Archie never returned to Angele and her children. Throughout his adult life he indulged a lust for women along with a thirst for alcohol and a mania for romantic falsehood. No doubt these foibles got him into trouble at Bisco as they had at Temagami, for in 1914 Archie bolted again. This time he left the north country altogether and went all the way back to the Atlantic Coast, where his odyssey had begun.

The First World War broke out that summer and Canada sent overseas an expeditionary force. If Archie had any immediate urge to enlist, he could have done so at Toronto or Montreal or almost anywhere on his way to the Atlantic Coast. Instead, he passed on down the long valley of the St. John River, crossed over the Bay of Fundy by the ferry steamer to Digby, N.S., and made his way to a shack at Bear River. On his way down the St. John he may have met the mysterious John McVail—McVaul —McVarn—McNeil who subsequently appeared in a scrawl as his next of kin on one of his army papers.

Some distance up Bear River from the white village of that

name a cluster of Micmac shanties lay in the woods. A casual traveler on the highway would never suspect its existence. In his long flight from Bisco, well over a thousand miles by rail and foot and canoe, Archie came exactly to that spot. So he must have known it before, in those vague two years after he first set foot in Canada.

During the winter of 1914, shacked up at Bear River, he made up his mind to enlist for war service. Perhaps under all his shallow pretenses, his indolence, his loathing of all discipline and authority, lay a dim but rooted love of England that made him offer himself. More likely he itched to get back to England for a time, to see his aunts in the old home at 32 St. James Road, to boast of real or imaginary adventures in the Canadian wilds, and elsewhere to indulge his appetites in the flesh of English women and the spirit of English pubs.

Whatever it was, when the snow had gone and the sun was warm in May 1915, a tall lean man about twenty-seven years old, wearing the rough clothes of a woodsman, with long hair brushing the shoulders of his jacket, set out for the little town of Digby, ten miles away. The estuary of Bear River was a beautiful fiord in which the Fundy tides ebbed and flowed for a distance of four miles, and the road toward Digby gave lofty views over the water and the farms and cherry orchards for which the place was noted.

Digby was the nearest recruiting post of the Canadian Army, and in May 1915 the officer in charge of the post was busy picking up men for a new regiment, the 40th Canadian Infantry Battalion, then being raised in Nova Scotia for war service. The regimental headquarters was at Aldershot Camp, eighty miles up the Annapolis Valley from Digby. However, in the scurry of raising an army everything was scarce, from shelter to boots and equipment, and for the time being all recruits were held at their local stations like Digby, with makeshift board and lodging, and hours of foot drill to pass the time of day. One of the recruits was a young farmer named James McKinnon, from Smith's

95

Cove near the mouth of Bear River. He survived the war and never forgot those early days of his army experience.

"In March 1915 I went in to Digby and enlisted in the Canadian Army. Doctor Duvernet of Digby examined me for army service. Captain Earl Phinney of the 40th Battalion was in charge of the recruits. He had a small office in the Digby courthouse and every day he drilled us on the courthouse grounds. There were no barracks. Phinney placed his recruits in small wooden hotels and boardinghouses that catered to the summer tourist trade. I myself was quartered with several other fellows in the old Winchester Hotel—long gone now. At first we were dressed in old militia uniforms of blue serge, with blue puttees. In May we got new khaki uniforms, and flat-topped caps with the new brass badge of the 40th Battalion. Towards the end of May we moved by train up the valley to join the main body at Aldershot Camp.

"Shortly before we left Digby I heard some of the fellows laughing at a new recruit, and I took a look at him. He was about my age, twenty-five, or maybe a year or two older. He was tall and wiry-looking, with a brown face and light eyes. But what caught everybody's attention was his hair. It hung right down to his shoulders, and all the fellows laughed. They said his first army order would be to get his hair cut. And so it was.

"The next day his hair was clipped as short as ours. He said his name was Archie Belaney and he had been 'out West.' He had a revolver and he liked to show the fellows how good he was with it. He would get them to chuck sticks and cans up in the air, and he would shoot and hit them pretty well every time. Eventually we were all drafted to other regiments, so I never got to know any more about Archie Belaney. After Aldershot I never saw him again."

Another who remembered Archie Belaney at Digby was the man who examined him for army service, Doctor Duvernet. Long afterwards, when Belaney's imposture was revealed by Canadian newspapers, Duvernet told of his enlistment, the first authentic detail of his long and bold deception.

Archie signed up on May 6, 1915, giving the date of his birth correctly but the place of birth as Montreal. In filling out his Attestation Paper he wrote the word "brother" on the line for next of kin, and then scratched it out with a stroke of the pencil, leaving nothing. On the same paper he wrote that he had previous military experience in "Mexican Scouts and 28th Dragoons."

Duvernet's clerk jotted down these particulars: "Apparent age: 27 years 9 months. Distinctive marks: slight scar left side. Height: 6 feet 1 inch. Chest girth: 36 inches. Expansion: 2 inches. Complexion: light. Hair: light. Eyes: grey."

Actually, Belaney's hair was dark brown, and in later years he was said to have used a black dye. His eyes were grey-blue, usually more blue than grey. His true age was a few months short of twenty-seven. Recruits were pouring in from all the countryside about Digby, and no doubt the amateur military clerk was in a hurry.

Archie did not stay long at Aldershot Camp, which then was a sandy clearing in pine woods near Kentville, N.S., nothing like the famous English camp of the same name. Like many another Canadian battalion raised urgently in those early years of the war, the 40th was fated never to reach France as a unit. It got as far as England, and then melted away in drafts to battle-worn regiments on the Western Front. Indeed, the first draft was taken while the utterly raw 40th was getting its basic training at Aldershot, N.S. One of the drafted men, picked undoubtedly for his boasted "previous military service," was Pvt. Archibald Belaney, who was promptly promoted to lance-corporal. A short run by train took the draft to the bustling port of Halifax, and on June 15, 1915, Archie sailed for England aboard the transport *Caledonia*.

He had been just forty days a soldier.

On June 24 the ship arrived at Devonport, England, and in his characteristic fashion Archie promptly vanished. He did not turn up again until August 11, when he reported for duty with the 23rd Canadian Reserve Battalion at Shorncliff Camp, near Dover. For absence without leave his lance-corporal's stripe was taken away, and within a few days, as a buck private, Archie was sent over the Channel to join a front-line regiment. It was the 13th Canadian Battalion, a unit of the Royal Highlanders of Canada, nowadays known as the Canadian Black Watch.

Thus the moody lad from Sussex, the greenhorn trapper of the north woods, the "lousy cook" of the sportsmen, the veteran of service in those mysterious forces the "Mexican Scouts and 28th Dragoons," found himself an actual warrior at last in the kilt and balmoral of the Canadian Scots.

The 13th Battalion had lost heavily in a savage battle at Ypres in April, and later in bloody bombardments at Festubert and Givenchy. Now it was refilling its ranks with drafts from Canadian reserve battalions in England, and training these new bodies on a quiet sector of the front just below the notorious Ypres salient. In this position there were occasional casualties from German shells or snipers, but when the autumn came the main wastage was in sick. The dreary fall rains of Flanders poured into every hole and trench, and in the low-lying region of Ploegsteerte ("Plug Street") Wood, where the 13th were, the soggy conditions produced a lot of influenza, rheumatism and "trench feet." Few of these cases were serious, and nearly all were treated at field ambulance stations just behind the line.

In the Canadian wilds Archie Belaney had learned to live in the Indian fashion with scant shelter and a certain fortitude; but the ceaseless wet and mud of Flanders in fall and winter were like nothing in the Canadian north. Worse than the weather for a man of Archie's indolence were the army "fatigues," especially carrying rations and ammunition up to the front line at night.

On December 12, 1915, Pvt. A. Belaney reported himself sick with influenza, and he was sent to No. 3 Canadian Field Ambulance, in the immediate rear. He complained of abdominal pains at the same time, for a medical officer scribbled "appendix?" on the Casualty Form. However, Archie had nothing worse than a bad cold and he was "discharged to duty" on December 20. He did not turn up for duty until the day after Christmas.

He was a member of B Company's sixth platoon, and his platoon commander, Lt. W. E. Macfarlane of Montreal, well remembered him afterwards.

"He was quite striking looking, with well-chiseled rather aesthetic features. He had certain Indian characteristics . . . and rather took pride in his Indian origin. Like most drafts at that time his military training was rather sketchy, but Belaney was good material and I took more than usual interest in him. He was, however, strangely reticent, and it was with some difficulty that I could judge his capabilities. It took a direct order to get his hair cut to regimental standard. He held himself aloof, even from his comrades, but was not disliked or unpopular. He was just a lone-wolf type.

"He had a considerable knowledge of fieldcraft, and was a good though not a remarkable shot. I made Belaney a sniper-observer. He had infinite patience and the gift of absolute immobility for long periods. His reports as an observer were short, to the point, and intelligent. Unlike many snipers he did not make exaggerated claims of 'kills.' Belaney was a dependable if not an outstanding soldier, and I have often wished that I had had him longer under my command, to see if I could really have got 'inside' him. I never felt that I did, although I think he opened up to me more than to anyone else. I was injured by shellfire on April 19, 1916, and never saw Belaney again."

One of Belaney's fellow sniper-observers, Pvt. Albert Chandler, lived after the war at Melfort, Saskatchewan. He recalled: "I drafted to the 13th Battalion and spent a year in the trenches as a sniper. We always worked in pairs, with rifles and telescopes. My partner was a fellow named Ellison. We seldom shot from the front line because it might draw fire from the Germans. We built our sniping posts mostly in the communication trenches. Then, if spotted, the fire would be away from our own men.

"I remember Archie Belaney very well. His partner was a short French fellow, a *métis* (half-breed) I am sure. I remember an incident. Belaney and his partner had a dugout next to ours at Messines, a trench called Well Walk. There was a farmhouse about fifty yards in front, in no man's land. Belaney and I crawled on our bellies to this shelled house just to see what we could find. We came back with a lot of vegetables. Ellison and I made some soup, and so did Belaney and the Frenchman. Not long after, they were sick. They said the Germans had poisoned the vegetables. Ellison and I weren't sick, so we investigated. The Frenchman liked a lot of pepper in the soup, and in the poor light of the dugout he had used a can of Keating's Louse Powder by mistake. Luckily they both vomited a lot. The four of us were together a lot in the trenches, but out of the trenches Ellison and I did not associate with them. They drank firewater, as they called it, and then acted like half-crazy *métis*."

On January 18, 1916, Pvt. Archibald Belaney reported a gunshot wound in his left wrist. It was slight and was marked "accidental" in the casualty list. It happened when the battalion was in a reserve position and preparing to move up to the front line the next day. Apparently the medical officer bandaged the wound and considered Belaney fit for duty, for he went to the front with the others. Ten days later, when the battalion came out of the line, Belaney reported at No. 1 Canadian Field Ambulance for treatment of this wound. He remained there a week and was again "discharged to duty."

The Flanders winter was trying to all troops, friend and foe, and life in the sodden trenches was a miserable existence. Like other Canadian units the 13th Battalion spent a regular round —so many days in reserve trenches, so many days in the front line, and so many at rest in camps or villages in the rear area. Sometimes the 13th relieved another Canadian battalion in this round. Sometimes it relieved British units, and one of them was the Royal Sussex Regiment. In view of Private Belaney's origin, the men of Sussex must have interested him in passing, for some were bound to be from Hastings.

The trench positions of Archie's regiment had such names as Souvenir Farm, Scurry Lane, Well Walk, Gabion Farm, Lover's Lane, New Year Trench, and Gordon Post. There were reserve positions known as Larchwood Dugouts and Railway Dugouts. When they came out of the line for a rest they marched back to billets or hut camps at Bailleul, Meteren or Dickebusch, and to the luxury of shower baths at Poperinghe.

Belaney's enterprising platoon commander, Lieutenant Macfarlane, was soon given a new and livelier duty. "During the winter of 1915 until about mid-March 1916, the 13th were in the Messines-Ploegsteerte Wood sector, where no man's land was from a quarter to half a mile in width. When we first went there the Germans were quite cock-a-hoop and raided several listening posts. I was given the job of stopping this, and had a free hand in organizing a scout section, quite distinct from the sniper-observer people I have already mentioned. (I did NOT select Belaney!) I was completely detached from company and platoon duties, so I recall nothing of the accidental wound to Belaney."

Macfarlane and his patrols had several clashes with the Germans in no man's land during the early months of 1916. Apart from these affairs there was no actual fighting, but in the course of trench duty there were daily casualties from German snipers or shellfire. Each day the officer writing the battalion's official diary noted the casualties by name and regimental number, and the exact nature of the injury—"shell fragment," "bullet in head," and so on.

In this second winter of the war (the first for the Canadians in the battle zone) the morale of the men in general was high, and among so many raw troops a wound marked "accidental" was probably just that. The wound deliberately self-inflicted, made by men of poor moral fiber to get themselves out of all this unending danger and hardship, began to appear in the spring of 1916. As the war dragged on, the "S.I.W." became more frequent, and medical officers regarded with sharp suspicion any wound that might have been contrived.

It was noted that the self-inflicted wound was usually in the hand or foot, and in a position where it would injure only the trigger finger or the lesser toes. To avoid telltale cordite burns, the more artful dodgers put an empty bully-beef tin over the rifle muzzle and shot the bullet through it. A shot in the hand required much contrivance with the trigger. It was much easier to shoot through the foot, preferably just behind the small toes, where the injury would prevent a man from marching to war, but not from walking fairly well when the war was over.

His appointment as a sniper-observer took Archie out of the front line from March 17 until April 14, while he and others took a special course in the rear. He came back to the battalion at an unfortunate time. It was still posted in trenches dominated by German artillery on Messines Ridge, and now, after long bestowing their chief attention and fire on the British trenches of the Ypres salient, the Germans had decided to deliver a "hate" on the Canadians to the south of it.

On April 18, 1916, a sudden concentration of shells fell on the trenches of the 13th Battalion, and the bombardment continued with great violence all through that night and the following day. Lieutenant Macfarlane, wounded and almost buried by a shell, was one of many casualties. He was one of the original officers of the battalion, a survivor of the terrific battle at Ypres and the heavy shellstorms at Festubert and Givenchy. However, for some of his company this was the first experience of heavy and accurate bombardment lasting day and night, a frightening ordeal for any man. One of these was Archie Belaney.

On April 23, the battered battalion was relieved and marched to the tune of drums and bagpipes to a hut camp at Dickebusch, a small Belgian hamlet southwest of Ypres. It was about three and a half miles from the nearest German trenches, beyond reach of rifle and machine-gun fire, but within the range of random shells from the German heavy artillery.

On the next day (April 24) the battalion's war diarist wrote: "Weather bright and fine. Being the first day out of the trenches, the greater part of the day was devoted to cleaning equipment, clothing, etc. and resting. Officers commanding companies were instructed to pay particular attention to the condition of the men's feet after their tour of the trenches." He then recorded the day's casualties: three sick, one dead, one wounded. The wounded man was Pvt. A. Belaney. According to his Medical Case Sheet, he was "struck by a bullet which perforated right foot near its external border." Later examination by X-ray showed that the bullet had damaged the bones at the base of the little toe and the toe adjoining.

The regimental diarist wrote no explanation of this wound. The camp was out of range of German bullets in the accepted meaning of the word. A shell fragment was something else, and the diary said nothing of shellfire on that day, the day before, or the day after. Lieutenant Macfarlane, suffering from his own injuries sustained in the front line, knew nothing of Belaney's wound. Writing long afterwards, he took a charitable view of it:

"When in reserve at Dickebusche Huts (usually for eight days) the battalion supplied carrying and working parties to the forward trenches every night. Tracks, roads, etc. were well known to the Bosches, and the mud confined us to these routes. They were covered by fixed rifle and machine-gun fire. I shall be surprised if the war diary does not show a number of gunshot wound casualties when the battalion was supposed to be "resting" at Dickebusche. However, I was excused ordinary duties while having my wounds attended to, so I am naturally vague about what happened to whom."

Whatever the manner of his wound, Archie Belaney was out of the war for a time at least. He was conveyed to a Canadian general hospital at Boulogne and thence over the Channel to England. A surgeon performed an operation to adjust the damage to his toes. It was not a difficult operation, and it began to look as if a month or two in hospital would make Pvt. A. Belaney fit for war again. Archie soon made an additional complaint to the doctors—"defective eyesight owing to previous attacks of snow blindness." So as Archie's wound began to heal, his eyes had to be fitted with glasses. This was the man whose sight had so impressed Lieutenant Macfarlane in the trenches, and who, only a few weeks ago, had passed a rigorous course for sniper-observers.

On June 28, 1916, a hospital report on Belaney concluded: "Has been up and about for the last six weeks. Wound healed. Fracture united. Glasses suitable. Walks with a slight limp. Requires no further treatment."

Discharge to duty loomed before Archie again. Not to the fighting line, of course, what with his bad sight and the limp, but still to some rear echelon with the army's irksome restraints and discipline, its choredom and boredom, going on for the duration of the war.

Suddenly he began to complain of agony in his wounded foot. Whenever he walked he hobbled terribly, taking the weight on the inner side of the foot from heel to big toe, and curling the outer side until it seemed deformed. Puzzled surgeons made another slight operation on the small toe bones but it made no difference. The X-rays said one thing, Archie said quite another and suited his actions to the word. The doctors shifted their problem from one convalescent hospital to another, all over southern England. This medical form of the old army game called passing the buck went on for almost a year. To mention only three passes: In the summer of 1916 Archie was sent to a Canadian convalescent hospital at Bromley; in September he was transferred to another at Woodcote Park, Epsom; and on February 24, 1917, probably at his own request, he went to a Canadian military hospital at Hastings. Thus he came back to the scene of his birth and of the first fifteen years of his life.

During this long game of hospital shuttlecock in England, Archie managed to get away frequently for a few days or a week as a convalescent needing outside interests. One of these interests proved to be another "wife." On an army form filled out in this period he named his next of kin as "Mrs. Ivy Belaney," giving an address in the Bayswater district of London. Later he changed the address to one in Hastings—not the address of his aunts.

In Flanders he had chosen a French-Indian *métis* for his sole companion, and he had given Lieutenant Macfarlane and others to believe that he was a half-breed himself; but in these hospital days, with the tan bleached from his face, with his hair clipped short in the hospital routine, Archie looked very much the white man that he was. As "Mrs. Ivy Belaney" moved from London to Hastings and undoubtedly met his aunts, he could not have posed as a half-breed to her or anyone else, and apparently he did not try.

During the spring and summer of 1917 the Canadian troops were fighting hard at Vimy Ridge, among the coal mines and slag dumps of Lens, and along the Scarpe River. It was trench warfare at its worst, and wounded men poured into the Canadian hospitals in England. At the summer's end another bloody prospect loomed before the Canadian Corps. It was sure to be drawn into Field Marshal Haig's blind and stubborn battle to break out of the Ypres salient—the bitter autumn road to Passchendaele. To make room for a new flood of wounded, the Canadian hospitals in England were ordered to clear out all hopeless or baffling cases and send them back to Canada.

One of the baffling cases was, of course, Pvt. A. Belaney. In March the X-ray technicians of the Canadian hospital at Hastings had examined him again, and once more reported: "Fracture of the fifth metatarsal seems well united and unlikely to cause further trouble." And again Archie refuted the medicos with a continued hobbling and complaint of pain. Finally he won, or rather the approaching shadow of Ypres won for him. Three army doctors signed a form stating that his injury was incurable, that his foot was in fact "deformed," and that he would have a 20 percent disability in earning a living as a "laborer."

So Archie was packed off to Canada for final therapy and discharge. On September 19, 1917, he sailed from Liverpool for Halifax, N.S., retracing his old track of 1904. In all ways he was lucky. His hospital ship, the *Llandovery Castle*, was torpedoed and sunk with most of her crew and staff in the following year.

Although he had enlisted in Nova Scotia, he asked for discharge at Toronto, and he traveled there by hospital train from Halifax. On November 30, 1917, he got his release from the army at last. It was a triumph. He had loathed the army from the hour of his enlistment, when the recruits at Digby laughed at his long hair, and he rarely spoke of his service afterwards except

105

to claim favor or notice for himself as a wounded veteran of the war. The military clerk who scribbled Archie's discharge certificate took Pvt. A. Belaney entirely at his own word, writing that he was a "teetotaler" and that his military character was "very good." So the artful dodger of the 13th Battalion emerged from army service with a well-mended foot, a clean sheet in the record, and a pension of $20 per month.

Up to the time of his discharge, about two thirds of his pay had been assigned to his "wife" Ivy in England. That of course ceased with his army service. He stayed the winter in Toronto, receiving foot therapy as an outpatient of Christie Street Hospital. He soon banished "Mrs. Ivy" from his thoughts. On January 6, 1918, he made out a new pension form stating that he was single, and that his next of kin was someone named Louis Legacie of Biscotasing, Ontario. About four months later a pensions clerk wrote on Belaney's active-service casualty form the words "marriage approved." Apparently Archie got himself another "wife" during the spring months of 1918. Whoever she was, her name was not shown and she drifted off into the shadows of Archie's amatory history, which unlike his military history left no documents.

In the early summer of 1918, when the Canadian Corps was preparing its all-out attack at Amiens, the beginning of the war's end, Archie threw off the dust of Toronto and left for his old stamping ground at Bisco. He threw off his limp and the eyeglasses at the same time. After that he walked the woods with ease, and later the streets and lecture platforms of great cities, where newsmen never failed to remark his "long loping stride." His superb eyesight enabled him to recognize afar the creatures of the wild, and when he came to the lecture platform he could read his notes, in ordinary type, at any distance up to an arm's length from his face.

Since his sudden departure from Bisco in 1914, the war had made great changes in the life of the north country. Many of its most adventurous trappers and prospectors had gone overseas with the Canadian Army, and a migration of draftdodgers and other furtive characters from the towns had drifted into their cabins, hiding from the law, and for easy money raiding the trap lines of the Indians.

For the next seven years Archie roved about, sometimes with sportsmen, sometimes with one or two Ojibwas or *métis,* sometimes alone. Bisco was his base. One man who met him there in 1918 found him loafing about, boasting of his prowess as a canoeman, as a hunter, as a trapper, and as a buck among the squaws. Everyone in Bisco regarded him as a backwoods Munchausen and believed not half he said. It was noted that he never boasted of his service in the army.

When he got money for a good catch of fur he traveled to various towns along the railway for a spree. Afterwards there were picaresque tales of these adventures, some told by himself, some by eyewitnesses. One item appeared in many. In his rages, real or faked—and Archie could fake a dramatic rage at the drop of a hat—he had a habit of hurling a hunting knife which had a six-inch blade and was carried in a handy sheath at his belt. At twenty feet he could stab a spot the size of a fingernail. It was a trick he had practiced in idle hours for years. Done in earnest, it could kill or maim, and it may account for some of his quick departures and far flights in Canada. But usually these episodes were faked. He enjoyed frightening men of small courage, even in casual encounters in hotel foyers during his romantic masquerade in Britain and the United States later on. In all these affairs the observers noticed that the knife always missed the human target but stuck in the woodwork close by.

Eventually his postwar wanderings in the north bush took Archie back to the scene of his marriage to Angele Uguna, fifteen years after he deserted her. In the migratory way of her people it was probable that she had left the place long since. Archie felt safe to venture there for a look, at any rate.

In May 1925, he boarded the little steamer *Temagami Belle* for a voyage up the familiar lake, and on deck among the passengers heading north for the season he noticed a young Indian girl who caught his fancy at once. She was of Mohawk blood, from Mattawa on the Ottawa River, and she was on her way to a summer job as waitress in a Temagami hotel. She wore sensible khaki breeches, shirt and boots for the journey, but like the other girls at Mattawa she liked to "doll up" when she could, and in her suitcase she had attractive dresses and sheer stockings and high-heeled shoes.

It did not take Archie long to engage her in chat. He was thirty-seven, as tall and lean as ever, and as glib. She was a small creature in her teens, naive, flattered by the attentions of this handsome stranger with the bronzed face, the bold nose, the dangling black hair and intimate grey-blue eyes. She told him her name, Gertrude Anahareo, and added, smiling, that her friends sometimes called her Pony. And indeed she was like a charming little mare, tossing her mane and regarding Archie and the world with inquisitive black eyes. Thereafter in their private conversations Archie always called her Pony. He told her his name was Archie McNeil, that he was the son of a Scotsman and an Indian woman, and that he was looking for a new place to hunt and trap.

Archie had to be careful about Temagami, where some people remembered his marriage to Angele, but he arranged to meet Pony frequently, and they exchanged letters when she went home to Mattawa for the winter. At last he found the place he had been looking for, a small lake in the Laurentian hills near the little whistle-stop called Doucet, where the Transcontinental Railway plunged through the north woods of Quebec on its way to Quebec City. This was not only a fresh trapping ground. It was a safe distance from the chance of meeting Angele or any other of the people in his past whom he wished to avoid. In all Archie's wanderings, characterized by sudden departures and far removes, there was always the mark of a fugitive as much as a vagrant, the furtive shifts of a man always trying to run away from his own shadow.

In 1927 Pony traveled by rail to Doucet, Archie met the train, and they walked to his cabin ten miles back in the woods. She had come to stay. Years later Archie said: "I sent the lady a railroad ticket, she came up on a Pullman, and we were married according to plan." Who married them in that remote spot he did not say. Pony knew nothing of Archie's past except the romantic things he told her, and like all his women she believed whatever he said. She had been educated in the school at Mattawa, she could read and write well, and she could draw simple pencil sketches of Indians and canoes and beavers, in a setting of lake and forest. Archie put this skill to good use later on when he wanted just this sort of thing to illustrate his writings. In fact, Archie had found an ideal companion for the years ahead.

He was an avid reader himself. He always was, from the time he was a boy in Hastings; and in the sporting camps and hotels of northern Ontario he had picked up and devoured all kinds of books and magazines. In the time to come he would reveal a surprising acquaintance with Shakespeare, Walt Whitman, *The Arabian Nights*, the novels of Sir Walter Scott and of Fenimore Cooper. He could quote from such oddly assorted works as *The Wizard of Oz, Hiawatha, Songs of a Sourdough,* histories of the Union Pacific Railway and the Seminole war in Florida, the philosophy of St. Francis of Assisi, and the spellbinding modern sermons of England's fiery evangelist "Gipsy" Smith.

And now, in another odd lot of reading matter picked up at Temagami, Pony had brought two items that were to change his life and lead him on to the greatest hoax of the century. One was entitled *The Power of Will.* As Archie wrote later: "I had always felt that if a man believed himself capable of anything, put into his project all the best there was in him, and carried on with absolute sincerity of purpose, he could accomplish nearly any reasonable aim." The second item of Pony's gathering consisted of five small tattered booklets entitled *The Irving Writing System,* which dealt with the art of English composition. Their subtitles were "Setting," "Dialogue," "Point of View," "Unity of Impression," and "Style."

To Gertrude "Pony" Anahareo, accustomed to town life at Mattawa, this plunge far into the bush with no company but that of a man, summer and winter, was a violent change. Unlike the wandering Ojibwas, the Mohawks were a people of settled habit. Even in their old savage days they had lived in large villages of long houses, where the women cultivated corn, beans and pumpkins in the surrounding fields, leaving the men free to hunt, fish or go away to war as they chose.

Nevertheless, the civilized young Pony adapted herself to the life of the lone wolf Archie, even traveling with him on his trap lines, although she was squeamish about the suffering of trapped animals and the bloody business that silenced them. Archie himself had no qualms at all. But later, according to his own account, Pony converted him to a tenderness for one of the species he trapped. It was the beaver, and it happened in this wise.

Beavers usually live beside a lake or pond raised artificially by their dams. The "lodge" is made of heaped sticks and mud, and it contains a wet chamber and a dry one. The sole entrance is under water by way of the wet chamber and thence up to the dry one, where in May or June the young are born. The trapper's practice was to fasten steel traps under water around the entrance. When caught in them, the beaver, unable to surface and breathe, perished by drowning. If this happened after the young were born, but while they were still too small to forage for themselves, the "kittens" died of starvation in the dry chamber. If they were old enough to dive through the lower chamber and come to the surface of the pond, they were an easy prey for mink and other predators.

One day Archie was checking over his beaver traps, with Pony paddling in the woman's place at the bow of the canoe. Like humans, a beaver household may contain grandparents as well as parents and infants. One such house yielded three adult beavers, all drowned in Archie's traps. A fourth trap was gone. Obviously, a fourth adult had got caught in it and dragged it away from the fastening, only to die somewhere else on the bottom of the pond. Archie and Pony could hear the voices of hungry "kittens" crying inside the lodge. They searched about the pond all that day and part of the next, looking for the missing adult, whose pelt was valuable. The "kittens" were worthless. At last they were ready to give up the hunt.

As Archie wrote it: "So we turned to go, finally and for good. As we were leaving I heard behind me a light splash, and looking saw what appeared to be a muskrat lying on top of the water alongside of the 'house.' I threw up my gun, and standing in the canoe to get a better aim, prepared to shoot. At that distance a man could never miss, and my finger was about to press the trigger when the creature gave a low cry, and at the same instant I saw, right in my line of fire, another who gave out the same peculiar call. . . . They were young beaver! I lowered my gun and said, 'There are your kittens.' The instinct of a woman spoke out at once. 'Let us save them,' cried Anahareo excitedly, and then in a lower voice, 'It is up to us, after what we've done.' And truly what had been done here looked now to be an act of brutal savagery. And with some confused thought of giving back what I had taken, some dim idea of atonement, I answered, 'Yes, we have to. Let's take them home.'"

This was one of Archie's first and best-written stories, and maybe it was true. Gertrude Anahareo was that sort of woman, even if Archie was not quite that sort of man. His new spirit of mercy and atonement did not extend to the fox, marten, lynx, fisher, weasel and mink he also trapped for their pelts, nor to the moose, deer and wild fowl he hunted for the pot. Man must live, and so must woman.

He and Pony carried the two young beavers to their cabin and kept them alive with tinned milk until they were able to eat the tender inner bark of poplar saplings, their natural food. Each weighed barely half a pound. As they grew they made themselves at home, building their own "lodge" of sticks inside Archie's cabin, crawling sometimes into the sleeping bunk with him and Pony, and gnawing away at the table legs in an effort to find out what delicious stuff was on the top of it. They were very like humans, standing upright with their forepaws on each other's shoulders and chattering softly together. Archie whimsically named them McGinnis and McGinty, after two characters in a story he was reading.

Within a few weeks Archie determined on another far flight. According to the tale he told much later, he was seeking a place where in his new role he could protect and encourage wild beavers, and a passing Micmac Indian had told him of wonderful beaver country at Lake Temiscouata, near the border between New Brunswick and the province of Quebec. This meant a journey of nearly five hundred miles by rail. It would take him over the St. Lawrence River at Quebec, and thence over the height of land to the little sawmill town of Cabano, on Lake Temiscouata.

A Micmac was most unlikely to be wandering so far from his own habitat as the remote northern bush of Quebec. In any case, Archie himself was thoroughly familiar with the Micmac country, and he had passed Temiscouata on his way down the St. John Valley in 1914. The only logical explanation of this move is that something had happened to make another long flight desirable, and as in 1914, it had to be toward the east. Northern Ontario and now northern Quebec had become hostile territory for the man who called himself Archie McNeil.

He and Pony packed up their belongings, including the two beavers in a ventilated box, and caught the first train through Doucet for Quebec City. There they changed trains and went on to Lake Temiscouata. When they arrived at Cabano, Archie knew exactly where to go. Across the big lake from the town stood a bulky green hill shaped like an elephant, and behind that was a stream and a chain of small lakes and ponds in the cedar forest. It offered an excellent retreat. Archie had shipped his canoe by freight to Cabano, and he and Pony now paddled over the lake and up the stream to the first of its small ponds. Its name was Touladi, and in the time to come Archie was to make it famous.

In his book *Pilgrims of the Wild* he described a terrible journey of "forty miles" up this stream, amid snow and ice. According to him the canoe upset in the rapids, he and Pony were nearly drowned, they lost much of their supplies, and after a lot of wandering in frightful conditions he built a cabin "beside a small nameless pond" and settled in for the rest of the winter. But no experienced woodsman would set out on such a journey after the onset of a Canadian winter. In truth, Archie and Pony were never far from Cabano, and a road much used by logging companies ran past Touladi and followed the stream closely for more than twenty miles. In spite of the "upset" canoe they settled miraculously in a cabin equipped with window, stove and chimney, with their pets and baggage, their books, magazines, a camera, and a good supply of films.

The hazardous journey so bravely described was only the first of Archie's fables about his two-year stay at Temiscouata. He had now determined to shed his real identity altogether, dropping the McNeil name as he had previously dropped the Belaney. He would pose as a half-breed and call himself Archie Grey Owl. One of the magazines at hand was Britain's famous *Country Life*. He read it carefully and decided to write an article dealing with backwoods life in Canada. He would illustrate it with carefully posed photographs of himself and his Indian wife in buckskins and feathers, with their beaver pets. His companion's name henceforth would be simply Anahareo. Gertrude and Pony were abolished. He felt confident that *Country Life* would buy his article and ask for more. He had not studied *The Power of Will* for nothing. And now he began to study more carefully those booklets of *The Irving Writing System*.

He finished the article and sent it off to England in January 1929, together with fifty photographs, and signed his manuscript and letter simply "Grey Owl." According to him this name had been given him by the Ojibwas in a formal ceremony. His tale went like this: On a lone winter journey in the Mississagi Forest he had been smitten by snow blindness. It happened, he said, while crossing the ice of a lake at night. He managed to reach the shore and the shelter of trees, but he was lost and blind, doomed to a miserable death. Then he heard a voice saying in Ojibwa, "I am Neganikabo, The-One-Who-Stands-First. I will make a fire." In the warmth of the fire his eyesight recovered. He had heard of Neganikabo, a famous figure among the Ojibwa people, very old, and a walking encyclopedia of life in the northern forest. His gun was an ancient muzzle-loading musket. Slung at his side was a "medicine bag" decorated with dyed porcupine quills. It held some bones and other items of magic power.

From that time, Archie said, he traveled four years with Neganikabo, learning all that the old man could teach. At the end of this apprenticeship he was taken into the Ojibwa tribe as a blood brother, with Neganikabo his sponsor. The ceremony was performed at night, with a chanting of "Hi-heeh, Hi-heh, Ho, Hi-he, Ha!" and so forth, by a band of Ojibwas squatting about a fire in the forest. The name they gave him was Wa-Sha-Quon-Asin, which in one of Archie's tales meant "Shining Beak" and in another "He-Who-Walks-By-Night." In either case, it referred to the bird known to naturalists as the Great Grey Owl.

Archie's account of all this was colorful and charming in print, and still more when he appeared in person in a dramatic Red Indian costume and told it to rapt gatherings of city folk. Yet there was always the ghost of a mischievous grin, somehow, behind this and much else that Archie told about himself. Of all the birds and beasts in the forest, why Grey Owl? Was it because, whenever he looked in a mirror, Archie saw in his own bold eyebrows and sharp curved nose a caricature of that terror of the wood mice? Or because he knew that the grey owl is only a winter visitor to the settled parts of Canada, and he relished his own winter forays in towns from Bisco to Toronto? Or was it because he knew that the so-called Great Grey Owl was absurdly small and insignificant when stripped of its imposing mass of feathers?

His public explanation was that the Ojibwas had noted his habit of traveling at night. He liked to boast of long nocturnal journeys in the thick of the forest, or hurtling down dark rivers in a canoe, regardless of rocks and waterfalls. If the Ojibwas gave

114

him the name at all, it was probably in jest at Bisco, when they saw the nightly revels of Archie and other trappers and canoemen in town for a spree. Toward the end of his life he remarked that among the things he would like to do again was "to enter Bisco as I left it, in the nighttime by canoe, and give the long loud whoop of the laughing owl, and hear it answered from the dwellings of a dozen Bisco men."

Much of the lore that Archie said he acquired from The-One-Who-Stands-First has an obvious smack of the tall tales with which all the Algonquin tribes amused themselves about their winter fires. For example, how does one get snow-blind while crossing a frozen lake at night? For another, there was the art of following a moose track made a month past and hidden by subsequent snows. The tracker had to pause frequently, peel off a mitten, and thrust his naked fingers down through the snow to feel the pressed outline of the old track. Sometimes it took as much as fifteen minutes for those bare fingers to find which way the bygone hoofs had pointed. Then he could go on to the next.

Anyone interested in finding where a moose has been long since, and willing to lose a hand by frostbite, may try this any winter in the subzero cold of the north woods. To his lecture audiences Grey Owl recited this sort of stuff with the solemn face of his name-bird, and like that bird he probably made little chuckling sounds to himself now and then, quite apart from his public voice.

The Micmacs, whom he knew quite as well as the Ojibwas, had fireside tales of a whimsical spirit named Glooscap, who created the earth and all the creatures in it, including the Indians. Glooscap could transform men into fish or birds or animals, or *vice versa*, and he was fond of playing tricks and jokes. There was a whole mythology of his adventures. Translated, his name meant "The Fibber." It would have fitted Archie just as well.

In March 1929, Archie called at the Cabano post office and found a letter awaiting him. It was from the editor of *Country*

Life, accepting his article and some of the photographs. Enclosed was a check in pounds sterling to the value of about $150. It paid Archie's debt at the store and told him clearly that his knowledge of the wilds and his flair for words were about to pay off.

He and Anahareo were still living as squatters in a cabin built by a logging crew who had cut the best of the timber nearby and moved on. It stood beside Touladi Lake, only five miles from the town of Cabano. As he said, "With set purpose and design I commenced to write again, and got away another article." Then, mysteriously, their pet beavers swam away into the lake and never came back. Anahareo managed to live-trap another small "kitten," a female they called Jelly Roll because it liked that delicacy from the Cabano baker's shop. As summer came they moved again, and this time pitched a tent just outside Cabano on the shore of Temiscouata. "The proceeds of my second article arrived, and with all bills paid and a well-filled cache beside the tent we had no immediate worries."

Archie's fountain pen was busy with stories and articles. The townsfolk of Cabano were almost entirely French-Canadian, and although Archie and Anahareo knew little French, they had friendly visitors curious to see "*les sauvages*" and their beaver pet. Two of the visitors suggested that Grey Owl and his woman take the train to Métis Beach, on the south shore of the St. Lawrence, where in summer the hotels were full of rich tourists, bored and avid for novelty. Grey Owl might give talks there on life in the forest and get paid for doing it.

Métis Beach was two hundred miles below Quebec City, and the water of the St. Lawrence estuary there was mostly tidal Atlantic. During the past winter, as props for their photographs of each other, Anahareo had made new elaborate costumes of buckskin, with long fringes of leather dangling across the breast and along the seams. Archie himself had shot an eagle and made a war bonnet of the kind familiar in Western movies but never worn by the forest Indians of the East.

Grey Owl resolved now to put his new role to a public test.

He and Anahareo packed up their tent and baggage, carried Jelly Roll in a ventilated box, and moved by train to Métis Beach. The climate by salt water was chillier than that of Temiscouata —"we cringed in our tent alongside the unfriendly Atlantic Ocean." Despite the ancient name of the place, there were no Indians or half-breeds at Métis, and a pair like Grey Owl and his woman, dressed in their moving-picture costumes, were a sensation from the moment they stepped off the train. The tourists clicked their cameras busily, and it was not long before the manager of one hotel engaged Grey Owl to give a talk for the entertainment of his guests. One of the guests, an American lady, made invitation cards, drummed up an audience, and gave Archie some advice on the art of elocution.

When he got up to speak in the hotel ballroom Archie felt "like a snake that has swallowed an icicle, chilled from one end to the other." But he found a good audience and he warmed to his subject. At the end, "these people crowded around us, shook our hands, congratulated us." This led to other bookings in hotels, in halls, at private parties in the summer colony. Anahareo played her part, addressing herself to the children, telling folk tales of the Iroquois, and making pencil sketches of Indians, animals and birds. And Jelly Roll delighted everybody. Money rolled in.

At the end of the summer Archie and Anahareo returned by rail to their camp site at Cabano. Here they had an unexpected visitor. According to Archie, he was an Indian from the Ottawa Valley, an old acquaintance of Anahareo named David White Stone. As Archie told it, David had been smitten by the gold fever and he told Anahareo of a fabulously rich deposit in the wilds of Chibougamau, in northern Quebec. She caught the fever herself and went off with David to that remote region, with Archie's canoe and apparently Archie's tacit consent. After a time, in Archie's story, he got a letter from Anahareo, describing how David had gone on a wild spree in Quebec City, how she had sought him from tavern to tavern, and found him at last, and got him to travel on. After about eighteen months Anahareo came out of the north bush by airplane and thence by train back to Temiscouata. All this Grey Owl set forth in his book *Pilgrims of the Wild.*

Gertrude Anahareo, who knew the truth about this and many other yarns of Grey Owl, never revealed what actually happened. She truly loved the man she knew as Archie McNeil and she was loyal to him. Why did she leave him for eighteen months? Probably because most of his money was going into booze, and in his drunken spells Archie was a bad companion. Tired of this squalid life in shacks and tents, Anahareo probably went home to her folk at Mattawa, there to remain until Archie turned sober and offered her a decent home. David White Stone, if he existed at all, had nothing to do with it.

So Archie lived a year and a half alone, except for the young beaver Jelly Roll. He had moved from the tent to an empty shack near Cabano, and frequently he went into the town, calling on families he had come to know and staying for a good square meal. One day he found a copy of *Canadian Forest and Outdoors,* a magazine published by the Canadian Forestry Association. During his sober hours in the shack he did a lot of scribbling, and one result was an article entitled "The Vanishing Life of the Wild," which he mailed to *Canadian Forest and Outdoors.* It was accepted and published, Archie's first appearance in a Canadian magazine. The editors asked for more, Archie obliged, and the magazine published articles and photographs by Grey Owl for the next three years.

Also in these months at Temiscouata ("during fits of loneliness") he wrote long rambling letters to the editor of *Country Life,* hoping for further publication and keeping up his English contact. The outcome of these was a suggestion from London that he write a book about his life and observations in the backwoods. Archie set to work at once. He was still studying *The Irving Writing System.* He had bought a dictionary and a book of synonyms. And now came something else.

In the first few years after the war he had shared with the Indians a superstitious hatred of the newfangled radios, then beginning to appear in backwoods towns. "We all had an idea in those days that radio caused electrical disturbances that had a bad effect on the weather, so that on account of some gigolo singing 'Ting-a-ling' or 'You've Got Me Crying Again' in Montreal or Los Angeles, a bunch of good men had bad snowshoeing all winter."

Now to his lonely hut came a benevolent townsman of Cabano, bringing a small radio set with batteries and an aerial wire. "Here, I soon discovered, was a word mine all by itself. From then on, radio announcers, authors, book reviewers, news reporters, politicians and others whose trade is words became my nightly company. These people and the works of Emerson, Shakespeare and the Bible each made their unwitting contribution to my omnivorous appetite for the means wherewith to express myself."

He managed to trap a male beaver alive, but with a cut scalp, and consequently named him Rawhide. Rawhide and Jelly Roll built a "lodge" half in and half outside the cabin, where they could go back and forth as they pleased, and Archie watched their antics and wrote about them with increasing skill. His articles and photographs in *Canadian Forest and Outdoors* soon came to the notice of the National Parks Service at Ottawa, and an official of the Department, J. C. Campbell, took train for Cabano to see for himself. He stayed two days with Grey Owl, watching the beavers and their owner. Then he sent for a movie-camera crew and made a film, which was called *The Beaver People* and was shown widely in Canada.

Later in the year Campbell came back to Cabano with a proposition. The Department was interested in Grey Owl and his beavers as a new means of publicity for its conservation of wild game. One immediate project was the introduction of beavers into Riding Mountain Park in Manitoba. Would Grey Owl move his own beavers there and keep careful charge of them as he was doing now? Other beavers would be live-trapped elsewhere and brought to Riding Mountain to add to the colony. For his services as keeper, Grey Owl would be paid forty cents an hour, and he would have the free use of a dwelling for himself, to be built to his own design.

Grey Owl was only too happy to oblige. Life without Anahareo had been lonely and dull. Now he could offer her a regular income and a comfortable home at a far remove from all the old associations of Ontario and Quebec. Once she knew this, she would surely return to him. Later, tongue in cheek, Archie described her returning to Temiscouata as a penitent. "One day I returned to find sitting in the cabin . . . Anahareo! She had come out to civilization by plane. Her tale was quickly told. The mining business was not what it was cracked up to be. Her claims were unsalable. She had got out of the country while she still had the price to do so. She had had what she called her 'fling' and was satisfied. But there was a note of sadness when she spoke of David. The spring of his vitality had dried within him and he had seemed to wilt and wither . . . a weary unhappy old man. One night, not long before the falling of the leaves, he had bid Anahareo goodbye. He was going home."

This nonsense, with its malicious innuendo, was as far from the truth as any of the tall tales Archie told about himself. The fact seems to have been that Anahareo remained with her own folk on the Ottawa River until Archie put away the old life and offered her a new and better one in the West.

Meanwhile his book was published in England. The editors had changed Archie's title to *Men of the Last Frontier*, and they had made changes in the text, untying the knots in Archie's syntax and cutting down the profusion of capital letters that he loved. Grey Owl resented this reflection on his handiwork. He called it "tampering" and reckoned it dishonest. His connection with the *Country Life* publishers ended soon after. Later Archie declared that he broke it off himself, but apparently it was a mutual affair. *Men of the Last Frontier* had only a modest sale in Britain, and by that time the publishers felt that they had done their best for the remarkable scribbler in the wilds of Canada.

In his last months at Temiscouata, according to himself: "I was having the time of my life. My writings began to appear in different publications. I received numbers of press notices. Most reviewers were kind and let me down easy, even praised me. Letters came from Germany, Australia, London, New York. I felt elated yet somehow apprehensive. I had started something. I had fired an arrow wildly into the air and it had come home to roost, and in great feather. One critic, mildly scandalized apparently that an uncultured bushwhacker of acknowledged native blood should so step out of character, was more severe. Unkindest cut of all came an accusation that most of the text had been the work of a ghost writer—after all my sweating, conniving, contriving and conspirating with that dictionary, the synonyms and the System!"

In the spring of 1931, Archie left the shack at Lake Temiscouata and with his small possessions went off by rail to his new job, nearly two thousand miles away in the West. In a baggage car of the train rode Rawhide and Jelly Roll, in a ventilated water tank provided by the Department. Within a few weeks Archie's itchy foot was eager to be on the move again. He did not like "the great high oasis of Riding Mountain, with its poplar forest and rolling downs covered with flowers, that stands like an immense island of green above the hot dry sameness of the wheat-stricken Manitoba prairie."

Jelly Roll and her mate took it happily enough. Beside a small lake they built a great "house" of sticks and mud, eight feet high and more than sixteen in diameter, and there Jelly Roll gave birth to her first "kittens," a litter of four. She brought them to Grey Owl like a visiting neighbor, and at the end of a month they would follow him around and answer his calls. A movie-camera crew arrived and took more films. Meanwhile the Department was considering a report from Grey Owl stating that Riding Mountain lacked sufficient open water for a large increase of beaver and therefore was useless for their purpose. In reply the

121

Ottawa official suggested a removal to Prince Albert Park in Saskatchewan, about three hundred miles to the northwest.

As the summer waned, Grey Owl made a quick trip by train to the city of Prince Albert, and thence by road to the town site of Waskesiu in the heart of the park. The park itself proved to be a huge expanse of forest and hills and lakes, stretching up into the north. Waskesiu Lake formed a bright finger twenty miles long, pointing into the forest toward Kingsmere Lake. On the portage trail from Waskesiu to Kingsmere, Archie paused to look at a quiet pool known to the wayfaring Cree Indians as Ajawaan. It lay in a hollow of tall-timbered hills, lonely and beautiful, the kind of place he liked, the kind he had always chosen for himself, secluded yet within easy reach of a railway line. He wrote the Department and the thing was done.

The park wardens built a home for him at the north tip of Ajawaan. It consisted of two log cabins, one at the water's edge, the other up the slope in the shelter of the jack pines. The higher one was to satisfy Anahareo. For all her interest in beavers, she did not delight in them slithering into her bed or in watching them chew the furniture, as Archie did. The lower cabin had a hole in the floor and a tunnel to the lake, so that the beavers could come and go whenever they felt inclined. Here the busy little animals built a lodge of sticks and mud, half in and half outside the cabin, while in the lake they gathered a tangle of poplar logs and twigs for a winter's food. In this lower cabin were a table, a chair, a bunk and a stove, so that Archie could spend days and nights watching what he fondly called his Beaver People, and writing his notes.

The cabin higher up the slope was equipped entirely for human living, and its furniture included naturally a good kitchen stove and a radio. Now Anahareo came to stay. Her reunion with the man she still knew as Archie McNeil was happy and complete, and by spring she was pregnant. In 1932 she went to a Prince Albert hospital and gave birth to a girl baby. The proud father, busy cultivating a legend as well as his beavers, named the child Rita Grey Owl. Later Anahareo changed the name to

Shirley Dawn McNeil. She never knew Archie's real name until the revelations after his death.

By 1932, Archie had decided firmly on a family history that he had been hinting about for years. He was the son of a Scotsman named McNeil and an Apache woman named Kitty Cochise, a neat twist of his mother's real name. (Cochise was of course a famous Apache chief.) Archie had been born "near Hermosillo in Sonora," a Mexican state facing on the Gulf of California. Occasionally, however, he was born "near Jacarillo," which actually was the name of an Apache band living in United States territory. Undoubtedly he chose these names in the far southwest for their romantic sound, which he had heard first from his English aunts in their thrice-told tales of his father. But they had another virtue. They were two thousand long miles from Canada. No Canadian was likely to track down his "Apache" blood.

His government employers classed Archie as "temporary labor," but in fact he had a steady job at a wage rate of $1320 a year, with no rent to pay, and most of the time his own. A Department memo in 1933 defined his duties thus: "Mr. Archie Grey Owl: in charge of beaver colonies in Prince Albert Park; to protect and study the life of the beaver and to gather information regarding same; to write articles dealing with the wild life of the National Parks from personal knowledge gained by close observation."

Several groups of wild beaver existed in the wide reaches of Prince Albert Park before "Archie Grey Owl" came there with his six pets. As an experiment the park wardens had trapped a pair of beavers elsewhere and released them in the park as far back as 1927. However, after Archie's death a legend spread among Canadian city dwellers that the romantic and mysterious man who called himself Grey Owl had been the prime mover in restoring the beaver to most of the forest between the Rockies and the Atlantic. This godlike power was quite in the tradition of Hiawatha—or Glooscap, say—and Archie's ghost must have loved it.

The new job at Ajawaan suited him, literally, down to the

123

ground. He was now forty-five and tired of a wandering hand-to-mouth existence. A comfortable dwelling and steady pay for little work were new in his existence. His taste of authorship and the money and fame it could bring made him eager to go on with it. During 1934 he finished the manuscript of a book, purporting to be sketches from his own life, which he entitled *The Pilgrims*. He signed the manuscript Grey Owl and inquired hither and yon by letter in search of another English publisher. One inquiry brought him in touch with Hugh Eayrs of Toronto, manager of the Canadian branch of Macmillan. Eayrs knew about the *Country Life* articles and the book that came out of them. He wrote a suggestion to his friend Lovat Dickson in London, and at the same time sent Dickson's address to Grey Owl.

Dickson, a young Canadian, had started a small publishing business in London in 1932. It took courage to do that just when the Great Depression was sinking into its depths, and by 1934 Dickson was still in business and even making a modest profit. Just after Christmas of that year he got the letter from Eayrs. Within a few days he had one from Grey Owl, which began: "Dear Mr. Dickson. Mr. Eayrs the head of Canadian MacMillans writes me that you are a good Canadian and known to be an honest man. I am looking for such a man to be my publisher."

Grey Owl went on to say he had written a book called *The Pilgrims* and was sending the manuscript. He was the son of a Scotsman and an Apache woman, but he had spent most of his life in Canada. One thing he insisted on. The style and wording of his book were not to be changed in any way. Then came the manuscript.

Strictly speaking, it was a typescript, for Grey Owl had found friends who owned a portable typewriter. They were Mr. and Mrs. Herbert Winters of Prince Albert, who sometimes visited him in the park at Ajawaan, entertained him in the city, and spent many hours discussing his book with him and getting it ready for a publisher. As Winters said: "He was a terrible one for insertions. It was my job to collect all the bits and pieces and get it typed out for him."

As Lovat Dickson recalled: "His letter appealed to me. I was a Canadian, and this was the first time a Canadian had turned to me. Besides, I knew half-breeds. I had seen them and talked to them often in the Alberta foothills country. I knew their weaknesses and their extreme sensitivity. My simple heart—I think it really then was simple—responded to him. I wrote back to welcome him into my little fold. The story seemed to me to have a most moving simplicity. I had always been a lover of animal stories, but this account of the partnership of a man and a wild beast in the loneliness of the forest, of their joint struggle for survival, seemed to me a classic of its kind, and it would have been sheer effrontery to touch it up. I let it go forth unblemished" (but under the title *Pilgrims of the Wild*) "and my wildest hopes were fulfilled. The book became overnight a best seller. We published it first in January 1935, and by December of that year we had reprinted it seven times, each reprint larger than the one before. It became a new experience to me, to go to my office each morning and hardly be able to push back the door because of the hundreds of orders from all over the United Kingdom which poured in by every morning's post."

It was the custom of British publishers to hold an annual exhibition of their books in London, and in 1935 Dickson was chairman of the lecture committee, a very important part of the show. In booking lecturers he got Winston Churchill, then in the political shadows, whose history of Marlborough was just out. For a bit of exotic color he booked Sabu, the young actor from India who had made a hit in the movie of Kipling's *Toomai of the Elephants*.

Now came a notion of adding Grey Owl, straight from the wilds of Canada. Dickson had seen convincing photographs of the man, of Anahareo and the beavers. The cost would be heavy, but he thought he could arrange other lectures in London and elsewhere in Britain, charging an entrance fee. He wrote the author at Ajawaan setting forth his idea, and guaranteed the fare to Britain and back, plus half of any profit from the lecture tour. At that time, before the days of airmail, it took at least three weeks for a letter to cross the Atlantic and so long a stretch of Canada. In the woods at Ajawaan, Archie was scribbling away at a new book, to be finished by the end of 1935. Two months had passed before the busy London publisher got a cablegram in reply, and by that time he had half forgotten his idea and the impulsive invitation.

Actually, the idea was not so new as Dickson supposed. When Archie Belaney was a small schoolboy at Hastings a real Canadian half-breed had appeared in England and given public recitals of her poetry. She was the talented and beautiful Pauline Johnson, whose blood was half Mohawk and half English, and whose Indian name was Tekahionwake. In her full costume of buckskins, with beaded moccasins, with two or three eagle feathers in her long black hair, she made a striking figure on the stage. London was impressed, and John Lane of the Bodley Head made an immediate contract to publish a volume of her verse entitled *The White Wampum*. She made further tours of Britain in later years. One member of her audience in London's Steinway Hall was the respected English *littérateur* Theodore Watts-Dunton, who had noticed and praised her poetry as far back as 1889.

Archie Grey Owl knew of her career and he must have read some of her poetry. In 1912 her Toronto publishers had brought out a volume of her verse called *Flint and Feather,* which contained a description of her life and travels and a handsome studio photograph of her in Indian dress. Archie's companion, Anahareo, was a Mohawk herself, intelligent and literate, and she too knew about Tekahionwake, whose father had been chief of all six nations of the Iroquois and was even said to be descended from Hiawatha.

Archie's metamorphosis was now complete, and in his own buckskins, moccasins and feathers he was about to follow in Pauline Johnson's tracks. Over the years, with care, he had cast off the last betraying trace of English accent and now spoke in the drawl of a Canadian backwoodsman. When he chose, he could speak in deep, thrilling tones, articulating every word with the clarity of a trained elocutionist. Long leave of absence from his job at Ajawaan was obtainable at the end of the summer season. Meanwhile he wrote a letter to follow his wire.

Beaver Lodge,
July 2nd, 1935

Dear Mr. Dickson and Mr. Eayrs,

I have just now cabled you to the effect that I will, after all, undertake the lecture tour this year. The difficulties will be immense, and I am not sure but what I will have to reduce the number of lectures, as my time is all broken up. I am away behind in my correspondence, and with that, the continuous running in and out of the beaver, and groups of visitors, and patrolling against predators, I have no time to myself, going often without meals and snatching my sleep in the forenoon.

Yet I see plainly the great advantage of making it this year, with two books on sale, and striking while the iron is hot. So I must do something if, as I said before, it kills us all.

All this writing and phoning and telegraphing and business, and worrying about mail, all things that I detest, are slowly estranging me from my environment, which with my beaver is paramount. Beside them all other things (my family of course excepted, naturally) are side issues. Now, somehow, these detestable affairs seem to be on the point of usurping my whole life. I even dream of them. Sometimes I feel like dumping the whole thing overboard, books, lectures, everything, and dropping back into the obscurity to which I belong, back in the woods. I dread the ocean voyage, the English climate, the crowds. Not stage fright by any means, but the invasion into what has been habitual solitude for over 30 years.

Of course I will stay with it and do my best. All those of you who have worked so faithfully and loyally to advance me (push, I guess, is the word, I'm a first class hanger-backer) can not be so let down. But when in England I hope that my inexperience, my deep-seated attachment for my environment, for which I am going to be mighty lonesome, and my absolute ineptitude at smart conversation, and entire lack of social graces, will be taken into consideration.

This is going to be a hard row for me to hoe, especially without the time for the preparations I figured on. I will do my best, and

I know I can depend on the cooperation of Mr. Campbell, and Major Wood, superintendent of the Park, in every way.

Now that's over, we'll discuss sensibly one or two things which I consider to be of the utmost importance.

I will, as you suggest, read a paper before the Royal Humane Society (is it?). Yet although I am over there on what is really a humanitarian mission (and please be guided by my instinct in this) this must not be unduly stressed, either in advertising or in any publicity.

It must appear naturally, as in a novel the hero's and other characters' ideas and character are unfolded in the action of a story, rather than by descriptive explanation. Humanitarianism, though really my chief object, will be presented indirectly. I give what I hope will be interesting, lively, and altogether vigorous talks, tell the tale, so to speak, guide the audience to see things as I do, and then leave them to their own thinking.

I do not want to go down as a softhearted missionary type, or animal evangelist, but a man of action having a story to tell— yet a man of understanding and intimate acquaintance with the Wilderness and its people. Adventure, comedy, tragedy will appear, if I am man enough to make them do so. I will not bemoan or preach or hand out any soft stuff, yet I will miss no chance to enlist the sympathies of the audience.

They want to know about the Romantic North. I will give them Romance; the Beaver People, the Indian, the North, harsh, savage, yet beautiful. They cannot but love my Beaver People as I tell of them. Yet the appeal must not be too obvious or forced. I think the public like to think they are forming their own conclusions.

In publicity and advertising, lay little if any stress on my humanity, benevolence etc. (I am really considered a rather tough egg by those that know me) but more on my experience and accomplishments as a woodsman, including canoeship, snowshoeman, travelling by day or night, Indian accomplishments, and exponent (in later years) of the natural brotherhood between men and animals.

In fact I think the truest definition of my status (though I do not of course estimate myself his equal) is that of a modern Hiawatha and perhaps an interpreter of the spirit of the wild. Read Longfellow's *Hiawatha*. Use it in your publicity; not too much of the saintly St. Francis of Assisi. I am not gentle nor religious, and am not even a Christian. Neither do I want to be a kind of

Gypsy Smith. It would attract the more fanatical and generally impracticable people. They can do nothing for us.

In any advertising given out, please stipulate that there are no quotation marks attached to my name, as these detract from any dignity that it may have as a name that I earned and did not come by, by accident. I use it in all business, banking, etc. and it is quite legal, being generally accepted as my signature on all legal documents and Government correspondence.

I fear that you will find me very bothersome in all this, but it is so hard for us to get together at this distance that I am, thus early, getting it all lumped together, so as to avoid complicating matters at a critical time.

Your terms I find exceedingly generous, and thank you. Yet the chief gain to me will be the long sought opportunity of meeting all you people, and knowing you; besides the chance I will have to confer with you and improve my literary experience.

Do not bill me as a full-blooded Indian; let it be known that I am of mixed parentage. I favour the Indian in build, action, mentality, and to a large extent facially, but am not very dark skinned, about a rather light bronze, have blue eyes and black hair worn in braids.

I do not speak English quite as fluently as I write it, hence must partly read my lectures. From you I hope to get a slant on the English public and what they expect.

As to dress, I will bring two suits of buckskin. Also I will wear one plume on the platform, but very little if any beadwork, but be what I am—the hunter-scout type, and leave the ornaments to younger men. Perhaps I may wear my buckskin on the street, but there will be times when I will be less conspicuous in civilian clothes, with my braids tucked up under my hat, and only my moccasins as a trade mark.

Owing to an injured foot, a shrapnel wound, I can walk no distance on a cement sidewalk and must taxi distances of any length. But my gadding will be negligible.

I am mighty glad that it is possible for me to meet your wishes in this affair. It will be a strange unsettling time for me, but will accept it as the boys did their war experience, and meet it. There will be times when I will feel like poor Chikanee in his pen.

But I will do my utmost to merit the confidence you all are showing in me; also I will speak to whatever gatherings you may select, besides regular attendances, also to microphone or newsreel, anything at all to further the aims of all of you who, to the benefit of the Little People, are endeavouring to show me the road to success.

I am willing to work hard and faithfully, but may need some moral support, not so much around lecture times as in my adjustments to a mode of living that I am not at ease in.

With kindest regards and best wishes to you both,

Yours sincerely,

Grey Owl

Say hullo to the office staff for me.

P.S. My hotel bills will be small, as I do not want to live very high. I want to stay at quiet homely places where a fellow can be himself.

Please cause it to be known that my role is not that of one who has conquered nature, but of an interpreter of the true spirit of the Wilderness and its dwellers (by no means in a religious sense).

To avoid conflicting ideas and confusion, it would be well not to, in fact I would rather not be referred to as specifically Scotch and Apache. I am not consciously Scotch or Apache. Half-breed trapper I am, and far more closely identified with the Ojibway Indians than any other people. I want the Ojibways to get their share of any credit that may accrue. I am their man. They taught me much.

G.O.

Behind the first dissembling paragraphs of this long screed, here was the cunning actor behind the mask, setting forth exact plans for "putting it over."

On a chill day in September 1935, Lovat Dickson scrambled aboard the *Empress of Britain* at Southampton. "I was young and inexperienced, and I had very little money. I was really putting up a bluff as a publisher and an entrepreneur. I had been publishing only three years, and I had never arranged a lecture tour before. I was afraid that my best and most successful author was going to find me out, and I began to wish that I had never started this thing.

"I found my half-breed surrounded by newspaper reporters and holding his own very well. He was what I knew from his pictures he would be like. He looked at me as I looked at him, weighing up how far we were going to get on with each other, each of us guilty, I see now, with the knowledge that we were acting a bluff. I the publisher, the entrepreneur, he the Indian."

Dickson took Grey Owl in his car, drove to London, and left him at a hotel in South Kensington. When Dickson called the next morning he found his guest standing at a chest of drawers and glooming down at it. The bed showed no sign of use. Grey Owl's blanket roll was on the floor. The man of the wilderness said, "Get me out of here, brother, I can never stay here. Haven't you got a home?"

Dickson was a newlywed with a little house in Chelsea. He wondered what his bride would say, but there was only one thing to do. He invited Grey Owl to stay with them. He had engaged the Polytechnic Theater for two weeks and had advertised the forthcoming lectures. When he took Grey Owl to the empty theater for a dress rehearsal he was dismayed. Grey Owl was utterly stage-struck, as he had been in that first performance at Métis, when he "felt like a snake that has swallowed an icicle." As Dickson put it afterwards, "Finding himself on the stage, with the footlights shining on him, he proved completely lost. Wooden phrases, half remembered, indistinctly articulated, came out in a strangled voice."

To Dickson clearly the enterprise was doomed, but he did not like to say so.

The next day, a Sunday, the Dicksons took their awkward guest for a motor drive into the country and stopped for a picnic in Epping Forest. Grey Owl himself cooked the steaks over a fire. Afterwards, relaxing in the familiar seclusion of a forest, he leaned back and began spinning yarns of the Canadian backwoods. As his deep slow drawl went on, his host found himself borne away across the sea on a magic carpet of words. Suddenly he aroused.

"What had we been worrying about? Destroy his lecture notes, tear up everything, forget everything that he had painfully and stiffly taught himself to do for this great ordeal. Be natural! That was the answer."

When the show opened next day, barely more than a fifth of the seats were taken. Dickson stood in the dark of the wings with a microphone, intoning an introduction. The stage lights, blazing up at just the right moment, revealed Grey Owl mid-stage, in full costume, with a hand raised high in salute to the audience. With his own lean height added to that of the stage, he made a dramatic statue twice as large as life. Then, deliberately, he broke his pose and *came* to life.

As Dickson said: "From that moment on, when he began to speak to them in his friendly drawl, telling story after story about the wilderness and its inhabitants, he had them in the hollow of his clever hand. Word of this performance spread quickly. By the end of the week the theater was nearly full at every showing. In the next weeks we were turning people away. The season was extended to six weeks, and it was necessary to have police there to marshal the queues which by then stretched down Regent Street above the circus; all of them longing to hear the message he was giving: 'You are tired of civilization. I come and offer you, what? A single green leaf.' It was a very simple message but it answered some hunger in people at that time, deafened by Hitler's ranting, dreading the onslaught of a new war, longing for the simple and good life which seemed to many of them to be epitomised in the life of this half-savage."

The success of the London engagement made certain the success of the subsequent tour through England and Scotland. However, Dickson's young assistants who accompanied Grey Owl into the provinces did not find it roses, roses, all the way. Whenever their *protégé* could get himself next to a supply of strong drink he was apt to gulp it down, with unfortunate consequences. If he overheard what he considered a slighting remark he would stage one of his dramatic rages. Sometimes he did the knife trick, and the police were called.

While in London at the Dicksons' home, the visitor "took over

132

the whole house, playing the gramophone deafeningly. He took over our pretty little Irish maid, and I had to move swiftly to protect her. He splattered the walls of our guest room with ink, the result, he explained, of arguments with his fountain pen. Sometimes the level in the decanters sank alarmingly, and Grey Owl became morose and lonely for his beaver people, and I was torn between a desire to keep our lecture engagements and the resulting cash, and a desire to kick him very hard in the seat of his buckskin pants. I would work myself up to such a pitch of fury that I had to loose my wrath on him. Then he would look like a hurt child. He would fall silent, he would pad away on his moccasined feet to his room, the door would close with a suicidal bang, and I would think, 'the bastard,' and tumble into bed worn out with the burden of controlling this child of the forest."

Despite these various embarrassments behind the scenes, at the end of three months the tour was a golden success. In addition to filling London's Polytechnic for weeks, the child of the forest had filled such famous places as the Usher Hall in Edinburg, the Free Trade Hall in Manchester, and many another through Great Britain.

On the tour Grey Owl was wined and dined by rich and famous people in various parts of the country. He was asked to pose in full costume for a portrait by the great Sir John Lavery, and Grey Owl was happy to oblige. Lavery saw an Indian and painted one, the Noble Red Man to the life. The face in the portrait revealed nothing of the cynical poseur who peered forth from so many of his photographs. Canadian diplomat Vincent Massey afterwards bought the Lavery picture and presented it to the Canadian National Gallery at Ottawa, where it now hangs.

When Dickson's staff counted up the cash returns of the tour they found that, after paying all expenses, there was a profit of roughly £4000 to be shared half-and-half between Grey Owl and his publisher. This at a time when the pound sterling was worth about five Canadian dollars. On top of that came a tremendous boost to the sale of his books. So Archie sailed back to Canada in triumph; not this time as an emigrant youth with just

£5 to his name, nor as a wounded soldier with a forthcoming pension of $20 per month, but as a reincarnation of Hiawatha, with a large and growing fortune in the magic wampum of the Bank of England.

When he got back to Prince Albert Park, his government employers had a new project, and in the summer of 1936 they sent Grey Owl with a movie-camera crew to make films of the new beaver colonies and other wildlife in the national parks. Grey Owl figured prominently in the pictures, wearing buckskin and feather, posing with the easy grace of the actor he was, paddling a canoe or moving along a forest trail with the now familiar "loping Indian stride" of the newspapers. When Hugh Eayrs, on Dickson's behalf, asked to use these films for publicity, the Department agreed.

Grey Owl's main occupation in 1936 was of course the writing of another book. His private diversions, however, remained what they had always been. From time to time he disappeared from Ajawaan without the formality of leave from his boss, Major Williamson. He had good and sober friends in Prince Albert, but he found other people with whom a newly rich author could command all sorts of high jinks. Williamson covered up for him loyally, as much as he could, and although word of Grey Owl's misdeeds reached Ottawa, the Department was still disposed to accept this untamed half-breed as if he were any other wild creature in their charge.

Not so Anahareo, whose experience with Archie was so much longer and sadder. During this year she came to the end of her patience. The new Archie, flush with money, was no Hiawatha in her eyes, and she well knew he was no Grey Owl either. She left him, this time for good. When Archie finished his new book his choice of a title had the sly touch that lay behind so many things he wrote and said. It was *Tales of an Empty Cabin*. The truth was that Anahareo's departing footfall had barely died away from Ajawaan when a fresh young creature came tripping in. She was part Indian, part French. Like those of most *métis*, her name was purely French, but Archie's theatrical fancy waved its wand over that. He informed his London publisher that he had a new wife named Silver Moon.

That winter a movie crew made yet another film with Grey Owl prominent in the foreground, and again Eayrs got leave of absence for the author to come to Toronto and help in editing the film for lecture purposes. Major Williamson had written to R. A. Gibson, Director of Lands, Forests and Parks at Ottawa, informing him that Grey Owl wished to lecture in England during the next two winters, coming back to Ajawaan each May and staying until September.

By this time, however, Gibson was getting restive about Grey Owl's off-the-reservation activities of all sorts. He wrote back: "As you know, Grey Owl has been rather difficult to handle, and this will not improve. His activities have encouraged interest in wildlife matters, and Prince Albert National Park has benefited to a certain extent. For the time being the seasonal arrangement seems to be about the only solution, but I think we should have someone in training for this job. In fact we could use the same feature in other parks as well. There are bright young Indians going through the schools who would be glad to take on a specialty of this kind."

A month later Gibson wrote again: "While there is every appreciation of the publicity which Grey Owl has given to the National Park at Prince Albert, at the same time it cannot be denied that Grey Owl has capitalized to the limit his connection with the Department, and used our films to create a background for himself. In this he is aided by his publishers, and it is questionable how much of this should be permitted. Unfortunately Grey Owl's personal conduct on certain occasions has not reflected much credit upon the Department and there is a certain amount of criticism."

Despite this, Grey Owl obtained leave of absence for three weeks to make a film in the Mississagi Provincial Forest of Ontario. It took him back to a memorable old stamping ground, and there was risk of meeting a number of people who might recognize Grey Owl as Archie Belaney and say so in voices loud enough to reach the public ear. But more than twelve years had gone by since he was last seen in those parts—and Archie was nothing if not a gambler. Throughout his gaudy career as a public figure he chanced his luck that people who knew the paltry body behind the feathers of Grey Owl were not the kind who wrote to newspapers. And he won.

Albert Chandler, his fellow sniper-observer in the Flanders trenches, who lived less than sixty miles from Prince Albert, had this to say long afterwards: "A lot of people around here took him for an Indian, and I had a job convincing them that he wasn't. He liked acting as one. I intended seeing him at his home in Prince Albert Park, for we could certainly talk over old times in the 13th Battalion, but never had the opportunity."

War veterans had a preference in most federal government jobs, and when he filled out his first application form Archie had been careful to mention his army service. Knowing that his military record might be checked, he also gave his real name. In the Parks Branch office a typist misspelled it, hence the heading in a memorandum from R. A. Gibson dated November 17, 1937:

"re Archie Bellaney (Grey Owl).

"We do not know how long Grey Owl will be available in the future, but he has a certain publicity value so long as he behaves himself. I agree with Mr. Williamson that for any time he is required it should be satisfactory to engage him as a labourer. It is my hope that we may be able to develop some young Indians of good character to undertake work of this nature in National Parks."

On November 22, 1937, Gibson wrote a last word on the subject: "I am advised that Archie Bellaney (Grey Owl), who was on leave without pay, returned to duty on August 9th and remained on duty until August 31, when his services were discontinued. He may be considered as separated from the Department as from September 1, 1937."

136

Far away in London, Dickson was preparing another tour of Britain for the wild man of Ajawaan. As he wrote in his own book of reminiscences, *House of Words:*

A return engagement was imperative; too many people had been disappointed by not seeing him on the first tour. Grey Owl was willing, perhaps a shade too willing. I was naturally eager to repeat so profitable a performance. But some faint shadow of a misgiving kept clouding for me the bright prospect that a second tour opened up. I could not get out of my mind a feeling that Grey Owl confident was infinitely less attractive a figure than the Grey Owl who had come to "bunk in" with us.

His simplicity, his childlike earnestness, his absolute belief in his mission to save the beaver from extinction, were all there still. But they seemed to me to have been overlaid with a certain unbecoming proficiency, a prima donna's tendency to be dictatorial and exacting in his demands, an inclination to take himself too seriously. I could smile at all this privately but I was anxious that the public should not discover it.

He was a man of extraordinarily good looks. The long hair, the buckskin clothes, the deep and thrilling voice, the wild mysterious background from which he came, all contributed to the disturbing effect he plainly had on most women, especially the kind who tend to follow and devote themselves to any new prophet coming on the scene. Grey Owl liked it. He liked their flattery and attention of course, but the ardent side of his nature, which was very well developed, would respond to any woman who cared to give a signal, and I had my hands full in defending him from ladies of all degree. Defending is hardly the word. I mean trying to act as an insulator to the magnetic sparks that flashed in both directions.

The second tour was an even greater success than the first. There was not an unbooked day . . . and the crowds were enormous and enthusiastic. The lights in the crowded theatre would darken, and from the wings would come a voice speaking the last paragraphs of *Pilgrims of the Wild.* And with those moving words the lights would blaze up, and there in the centre of the stage in buckskin and feather would stand that still and striking figure. You could almost hear the audience draw its breath with shock. Then, with his right arm raised in greeting, *"How Kola!"*

would come his voice. He would speak for a minute in deep and vibrant tones. Then he would move for the first time, and a sigh of relief at the breaking of tension would come from the darkened auditorium. Then, padding up and down the front of the stage, he would tell stories of animals and Indians, of summer loveliness in the Canadian wilderness, of winter harshness, and of the fight that man and animal must both make to stay alive. They were stories of heroism, of disaster, of humor, of strange predicaments and surprising outcomes. He was a born raconteur. And to prove that these were not fairy tales came the films.

The climax of the second tour was a command for Grey Owl to go to Buckingham Palace and give his lecture there to the King and Queen. Grey Owl wanted Silver Dawn [sic] to come, but I sidetracked that by saying that the King was no doubt as much an admirer of Anahareo as I was, and that I did not think it would be politic. He said aggressively that it wasn't a matter of politics, and I hastened to change the subject.

I had arranged for projectors to show the films, and at two o'clock we went to the drawing room at Buckingham Palace. At about 2:30 the King and Queen came in. With them were the two princesses Elizabeth and Margaret, looking utterly charming and plainly excited at the prospect before them. Queen Mary was with them, and the Queen's mother and father, the Earl and Countess of Strathmore. They settled themselves in their chairs, Grey Owl caught my signal, and off he went.

He was now a master of his art. He seemed quite undismayed by the splendor of his surroundings and the glamour of this particular audience. He fastened his intent gaze on the two princesses, sure of their childish interest. Then the films were shown, and when the lights came up again he moved in on his final peroration and brought the lecture to the usual dramatic close. But Princess Elizabeth jumped up clapping her hands. "Oh, do go on," she said. "Don't stop. Do go on!"

Grey Owl laughed at her fondly, and at me meaningfully, and I signaled him to continue; and so, with the satisfied smile of one who is at last appreciated for his true worth, he moved into a fresh discourse. It included some stories which, because they were about local characters whose behaviour was somewhat scandalous, we had decided ought not to figure in this talk. But confidently, and without so much as a glance in my direction, he now threw them in. Then he ended, and the royal party stood up clapping their hands. The King, with a small excited princess on each side of him, came up to Grey Owl to congratulate him on the work he was doing, and to ask some pertinent questions about it.

They talked for about ten minutes, and the King held out his hand to say goodbye. Grey Owl took it. Moved by what I thought at the time was native simplicity but which I now see was a daring improvisation, he clapped the King on the shoulder and said, "Goodbye, brother, I'll be seeing you."

Like the true grey owl in the treetops of the north, Archie must have chortled softly when he walked away with Dickson from the palace. His impudent imposture had reached its height and taken in the royal heads of the British Empire. He had even slapped the King's shoulder and called him Brother! If only some others could have seen that! His aunts, say, or his old school-masters in Hastings, or Bill Guppy, or the sergeants who bawled him out in the army, or the Mountie constables who had arrested him at Bisco and elsewhere for drunken and disorderly conduct, or the swells at Métis who had patronized him first—how all those eyes would have popped!

With a royal seal on his performance and his bank account fatter than ever, Archie and his new companion "Silver Moon" recrossed the Atlantic to New York in March 1938. There they separated, "Silver Moon" traveling alone to Saskatchewan while Grey Owl, in the expert charge of an American booking agency, went on to gather dollar-wampum with a lecture tour of the United States and Canada.

He was in his fiftieth year. Most of his life had been spent careless of his health, and the effect was showing now. Although he thoroughly enjoyed his masquerade, each public performance was a strain, as every actor knows. Between towns and shows he turned more and more to the bottle for ease of body and soul. He ate little and slept less. And now he learned that the shadows of his past were catching up with him at last. One of his deserted wives had seen and recognized a Grey Owl photograph showing him at Ajawaan, and in Prince Albert a rising lawyer named John Diefenbaker was taking up her case for support.

Archie made his way back to the cabin in the park. It was empty again, for "Silver Moon" was staying in Regina. Winter clung to the north woods, and the frozen length of Waskesiu Lake made travel easy. Spring was just around the corner, and then the ice would break up and his Beaver People would be free once more to swim about the lake shores in search of tender young poplar. For Archie Belaney, however, the sap of spring would come no more. A pair of park rangers called at the supposedly deserted cabin and found him in a state of collapse. They managed to get him over the snow and ice to Waskesiu town site, and thence by road to Prince Albert, but a stealthy slayer followed him into the hospital. It was pneumonia, and it killed him in the morning of April 13, 1938.

In the final words of his own book, "The Pilgrimage is over."

Major Williamson wired the news to Ottawa and to London where, at the request of the BBC, Lovat Dickson gave a brief eulogy of Grey Owl after the evening news report. On the next evening there was more startling news from Canada. A London newspaper printed a dispatch saying that "Grey Owl" was neither Indian nor half-breed but just an Englishman named Archibald Belaney. To Dickson this was preposterous, and when newsmen questioned him he was quick to say so. Moreover he wrote a letter to the *Times* asserting that Grey Owl was what he said he was, a man of mixed Scotch and Indian parentage. His loyal letter drew others in sharp reply, for the truth was coming out at last. Eager reporters were hunting down Archie's tracks—and not by fumbling for them with bare hands in sub-Arctic snow. It did not take them long to find Ada and Carrie Belaney, who said, yes, Archie was their nephew, born in Hastings, without a drop of Indian blood. They knew that he called himself "Grey Owl," he had visited them on one of his tours, but they did not think it of great importance and they were astonished at this hullabaloo.

Archie's publisher was dismayed. Whatever his irritations with the wild man of Ajawaan, he believed him genuine, and now in the flood of newspaper comment there were hints of fraudulent conspiracy. These were false and unjust. Dickson had been deceived by Archie's clever and well-studied imposture like everybody else, and as far as the books and lectures were concerned the public had got good value for its money. Entertainment has its price, and the actor who puts on a good show is not called a fraud because he wears a robe and buskins. Archie gave a very good show indeed, and he succeeded mainly because the public were eager to be deceived, because he made real and immediate for them the image of the Noble Savage first portrayed by Fenimore Cooper and long later blown up to giant size on moving-picture screens the world around.

In retrospect, a great deal that "Grey Owl" wrote and said was palpable nonsense to any Canadian woodsman, white, red, or *métis*, but much else was good and true. The faculties that Lieutenant Macfarlane had noticed in Flanders—"A considerable knowledge of fieldcraft, infinite patience, and the gift of absolute immobility for long periods"—had enabled Archie to study the creatures of the north woods as an Indian does, and as few white men can. Archie's gifts of expression, with Dickson's honest and painstaking aid, had enabled him to describe what he had really seen and heard in the forest.

His books (*Men of the Last Frontier, Pilgrims of the Wild, Sajo and Her Beaver People, Tales of an Empty Cabin*) altogether sold more than a quarter-million copies, and a host of people, young and old, enjoyed them. Whatever he was not, Archie Belaney was a sharp observer, and when he talked about the creatures of the wild he had a stock of truth to draw upon. It was mainly when he talked about himself that he was false.

The really strange thing about the whole affair is that Archie regarded his gifts for speaking and writing merely as part of his act, just as he regarded the buckskins, the moccasins, the eagle feathers and the hunting knife. They had to be as perfect as he could make them, but all were theatrical props. Despite some sententious talk to his publishers about literary ambitions and the science of nature study, to others he denied with scorn that he was either a professional writer or a naturalist.

He liked to fancy himself as a reincarnation of Hiawatha, the simple and wise friend of all creatures great and small, the embodiment of the Good Spirit and the foe of all evil. His increasing absorption in his beaver pets gave him a peculiar familiarity with them and eventually an illusion in which they became people like himself, with a mutual language. Possibly this mental quirk began in his young and impressionable mind during his first years in Canada, among the Micmacs, with their tales of men and birds and beasts swapping skins in a trice and speaking one tongue. From his boyhood in Hastings he had held aloof from humans as much as he could, even from his aunts, and had given whatever affection he had to one or two animal pets. He was always more at home with animals, whether they swam, walked or flew. His human love affairs were like those of a buck deer in the forest, taking whatever females came into view while the heat was on him, and quite indifferent to them when the passion cooled. Morality and continence were things he liked to preach in pompous statements to the public, but he could not practice them himself. The well-worn pages of *The Power of Will* had taught him much, but never that.

After the revelations of the press, Lovat Dickson determined to get the truth about his astounding *protégé,* and he engaged experts to seek it in England and in North America. The truth about Archie's parentage was revealed when Margaret Anderson of Palatka, Florida, engaged on some other research in the public records there, came upon the entry of George Belaney's marriage to Kitty Cox more than fifty years before. From there the trail led back to England, and from there away to Canada. Many things they did not discover—the truth about Archie as a soldier, for example—but when they had gathered enough to show the real pattern of Belaney's life, Dickson revealed it and then closed his accounts on the whole affair. As he wrote afterwards: "He and I had known each other for only three years but we had become enormously engrossed in each other, and it was a good thing, I see now, that this partnership should have been broken. Grey Owl had played too large a part in my affairs."

And what became of Grey Owl, stripped of his imposing plumage and revealed as a petty body after all? The Prince Albert undertaker, preparing the corpse for burial, rejected the buckskins sent along by the hospital people, and dressed it in white shirt, collar, tie, socks, shoes and a blue-serge suit.

So Archie went to the Happy Hunting Ground dressed for a businessman's luncheon.

On his army documents he always gave his religion as Church of England, but in the role of Grey Owl he avowed himself a pagan. Nevertheless, Canon Strong of Prince Albert conducted the death rite of the Anglican Church in the undertaker's funeral chapel, and Mrs. Winters brought little Shirley Dawn McNeil to see the last of her father. Anahareo had gone back to her people like Angele Uguna and all the others.

Archie was buried on the spot he had loved best, by the quiet water of Ajawaan. The laden coffin went by road to Waskesiu. There two woodsmen, Alex Pease and Les Holden, took it on a horse-drawn toboggan a distance of twenty-four miles over the ice of Lake Waskesiu and up the rugged trail to Ajawaan. They buried Archie near the cabin—truly empty now. Later the park authorities placed a gravestone with the simple inscription:

GREY OWL
Died 1938

The two cabins at Ajawaan remained untenanted, and beside the lower one Archie's friends put up a wooden tablet saying:

This cabin stands as a memorial to Grey Owl, natural-

143

ist, author, and friend of the forest creatures. His work at
this site did much towards the restoration of the beaver
in this Park. Here in harmony with his surroundings he
wrote his stories of wild life.

Far to the eastward, in 1959, the Ontario Historic Sites Board set up a modest metal plaque, a mile south of the village of Temagami, in a camping ground for tourists. It was unveiled with ceremony, and in the little audience stood a son of Grey Owl and one of his daughters. The inscription was headed:

GREY OWL
1888–1938

But the text began: *Archibald Belaney, born in England . . .*

Mary Celeste

The deep thrusting tides of the Bay of Fundy almost cut away the peninsula of Nova Scotia from the Canadian mainland. One of the tidestreams, however, turns to penetrate Nova Scotia itself, filling a landlocked basin fifty miles long and twenty wide. Twice in each twenty-four-hour day Minas Basin rises forty feet or so to the high-tide mark and then ebbs away to its low-water level.

The north rim of the Basin is fairly low and straight from Truro to a promontory with a steep hill behind it, known to the Indians as Ke-no-me, "It-juts-out." From there westward again the shore runs evenly until you reach the passage into the Bay of Fundy. Here you meet an abrupt change into rugged wooded hills and rocky sea cliffs going on for thirty miles.

On this side of the channel the inflowing rivers and brooks have worn deep gullies through the hills, and where they emerge on tidewater there is a shelf of alluvial red soil. The seamen who first charted Minas Basin and its channel into Fundy noted these natural landing places and were careful to name the islands lying just offshore which marked them. Afterwards landsmen came to live on that shore, and named their settlements after the islands on the charts. So arose villages called Five Islands, Partridge Island, and Spencer's Island, all actually built on the mainland. Other settlers landed near the sheltering point of Ke-no-me, and with a frugal twist of the Indian name called their village Economy.

The Micmac Indians told weird tales of Minas Basin. According to them it was the home of a powerful spirit named Glooscap, whose magic powers had created the whole world and everything in it. He pitched his wigwam on the steep hump of Cape Blomidon overlooking the entrance to Minas Basin, but he roamed about a good deal. One tale concerned Spencer's Island. For a winter's supply of meat one fall, Glooscap chased a herd of moose out of the north-shore hills and down to a convenient half-moon beach. There he slaughtered them, cut up the meat, and dried it. Finally he boiled the tasty marrow out of the bones, using a huge stone pot or kettle which he conjured on the spot. Then, having no further use for the kettle, he tossed it into Minas Channel. It sank, bottom up, two miles out from the slaughter beach, so big that even with its brim on the sea floor a great part of it remained in the air. There it stands, tall and round, to this day. Sailors call it Spencer's Island. Indians know it as Ooteomul —"His Kettle."

In this place, haunted by Glooscap's spirit, within easy sight of his capsized kettle, and on the very beach once littered with his meat bones, a group of white men built a ship that was fated to misfortune. Indeed, she was a hoodoo ship from the day she was launched. The first name she bore was *Amazon*. Her second name, which was also her last, was *Mary Celeste*. Under that one she became notorious throughout the world.

One of the first settlers at Economy was an Englishman named Dewis, from Lancashire. After crossing the sea he got a Crown grant of land, probably with the aid of Benjamin and Joseph Gerrish, who were members of the Nova Scotia Council at the time. When Dewis built his little cottage on a knoll at Economy

146

he called it grandly Mount Gerrish. Years later, following the American Revolution, some refugee American Loyalist soldiers came with their families to settle on the north shore of Minas Basin and along the channel into the Bay of Fundy. One of them was Lt. Robert Spicer, who got a Crown grant of 500 acres in 1785 and built a home on the steep hillside overlooking the half-moon beach by Spencer's Island.

All these settlers on the north shore had to live by fishing as much as farming, because the shelf of arable soil at the foot of the hills was narrow. They had no market whatever for the forest trees standing on the slopes above. Fortunately, the twice-daily tides of Fundy brought in swarms of salmon, shad, alewives, herring, cod and other fish. With weirs of netting fastened on tall poles, the pioneers and their descendants were able to trap a rich catch when the tide was on the flow, and to gather it after the ebb. Except in winter these weirs were an unfailing source of food.

In 1815, the year of Napoleon's final defeat at Waterloo, a boy was born on the Dewis farm and named Joshua. The end of the long French wars brought the usual depression of trade, and Joshua Dewis grew up in hard times. He was a sturdy fellow with broad shoulders, strong hands, and a resourceful mind.

The easiest travel, in fact the only practical travel, between the north-shore settlements of Minas Basin and the market town of Windsor was by water. Consequently, in his teens Joshua began to earn a living by making small boats for the local farmers. In his twenties he progressed to his first ship, a modest little schooner built on the shore just below his home. By the age of forty-five Joshua (always pronounced "Josh-u-way") was well known about Minas Basin as a master shipwright, with many stout vessels to his credit. Like most Nova Scotia ships of the time, they were built mainly of spruce wood, with hardwood planking below the water line, decks of pine, and cabins well finished with maple, birch and beechwood.

In nearly thirty years of hard work Joshua had not been able to gather much cash, a scarce commodity in the Basin settlements, but his credit was good at Windsor and elsewhere about the shore, and wooden windjammers were still in demand. His only problem now was timber. The best available trees around Economy had been cut for shipbuilding or for export as lumber. There were plenty of trees to be had farther back on the hills, but it was easier to move along the shore to a place where timber still grew handy to the waterside. A shipyard could be set up anywhere, wanting only a sheltered launching place and a cheap wood supply.

In the year 1860, Joshua Dewis went (probably by boat) along the shore to the little village called Spencer's Island, inhabited by the descendants of Lt. Robert Spicer and his fellow pioneers. Their homes were perched here and there on the steep hillside, with a crooked lane dropping down to the beach. From the house built by Lieutenant Spicer the visitor could almost look down the chimneys of the lower houses. At the crest of the village there were fine views past Glooscap's "Kettle" to the farther shore of Minas Channel, and eastward past the high shoulder of Glooscap's home, Cape Blomidon, to the distant glitter of Minas Basin.

Joshua's errand was soon explained. He wanted to build ships on the beach at the foot of the village, using timber owned by Jacob and Isaac Spicer on the slopes just above the little creek. They soon came to a deal. Joshua would fetch his shipwrights and equipment from Economy. The Spicers would supply the timber and arrange to board and lodge the carpenters. For all this the Spicers would take their pay in shares of the vessels. Merchants in the market town of Windsor at the Basin's southeast end would supply the iron, rope, sails and other ship furniture, and they too would take their pay in shares.

Today the spot where Joshua Dewis built one of the most famous ships in history lies drowned forever like the ship herself. Since 1860 the constant scour of powerful tides and the storms of the winters have pushed the beach back into the creek, whose little stream has to seep its way through a high stony barrier to reach the sea. The stones have a mauve tint, and the beach

148

makes a sweeping mauve arc at the foot of the village, sheltered from north winds by the hills, and from the more prevalent westerlies by the jut of Cape Spencer. The wooden homes peer down on it through fine old hardwood shade trees.

Joshua faced his shipyard eastward, and his carpenters had a day-long view into Minas Basin between the massive portals of Cape Blomidon and Cape Sharp. It would be hard to find a more beautiful place to build a ship or anything else; and on calm autumn days, when the warm haze transformed the capes to wavering purple shapes, it would be easy to see through Indian eyes the images of Glooscap, the evil giant Kookwess, the Ice Man, the cannibal Chenoo, and the other characters of Micmac demonology.

Making the shipyard was a simple matter. The mauve stones at the beachhead were leveled for the laying of the first keel. The stream in the creek was too small to turn a sawmill, and Joshua could not afford a steam engine, so all the timbers were squared by hand with saw and adze and broad ax. The planks and boards were handmade too. For these the logs were drawn over a pit, in which one man stood to ply the lower end of a long saw. The other man, the top sawyer, stood on the log itself, pulling and pushing his end of the saw in open air. The pit sawyer had the hardest job in the shipyard, planted in a stuffy hole, working with his arms raised most of the time, and with the sawdust falling about his face.

All the sawyers, carpenters, caulkers and riggers were craftsmen, skilled in their work. Everything that went into the ship was fashioned with care and pride. Beside the pit saw at the beachhead Joshua built a shed to cover his carpenters' workbenches and tools, a smithy for ironwork, a wood-fired steam box to soften planks for bending to the curves required, and a storeshed for sundry fittings and supplies.

The first vessel was to be about 200 tons by measurement, and rigged as a brigantine. That is to say, she would have two masts, with "square" (actually rectangular) sails hung from yards on the foremast, and a big "fore-and-aft" sail on the mainmast. This rig, combining the sailing advantages of a schooner and a pure square-rigger, was a favorite type for small Nova Scotia shipyards, and about 200 tons was a common size. The ships offered no problems in building or launching, they were easily financed, and once afloat, they were handy for the North Atlantic or the West Indian trade. They were big enough to weather any storm, nimble enough to slip among reefs and islands and into small harbors where a big ship could not go, and a master mariner with half a dozen seamen could sail them anywhere.

The design for Joshua's brigantine was made by Gideon Bigelow, who lived across Minas Basin at the little port of Canning, surrounded by farms and apple orchards, and already famous for its fine wooden ships. Joshua started work in the autumn of 1860, clambering about the steep woods above the creek and choosing timber for the keel, the stem and stern posts, the frames, and the knees which would brace the timbers in their places. The Spicers and another farmer named Robert McLellan did the logging. The slopes were so steep that even before snow came to make perfect sledding it was possible to skid logs down to the beach, using yoked pairs of oxen in the awkward places.

When the onset of winter forced Joshua's shipwrights to quit work for the season, the new ship was "up in frame." In other words, they had made the keel and raised upon it the stem and stern posts and all the ribs. There was a reason for setting up a ship's skeleton like this and leaving it naked through the winter. The green timbers of keel and frame would be seasoned by months of exposure to the weather before the carpenters came back in the spring to put on the planking. This would help to forestall rot between frame and planking after the ship was launched.

The carpenters went back to their homes at Economy for the winter. Joshua and his pit sawyers remained; and the Spicers and McLellan, making full use of the snow with their oxen and sleds, went on felling and skidding logs down to the beach beside the sawpit.

When the sun comes up the Nova Scotia sky in the early months of the year, its rays fall with a certain warmth on the beach by Spencer's Island, which faces southward, with the hills to screen it from the cold winds of Canada. By the month of March the shipwrights could resume their work, pausing for vagrant snowstorms now and then. Joshua drove them hard, as he drove himself. Nothing went into the ship without some touch of his strong hands. The working day was from dawn to dark, and there were six full working days a week.

Before the plank could go on the frames, the matter of rot prevention had to be tackled. The frame had been seasoned through the winter. The planks had been sawed in winter, when little sap remained in the trees, but there was still some moisture in them. Wood-rotting fungi might spring up wherever raw plank touched the frames. In modern times the builders of wooden craft have developed copper solutions to daub on like paint to prevent woodrot. In 1861, shipbuilders had to use the only thing available, which was salt in large crystals, known as rock salt.

The principle was that of preserving meat in brine. Wherever wood joined wood, notably at a ship's beam ends and the sides of the ribs or frames, the carpenters bored holes or cut grooves and stuffed them with rock salt. In that coarse form the salt would dissolve slowly, year by year, "pickling" the wood around it and making it safe against mold. Hundreds of pounds of salt went into the average vessel of the time. It was so important that whenever a wooden ship came up for sale the buyer's first question was, "Is she salted?"

After the salting the planks and frames and posts had to be bored for the treenails, the stout wooden bolts which fastened the planks in place. Like everything else about the ship, this was done by hand, and powerful men worked day after day, twirling the old-fashioned augers, boring through the planking and into the timber behind it. Treenails (pronounced "trunnels")

151

in Nova Scotia were often made from wood of the hackmatack tree, which resisted rot better than any other.

Shipwrights drove the treenails home with sledge hammers, sawed off the outer ends flush with the plank, and split the ends with a chisel and mallet. Into these splits they then hammered small wedges of dry maplewood, to "key" the treenails tightly in the holes. After that the sea, or any wetting at all, would swell the wedges and make the treenails tighter still.

When the outer planks were firmly fastened, the seams between them were packed with oakum. This was done by specialists called caulkers, who went from shipyard to shipyard and village to village, working at their trade. Oakum came woven in long strands made of old tarred rope. The caulkers drove two strands into every seam by mallet strokes on an iron wedge called a "horsing iron." The third and final strand was tapped in neatly with a smaller wedge and mallet, and then covered with hot tar. Of all the sounds in a shipyard the clinking of the caulkers' tools made the best music, rising and falling in a natural rhythm through the day.

The forest above the beach supplied all of the brigantine's timber except her masts, which required trees exceptionally tall and straight. Joshua got his from mastmakers on the St. John River, across the Bay of Fundy. His sails were cut and sewn to Bigelow's design by a sailmaking firm in Halifax, shipped by railway to Windsor, and thence by a coasting vessel to Spencer's Island.

Toward the end of May 1861, the brigantine was ready for launching, fully sparred, rigged and equipped. The chosen name for her was *Amazon* and she was registered in the nearby port of Parrsborough on June 10, 1861. The entry read:

Official number 37671. Port of registry, Parrsboro, N.S. Nationality, British. Propelled by sails. Number of decks, one. Number of masts, two. Rig, half-brig or brigantine. Stern, square. Build, carvel. Galleries, none. Framework, wood. Dimensions: length 99.3 feet: beam 22.5: depth 11.7. Total tonnage, 198.42.

Names, residence and description of owners, and number of shares held by each:

George Reid, of Parrsboro, farmer	8
Joshua Dewis shipwright	16
Isaac Spicer, Jacob Spicer, Robert McLellan, farmers ..	16
William Thompson and William Henry Bigelow, of Economy, mariners	12
Daniel Cox and William Henry Payzant, Windsor, merchants.....................................	12
Total	64

Soon after launching, the *Amazon* sailed east along the Basin shore to the village of Five Islands, there to load a cargo of plank for Britain. Her captain was Robert McLellan, a son of the shareholder. The cabin boy for the short run to Five Islands was young George Spicer of Spencer's Island. It was his first voyage anywhere, and a brief one. Later on he was to sail regularly in the *Amazon* as a seaman and finally as mate. From that he went on to command big Nova Scotia square-riggers trading all around the world. His last and biggest command, which he held for nearly twenty years, was the full-rigged ship *Glooscap*, launched at Spencer's Island in 1891, thirty years after Joshua Dewis launched the *Amazon*.

The village of Five Islands had a pretty site on the shelf by the Basin shore. It was really a straggle of farmhouses, with a shop and a sawmill or two, all set in fields with low wooded hills in the background. The red soil of the shelf was carefully tilled, and in winter the farmers took their horses and oxen into the woods and hauled logs out to the sawmills. A small river wriggled through the pastures to the sea. The islands that gave the place its name lay just offshore, a row of bold humps and pinnacles, all with red cliffs and banks, and some with green woods on top.

Even on a full Fundy tide it was impossible to get a ship of much size into the winding creek of the river. The *Amazon* anchored near the islands, and the cargo came out to her in lighters from a small wharf at Sand Point. It was a slow process. The movements of the lighters depended on winds and tides. Aboard the ship every plank had to be stowed with care to get the largest possible cargo into the holds.

During these weeks of loading, Captain McLellan spent much of his time at his home in Economy, a few miles along the shore. It was only a short run with the ship's boat. He was not a robust man and he was feeling ill when the *Amazon* finished loading, but he determined to go, hoping to feel better in the air at sea. The brigantine sailed on the next tide, passed through Minas Channel and into the Bay of Fundy. There the wind came ahead and the *Amazon* had to make long tacks down the Bay. Meanwhile there was a problem in the cabin aft, where Captain McLellan lay sick in his berth. The end of one long tack brought the ship off Quaco Head, on the New Brunswick coast, and by that time the mate had recognized the Captain's illness. It was pneumonia, and McLellan's state was desperate. The mate put the ship about and headed back for Minas Basin.

With the wind fair the *Amazon* made good sailing back to Minas Channel and was soon abreast of her birthplace. To go on to Economy would take many more hours, owing to the tide, and clearly now the Captain was near death. The mate steered in past "The Kettle" to the village of Spencer's Island. The seamen took their skipper ashore in the boat, carried him up the beach still littered with chips and shavings from the *Amazon's* making, and on up the steep and stony lane to young George Spicer's home. George's folk put McLellan to bed and did all they could for him, but the nearest doctor was in Parrsborough, twenty miles away, and before he could be fetched the Captain was dead.

The next day his seamen carried the body, wrapped in a blanket, down to the ship's boat, and set out along the shore to the Captain's home at Economy. George Spicer went with them. It was a melancholy errand and the saddest part was the journey's end, for young Mrs. McLellan, seeing the *Amazon's* boat at the shore below the house, came running down eagerly to see her bridegroom again. In a long life's experience all over the world George Spicer never forgot that moment.

So the career of Joshua's brigantine began, with her maiden voyage interrupted a few hours from home, and her first captain stricken dead.

The owners moved quickly to find another qualified master, and they did not have to look far. In the course of much shipbuilding and shipowning the villages by the shore of Minas Basin and Minas Channel had produced a remarkable breed of sailors. As late as the 1890s one section of the Channel shore, from Advocate to Apple River, could count ninety masters of deep-sea ships, not to mention coasters and fishermen.

The owners chose Capt. John Nutting Parker. "Jack" Parker was a typical Bluenose skipper of his time, a hard driver of ships and men, and shrewd in all his port and cargo dealings. Also he was lucky, and so were the owners, in the years he commanded the *Amazon*. They happened during the American Civil War, when ships of every kind were in demand and ocean freights were high. It was the only bit of good luck in the *Amazon*'s whole history.

After the first voyage to Britain, Jack Parker took the brigantine back and forth across the North Atlantic, unloading in various Mediterranean ports. In November 1861, he was in Marseilles. Proud of his smart new ship, he got a waterfront artist there to paint her under full sail, with the entrance to Marseilles in the background. A union jack flew at the peak of her foremast, a long white pennant bearing the name *Amazon* streamed from the peak of her mainmast, and aft at the gaff flew the red jack of the British merchant marine. The painter showed all the sails filled with a wind on the starboard quarter, and to make the flags look well he had them streaming against the wind—a common license of marine artists. This painting changed hands several times in the course of years, and now hangs in the museum at Fort Beausejour, near Amherst, N.S.

155

The end of the American Civil War in 1865 brought a sharp decline in the prosperity of the windjammers. The war had promoted a rapid advance in steamships, notably in building the blockade runners, and when these ships turned to pick up freight in a postwar world the tramp steamer was born and the doom of the wooden sailing ship was sealed. Iron hulls were tighter against leaks, far more durable than wood, and so cheaper to maintain and insure. They held more cargo for a given size because iron beams were slim compared with wooden ones. On top of all that the steam engine, now hitched to screw propellers instead of paddles, could take a ship directly from port to port, regardless of winds and weather.

The year 1867, in which the British provinces of North America joined in the confederation called Canada, was long marked as a bad one for the people of Nova Scotia. It was followed by a withering of business and prosperity. The Nova Scotians blamed it on their union with the rest of Canada, but it had various causes, notably the waning of the wooden ships which had been so long the chief resource and occupation of the Bluenoses. Like others, the owners of the *Amazon* found that after 1865 a succession of losing voyages made them "eat with tin spoons." The climax for them came in 1867.

In the summer of 1865 young George Spicer had rejoined the crew, this time as a seaman, and sailed in the *Amazon* to Europe and the West Indies for two years. In the autumn of 1867 the brigantine carried a cargo of corn from Baltimore to Halifax, and Spicer left her for a well-earned holiday at home. The skipper at this time was William Thompson, a shareholder in the ship, and in the common fashion of those days he had power of attorney to make any deal for cargo or repairs, or even to sell the ship itself. Unfortunately for the other shareholders, Captain Thompson lacked the good judgment of Jack Parker and had none of Parker's luck. The shareholders were considering a change of captains, but they moved too late.

156

Captain Thompson had decided to sail from Halifax to Cape Breton for a cargo of coal from the mines at Glace Bay. It was November, a time of wild gales and heavy seas on the Nova Scotia coast, and the insurance underwriters had a safety clause in their contracts for wooden sailing ships in those waters. The insurance would not apply on any voyage to Cape Breton after the first of November. In spite of this, Captain Thompson sailed for Glace Bay, and there followed a bit of business as deep and dark as the mines.

On November 9, 1867, the *Amazon* went aground a few miles from Glace Bay. In that exposed position, at that season, her case appeared hopeless—and there was no insurance. Thompson quickly sold the ship for a small sum, just as she lay. The buyers were a pair of Glace Bay men. The records show that on the very day she went ashore, a Mr. Alexander McBean applied for registry as the new owner of the *Amazon*. On the same day a Mr. John H. Beatty registered a bill of sale on the *Amazon*, signed by Thompson, endorsed by McBean, and held by himself. Perhaps the Glace Bay men were taking a wild gamble. Maybe Captain Thompson really believed the ship a "goner." The one fact that emerges from the dark is that McBean and Beatty got the ship afloat and into shelter before a storm could spring up. They retained their ownership for the next twelve months. Then came another peculiar bit of business.

In November 1868, the *Amazon* was put up at auction in New York and a shipmaster named Richard W. Haines bought her for $1750. To avoid the United States import taxes and regulations he procured a customs broker to get American registry for the ship, and changed her name to *Mary Celeste*. Nobody knows where he got that name. Nobody knows what truth, if any, lay in his subsequent claim that he bought the ship as a wreck and gave her a new keel, bottom, stern, spars, rigging and canvas, at a cost of $8825—in other words, that he practically built a new ship of American materials, and therefore did not cheat the government at all. Again, one thing is sure. If the *Amazon* required all that repair, she could not have sailed 800 miles to

New York in the stormy autumn of 1868. It seems obvious that whatever repairs were necessary for such a voyage must have been made in Nova Scotia, and that Haines himself did little more than paint a new name on her counter with New York as the port of registry.

The new owner sailed the *Mary Celeste* himself for about a year, but he had no luck with her, and she was seized at New York and sold for debt. The next buyer was James H. Winchester, a former Nova Scotia sea captain who had set up business in New York in 1866 as a ship broker. He had gone to sea as a boy, with little education. In the years since, he had become a shipmaster and now a broker, and although his spelling was bad and his temper rather hot, he was a shrewd and capable businessman. (The firm he founded, J. H. Winchester & Company, eventually became one of the foremost ship brokerage firms in New York.)

The *Mary Celeste* was one of his first ventures in actual ownership, and she tried him severely, as she tried everyone who had anything to do with her. Winchester had her seams re-caulked, and to protect her underwater planking from damage by the teredo worms in tropical waters he had the hull sheathed with "yellow metal," an alloy of copper and zinc. For the next four years, under various captains, the *Mary Celeste* sailed between U.S. ports and the West Indies. There was little profit in these voyages, but Winchester was a stubborn man and kept his faith in her. In the spring of 1872 he had an unpleasant surprise.

A marine surveyor named Abeel, in the employ of the U. S. Government, walked into Winchester's office and told him the *Mary Celeste* was of British build, registered in Nova Scotia under the name of *Amazon*, and that her American registry was false. He added blandly that her case might be passed over without taking it into the courts. Winchester caught the scent of blackmail and bristled at once. If the ship's registry was false, then let the government seize her and prove it. For his own part he was prepared to prove his own good faith in the purchase. He cabled the captain of the brigantine, which was lying at

Saint Thomas in the West Indies, to sail at once for Boston. When the *Mary Celeste* arrived there she was duly seized by government authority, and the case went to the courts. Winchester won. He proved that he had not been party to the fraudulent entry by Haines, and he made clear that he was about to do what Haines had not done—to change the ship extensively with American labor and materials.

The *Mary Celeste* sailed from Boston to a New York shipyard, where the work began at once. Winchester had decided to change her to a two-decker, with a larger capacity. She needed some repairs as well. Long afterwards it was said that the Nova Scotia frames had rotted in spite of their salting, and had to be replaced entirely. But in that case the adjacent planks must have rotted too, and the keel wherever the frames joined it; it would have been cheaper and much easier to write off the whole ship and build a new one. The fact that Winchester chose to enlarge the *Mary Celeste* shows that most of the Nova Scotia frame was still sound. After all, she was less than twelve years old.

These changes increased the ship's tonnage to 282, but she retained the brigantine rig and in general appearance at sea looked much the same.

The repairs and enlargement cost $11,500, a considerable sum in 1872. When the work was done Winchester sold a one-third interest in her to a Yankee shipmaster named Benjamin S. Briggs, and placed him in command. Briggs was a steadygoing seaman of thirty-seven, a son and grandson of deep-sea captains. He was born at Wareham, Massachusetts, and went to sea in his teens as a seaman with his father. Before his purchase of shares in the *Mary Celeste* he had been master of four ships, two of them bark-rigged and probably much bigger than his new command. He had spent some time in the Mediterranean trade, calling regularly at Gibraltar on the way, and as a Freemason was a member of St. John's lodge there. The U.S. consul at Gibraltar said of him afterwards: "Briggs I had known for many years, and he always bore a good character as a Christian and as an intelligent and active shipmaster."

Ben Briggs was married, with two children—a boy of seven and a girl of two. Like many married captains in foreign trade, he took his wife to sea with him, and his cabin furniture included a sewing machine and a "melodeon"—a small foot-treadle organ which Sarah Briggs had learned to play. In those days when American and Canadian windjammers were still to be seen in ports around the world, many with the captain's family aboard, a melodeon was important. In port there was much visiting back and forth, and there were evening singsongs (hymns on Sundays) when people from the same part of the world, often from the same village in New England or the Canadian sea provinces, gathered together. In ports like Rio, where ships sometimes lay for weeks in the anchorage, awaiting a berth or a cargo, there was usually a round of parties in the Yankee and Bluenose ships, each captain playing host in turn, and if any ship had no music aboard it was easy to carry the little melodeon by boat from one to another. The melodeon in the cabin of the *Mary Celeste* was undoubtedly a much-traveled instrument.

Among the odds and ends in the cabin was a souvenir that Briggs had picked up on one of his visits to Italy. It was an antique sword with a cross engraved on the hilt. It was stowed away under his berth.

The *Mary Celeste* was loading for a voyage to Italy, and Ben and Sarah Briggs decided to take along the baby Sophy, leaving their son Arthur with Briggs's mother at Marion, Massachusetts, where he could go to school. They all stayed with old Mrs. Briggs for a time, but in the middle of October the Captain left for New York to take charge of his new investment and to see the final loading. About ten days later Mrs. Briggs and little Sophy came down to New York by a steamship of the Fall River Line.

The brigantine lay at Pier 50 in the East River, loading industrial alcohol in oak casks, amounting to 1701 barrels. Sarah Briggs, in one of her spritely letters, wrote: "There is such an amount of thumping and bumping, of shakings and tossings to and fro of the cargo, and of screechings and growlings by es-

160

caping steam, that I believe I've gone slightly daft." She amused herself and Sophy by playing the melodeon and making little games with the baby's dolls "Daisy" and "Sarah Jane."

They had a visit from Sarah's brother William and his bride, who knocked off her bonnet coming down the companionway and so met her new sister-in-law in a somewhat rumpled fashion. William was studying for the Congregational ministry, his wife was inclined to be sedate, and Sarah herself was rather shy with strangers, so the bride's entrance in this fashion set them all laughing and broke the ice.

On November 3, Briggs wrote his mother: "It seems real home-like since Sarah and Sophia got here, and we enjoy our little quarters. We seem to have a very good mate and steward, and I hope we shall have a pleasant voyage. We have both missed Arthur and I believe I should have sent for him if I could have thought of a place to stow him away. Our vessel is in beautiful trim and I hope we shall have a fine passage, but as I have never been in her before I can't say how she'll sail." On the next day he went to the New York Customs House and cleared his ship for Genoa.

On November 5, 1872, a tug took the *Mary Celeste* away from the pier, but within two miles Briggs decided to anchor. The weather was thick outside the harbor, with a strong headwind. On the morning of November 7 he sailed, with a fair wind at last. His wife sent off a brief letter by the pilot as he left the ship outside Staten Island. It was addressed to her mother-in-law Briggs, explaining the delay in sailing, and adding: "As I have nothing more to say I will follow A. Ward's advice and say it at once. Farewell."

The smiling quotation from the famous American humorist and that one final word were the last that anyone ever saw or heard from Sarah Briggs. Indeed, except for entries in the ship's log, nothing ever was seen or heard from anyone on board the *Mary Celeste* after she left New York.

There were ten of them altogether: the Captain, his wife and child, First Mate Albert Richardson, Second Mate Andrew Gilling, seamen Volkert and Boz Lorenzen, who were brothers, Arian Martens, Gottlieb Gottschalk, and the cook-steward Edward Head. Briggs was thirty-seven, Martens thirty-five. All the other men were in their twenties. Richardson, a Maine man, had sailed with Captain Briggs before. Gilling was a Dane. Martens, Gottschalk and the Lorenzen brothers were German sailors from the Frisian Islands in the North Sea. Head lived in New York. Martens and one of the Lorenzens were married, with children. Subsequent investigations showed that the whole crew, from captain to seaman, were known in their home communities as capable and reliable men.

There was one four-footed passenger, a cat.

When the *Mary Celeste* sailed out past Staten Island, another brigantine named *Dei Gratia* ("By Grace of God") was loading a cargo of barreled petroleum at Hoboken in the port of New York. Like the *Mary Celeste* she was built in Nova Scotia, and although somewhat larger, she was much like her in rig and appearance. The *Dei Gratia* was still under British registry and her captain and first mate were Nova Scotians. Capt. David Morehouse was a Digby man, of a noted seafaring family. First Mate Oliver Deveau was a capable and experienced officer, of Acadian descent, from Saint Mary's Bay. Their cargo was consigned to a Mediterranean port. Exactly which port had not been decided by the shippers, and Captain Morehouse was to stop at Gibraltar for final orders, a common procedure in the Mediterranean trade. As it turned out, the cargo was going to Genoa. She sailed out of New York on November 15, 1872.

So by the quirks of circumstance here were two ships sailing the North Atlantic, eight days apart, both Nova Scotia built, both rigged as brigantines, both carrying potentially dangerous cargoes, and both bound from New York to Genoa.

November and December are rough months in the North Atlantic, and those of the year 1872 were no exception. The *Dei Gratia* weathered gales and heavy seas on much of the way.

The only land on the sea route from New York to Gibraltar was the Azores Islands, which lie far from any mainland, a scatter of small green cones extending over 400 miles. The most easterly of these islands was Santa Maria, about 2300 sea miles from New York and 800 from the coast of Portugal. British and American sailors knew it as Saint Mary's Island.

The *Dei Gratia* passed to the northward of the Azores, and at 1 P.M. on December 4 (December 5 by ship reckoning, which starts each day at noon) she was about 600 miles from Gibraltar. A seaman named Johnson was at the wheel, and Captain Morehouse standing nearby, when they sighted a brigantine very much like their own. As they drew closer Morehouse noted through his telescope that the stranger "was under very short canvas, steering very wild, and evidently in distress." He sent for First Mate Deveau. As Deveau testified later, "I came on deck and saw a vessel through the glass . . . about four or five miles off. The master proposed to speak the vessel in order to render assistance if necessary, and to haul wind for that purpose. We did. By my reckoning we were 38° 20′ North Latitude and 17° 15′ West Longitude."

As they drew near, Morehouse hailed and got no answer. He and Deveau could see now the disorderly state of the stranger's sails. Some were furled, others were hanging loose, and two had blown right off the yards leaving just a few rags of canvas. Her boat or boats were gone. There was nobody at her wheel; in fact, there was nobody on deck at all.

Deveau and two seamen put off in a boat to the derelict at three o'clock in the afternoon. There had been hard wind and rain in the morning, and although the weather was easing the sea was still running high. Deveau, a strong and fearless fellow, climbed aboard by the main chains (the stays of the mainmast where they are fastened to the hull) and one of his seamen followed. They found themselves in the silent presence of a mystery that was to tantalize the minds of landsmen and seamen ever after.

The painted lettering on her stern showed that she was the

Mary Celeste of New York, and so did the logbook and other documents in her cabin. There was not a soul aboard, living or dead. Not even a cat. The hatches of the fore hold and the lazarette were open, with the hatch covers lying on the deck. The cabin skylight was open. So were the doors of the galley, the cabin companionway and the forecastle, where sea water was sloshing about inside. Yet the cabin windows had been covered outside and well battened in preparation for bad weather. Three and a half feet of water lay in the hold, surging among the barrels of alcohol, although the barrels remained well stowed and in place. The ship's pumps were in good working order. There was no sign of serious damage to the hull, although it was evident that her deck had been washed by large waves during the past several days' bad weather. Fresh-water casks lashed in chocks on deck had been shifted bodily, chocks and all. The binnacle had been smashed by a sea and the compass ruined.

The Captain's cabin showed signs of a hasty departure. The bedding in the berth was unmade, and the sodden mattress bore the impress of a small body, as if a child had lain there. The Captain's chronometer and sextant were missing, but most of his charts and books remained. The cabin table had the usual "fiddle" —a rack of wooden squares—to keep dishes from sliding about in rough weather; but there was no food on the table, and none prepared in the galley. All the knives, forks and spoons were in their place in the pantry. Most of the clothing of the Captain, his wife and child were still in the cabin, and one of the child's dolls. The melodeon and sewing machine were in place, and so was Mrs. Briggs's case of needles, threads, buttons and hooks-and-eyes. The storeroom held plenty of provisions. There was a good supply of fresh water. The ship's logbook showed regular daily entries up to November 24. The "working log," a slate kept by the mate, had these inscriptions: "Monday, 25th. At 5 o'clock made the island of St. Mary's bearing E.S.E. At 8, Eastern point bore S.S.W. 6 miles distant."

That was the easterly finger of Santa Maria, known as Castello Point, the last landmark on the way to Gibraltar. The *Mary Ce-*

leste had passed along the north side of the island, and her mate had taken a departure bearing on Castello Point for the next run of dead-reckoning to Gibraltar.

From Santa Maria to the spot in the ocean where the *Dei Gratia* found the derelict ten days later was about 800 miles. With hard westerly and southwesterly gales, always the most dangerous to the people of the Azores but a great help to ships bound eastward, this drift was not surprising.

Boarding seas leaping through the open door of the galley had pushed the stove askew, and the fire inside was dead and cold. The cooking utensils hung on their proper hooks. Water covered the galley floor to the height of the door coaming, about ten inches. In the forecastle the seamen's possessions were untouched. Their sea chests contained various things of value, including a British five-pound banknote. Their clothing, oilskins, boots, razors, and even their pipes had been left behind. As Deveau pointed out afterwards, "My reason for saying they left in haste is that a sailor would generally take such things, especially his pipe."

The masts and their stays were perfectly sound, although there was much disorder in the sails and their running gear. On the foremast the square foresail and upper topsail had blown away, and the lower topsail drooped by its four corners. The jib and foretopmast-staysail were set and intact. The main staysail was down and lying loose on the fore house, as if the crew had let it fall "by the run." The mainsail was down and properly furled.

The main peak halyards (ropes used to hoist the gaff peak of the mainsail) had been slipped out of their blocks, and an end dangled, broken off short. This had a special significance later on.

The cargo was intact and there was no trace of fire or explosion in the holds. So the hatch covers of the lazarette and fore hold had not been blown off. They had been taken off and laid on the deck.

Deveau reported back to Captain Morehouse and they discussed this strange find. The *Mary Celeste* and her cargo were

165

valuable, and if she could be brought into port safely there would be salvage money for the owners and crew of the *Dei Gratia.* However, Morehouse, like any prudent master, had to consider the safety of his own ship and cargo first. They were 600 miles from Gibraltar, and the weather was not likely to ease much at this season of the year. If he divided his own small crew to man the *Mary Celeste* there was a strong chance that both ships might be in trouble, for a severe gale would catch them both with insufficient hands. Deveau was for taking the chance, and the decision was made. Deveau and two seamen, with the *Dei Gratia's* small boat, some cooked provisions, and the mate's navigation instruments, went over to the derelict. Deveau also took his pocket watch, because the clock in the cabin of the *Mary Celeste* had been damaged by water. The winter afternoon was far gone. It was only half an hour until sunset, with a hundred things to be done.

The first tasks were to put the hatches on, close the doors and skylight, and pump the water out of the holds. The three men set to work. After three hours' hard labor they got most of the water out of the ship. Then they set the remaining sails and rigged a makeshift foresail. Fortunately, the weather was moderate for two or three days, while Deveau and his men worked with little rest to "set her to rights."

For six days the ships sailed in company, and on the afternoon of December 11 they sighted Cape Spartel on the coast of Morocco. Then came a wild storm of wind and rain, and during the night the ships lost sight of each other. Captain Morehouse in the *Dei Gratia* managed to claw his way into Gibraltar on December 12. Deveau in the *Mary Celeste* was blown through the Gibraltar Strait as far as Ceuta on the African side. From there he was able to work the brigantine over to the Spanish side and follow that coast back to Gibraltar Bay. He arrived there on Friday the thirteenth, an unlucky day to the superstitious but a memorable and hopeful one for the three men on the salvaged ship.

Deveau wrote his wife: "My men were all done out when I

166

got in here, and I think it will be a week before I can do anything, for I never was so tired in my life. I can hardly tell what I am made of, but I do not care as long as I got in safe. I shall be well paid, for the *Mary Celeste* . . . was loaded with alcohol . . . and her cargo is worth eighty thousand dollars besides the vessel. We do not know how it will be settled yet. I expect the captain will have to stop, and I will proceed on the voyage with the *Dei Gratia*."

In these few words Oliver Deveau dismissed a feat of seamanship and endurance still remarkable in the records of the sea. Three men, boarding a derelict late on a winter afternoon, had "set her to rights" and sailed her well over 600 miles to port, suffering their greatest trial toward the end, in their exhausted state, when they had to weather a great storm in the narrow waters between Africa and Spain. They deserved a generous salvage award for their risks and toils, but Deveau overestimated the value of the cargo by far, and he had no notion of the difficulties in the way of the salvage claim.

The *Mary Celeste* was taken into custody immediately by the Marshal of the Vice-Admiralty Court at Gibraltar, and the hearings began on December 18. It was all done with full British punctilio under the supervision of Sir James Cochrane, who was Judge and Commissary of the Vice-Admiralty Court there. Various "Advocates and Proctors" (marine lawyers in Gibraltar, a notable place for salvage cases) represented Captain Morehouse and his owners, the owners and insurers of the *Mary Celeste*, and the owners and insurers of the cargo. But the person who really dominated the case was a zealous and highly imaginative official whose name and title might have come from a jingle by Gilbert and Sullivan. He was Frederick Solly Flood, Esquire, Advocate and Proctor for Her Majesty the Queen.

The case of the *Mary Celeste* was strange enough just as it stood, but Mr. Flood declared there had been foul play. When he prowled over the ship and its contents he found rusty spots on the deck, and on the old Italian sword which Deveau had discovered under the Captain's berth. These he declared to be

167

bloodstains. His assertions, like the stone in the quiet pond, set forth ripples of wild speculation that spread away from the Gibraltar courtroom and engaged all sorts of minds and pens from that day to this.

The case dragged on and on. After an expensive delay of ten days at Gibraltar, Captain Morehouse decided to send the *Dei Gratia* on to Genoa in charge of Mate Deveau. This aroused further suspicion on the part of Flood; and even Judge Cochrane remarked: "It appears very strange why the captain of the *Dei Gratia*, who knows little or nothing to help the investigation, should have remained here, whilst the first mate and crew who boarded the *Celeste* and brought her here should have been allowed to go away as they have done." As a result, Oliver Deveau had to leave the *Dei Gratia* in charge of the second mate at Genoa, and travel back to give further testimony in the court at Gibraltar.

In reply to questions he said calmly: "I noticed no marks or traces of blood upon the deck. I found that sword under the Captain's berth. There was nothing remarkable on it. I do not think there is anything remarkable about it now. It seems rusty. It did not occur to me that there had been any act of violence; there was nothing to induce one to believe or to show that there had been any violence."

A Gibraltar chemist, Dr. J. Patron, examined the marks or stains on the deck and on the sword, and decided that they were not bloodstains. A Gibraltar diver examined the hull of the *Mary Celeste* and found not the least damage or trace of grounding or collision. The hull was tight, and the water in the holds when she was discovered must have entered through the open hatches.

The hearing was still dragging on when J. H. Winchester arrived from New York to claim the *Mary Celeste* and to act for the insurance underwriters at New York. He had brought a new captain for the *Mary Celeste*, George Blatchford, a Massachusetts man, and he was anxious to get the ship and cargo on to Genoa. F. Solly Flood at once demanded that Winchester guarantee all claims, including that of the salvors, the costs of Her

168

Majesty's Vice-Admiralty Court, and any claim that might be made if the missing Captain and crew turned up alive. Winchester refused. Flood was insinuating, not only in the courtroom but by letter to the powerful British Board of Trade in London, that someone had bribed the sailors of the *Mary Celeste* to murder their officers and to leave the ship and cargo intact in a certain position off the Azores, where it would be "discovered" by salvagers. None of this made sense in view of the evidence, but Winchester inferred that he was being accused. He walked out of the courtroom in a rage and returned to New York by steamer from Lisbon, leaving a Gibraltar lawyer to fight the case through, and leaving Captain Blatchford to await the ship's release.

When the court did release the *Mary Celeste*, Blatchford had to spend another ten days refitting the brigantine's sails and running rigging, installing a new binnacle and compass, etc. It was not until March 10, 1873, that he was able to sail with a new crew for Genoa. On March 14, Judge Cochrane awarded the salvors of the *Mary Celeste* the sum of £1700, about $8300 in U.S. currency at the time. This was less than a fifth of the estimated value of ship and cargo, and by the time it was proportioned and distributed to the owners and crew of the *Dei Gratia*, nobody got very much. Certainly Oliver Deveau and his companions had a meager reward for their pluck and endurance.

When the *Mary Celeste* discharged her cargo at Genoa it was noted that some leakage or evaporation had occurred in many of the casks, and the loss amounted altogether to about nine barrels. This was not unusual nor a large loss in a cargo of 1701 barrels, *but it offered the only reasonable clue to the ship's abandonment.*

In wooden ships with highly inflammable cargoes, seamen had a wholesome suspicion of the stuff under their hatches. Morehouse with his cargo of petroleum was well aware of it. The Captain and crew of the *Mary Celeste* with her much more volatile and dangerous cargo were also aware of it. Alcohol leaking in a confined space would produce fumes that might explode on contact with a flame of any sort, or even a spark in the right condition. Even if the alcohol caught fire, without an explosion, the ship would flare up like a box of matches. In moderate weather it would have been possible to remove the hatch covers now and then to release any fumes that had gathered in the holds. Evidently, Captain Briggs did not consider it possible in the rough weather between New York and the Azores.

Then on November 26, after passing the eastern point of Santa Maria, something happened. Capt. David Morehouse told the Gibraltar court his theory, which he held firmly all his life. The fumes of escaped alcohol, developing pressure in the warmer atmosphere of the Azores, suddenly invaded the living quarters, fore and aft. Probably everybody smelled it at once. Naturally, Captain Briggs would order the doors and the cabin skylight to be opened. Then he ordered the seamen to take off the fore and lazarette hatch covers. The main hatch had the ship's boat lashed on its top, and therefore could not be removed without much effort and time. It was left on.

With the opening of the hatches there may have been a rush of vapor, but nothing more, and actually the danger was over then. But the seamen must have panicked and insisted on putting off in the ship's boat. Captain Briggs had no choice but to go along with them, taking his wife and child, and hoping to reason with the sailors before they went far from the ship. Although the wind had moderated, there was still a heavy sea. To put the boat into the water and then get ten people into it, the forward movement of the ship had to be stopped or greatly reduced. Hence the hasty and careless reduction of sail.

Removing a section of the ship's rail, they unlashed the boat and slid it over the side. Then they got into it—eight men, a woman, a child, and the ship's cat. As a natural precaution, Captain Briggs took with him his precious sextant and chronometer; but just as naturally he would have no intention of abandoning his ship altogether, especially in an overloaded boat, in a high sea. The nearest land was Santa Maria, miles to windward, and there was little or no hope of making it. Briggs's object obviously was to persuade the men to move away only to a prudent distance from the ship, and wait to see what, if anything, would happen. If no fire or explosion occurred, they could go back aboard and resume their voyage to Gibraltar.

Although the wind was light and the *Mary Celeste* now had only a few sails properly set, she was still moving slowly along. Therefore, before leaving the ship they secured a long rope by which they could tow at a safe distance astern. The handiest line for the purpose was the main peak halyard, and as the mainsail was lying furled on its boom the seamen had no trouble in getting the halyard out of its blocks and fastening one end to the boom. Letting this line pay out to its full length, they fastened the other end to the boat's bow and towed along at the same speed as the ship.

How long this went on, nobody could guess. The records of the meteorological stations in the Azores show that a cold front passed over the islands on the afternoon and evening of November 25, 1872. During the morning of the 25th the winds were light, but in the evening they sprang up to gale force. Reckoning by ship calendar, this would be on November 26.

Although sail had been so hurriedly reduced on the *Mary Celeste*, she was still carrying the square foresail and two topsails on her foremast, as well as the jib and foretopmast-staysail. With a sudden increase of wind these would fill out to full strain and send the ship bounding forward, dragging the overburdened boat by the single line of the halyard. Eventually, the foresail and upper topsail split and blew away, showing that the wind had risen to gale force. At that point, or perhaps before, the towline must have parted where it was fastened to the ship, for Deveau found the peak halyard "broke and gone." No labor at the boat's oars, however desperate, could overtake the flying *Mary Celeste*, and a small boat laden with ten people could not have lived long in a stormy sea beyond reach of the Azores. It was bound to swamp or capsize. So they perished, while their ship went bounding on to her blind rendezvous with another whose name, ironically enough, meant "Grace of God."

These are a seaman's theories, and Morehouse drew them with a firsthand knowledge of the sea, the weather, and the evidence aboard the derelict. Ever since 1872, however, this strange misadventure of the *Mary Celeste* has been told and retold, sometimes by authors frankly weaving fiction into it, sometimes by men purporting to reveal the truth. Frederick Solly Flood started it all with his first hasty report to the Board of Trade, which he made without regard to the chemist's analysis of the "blood" stains or the diver's report on the hull. According to Flood: "My own theory or guess is that the crew got at the alcohol, and in the fury of drunkenness murdered the Master, his wife and child and the chief mate; that they then damaged the bows of the vessel with a view to giving it the appearance of having struck on the rocks, or suffered a collision, so as to induce the master of any vessel which might pick them up, if they saw her at some distance, to think her not worth attempting to save; and that they did, some time between the 25th November and 5th December, escape on board some vessel bound for some North or South American port or the West Indies."

The man who gave Flood's theories their first display in the eyes of the world was Arthur Conan Doyle, famous afterwards as the creator of Sherlock Holmes. In 1884, during his final studies for a medical degree at Edinburgh University, Doyle tried his maiden pen by writing anonymously for the *Cornhill Magazine* a story called "J. Habakuk Jephson's Statement." Apparently, he had read or heard about F. Solly Flood's report on the *Mary Celeste,* and he contrived a tale of hatred and bloody murder, with no more basis than Flood's but far more entertaining. Doyle had yet to invent Sherlock Holmes, but already he could make mistakes like Doctor Watson, for example, giving the ship's name as *Marie Celeste,* an error followed faithfully by dozens of imitators down through the years since.

The only survivor of Ben Briggs's little family was young Arthur, left behind with his grandmother at Marion, Massachusetts. For months the old lady kept the bad news from the boy; but at last the U.S. consul at Gibraltar sent home the relics turned

172

over to him by the Vice-Admiralty Court, and with them came knowledge and sorrow. The list makes melancholy reading even to a stranger at this distance of time; the little rosewood melodeon, still capable of ghostly tunes, two documents of the Freemasons, nightshirts, two lady's hats, a crinoline, two blouse pins, a doll, and so forth.

From Genoa, Captain Blatchford sailed the *Mary Celeste* across the Atlantic to Boston, where he arrived on September 1, 1873. The owner, J. H. Winchester, put the ship up for sale. Many people came to look at her out of curiosity. Others, not knowing the ship's history, came to bid for her, but on learning the tale lost interest at once. It was as if the *Mary Celeste* were bewitched —and New Englanders never had liked witchcraft. Winchester sent the ship to New York, where eventually he managed to sell her. On going over the accounts, he found that she had lost $8000 between the time of his purchase and the sale.

The new owners were the firm of Cartwright & Harrison of Brooklyn, N.Y., and they had a long and sad experience with the hoodoo ship. Talking to the New York *World* in 1886, Cartwright said: "We owned her for five years, and of all the unlucky vessels I ever heard of, she was the most unlucky. When we sold her we found we had lost some $5000. Most of the time that we owned her she was in the general West Indian trade, and sometimes she lost her deck load of molasses and sometimes she didn't, but generally she did. We sent her out to Montevideo with a cargo of lumber and of course she arrived there minus her deck load; but we had got to expecting this. She had heavy weather, lost sails and spars, etc. There, the captain got a charter for Mauritius to carry horses. He had dreadful weather off the Cape of Good Hope, and on arriving at Mauritius the few horses left alive were too ill to be worth anything. The captain then obtained a good charter to bring a freight from Calcutta. On the passage home he was taken sick. In consequence the brig had to put in to Saint Helena, where after a detention of three weeks the captain died, and the mate brought the brig home. We next sent her to the coast of Africa, and on this voyage she lost $1000. After this we kept her in the West Indian trade, and at the end of five years were glad to sell her at a low figure."

The *Mary Celeste* now passed into the hands of Boston men headed by Wesley A. Gove, who operated the ship unsuccessfully for four years. At that point they hired a new captain, Gilman C. Parker, and Parker contrived the last voyage of the notorious brigantine. It was a memorable affair, one that would have delighted Sherlock Holmes, although in actual fact the relentless sleuth in the case was a Yankee marine-insurance investigator.

At Boston the *Mary Celeste* loaded a mixed cargo for Haiti in the West Indies. It was supposed to contain 475 barrels of salt fish, many barrels of bottled ale, and sundry cases and packages of cutlery, boots, shoes, paint, varnish and other dry goods and hardware. Actually, most of the items were of another description and worthless, and their entry on the ship's manifest was fraud. Capt. Gilman Parker, in collusion with the shippers, placed insurance to the amount of $25,000 on his ship and cargo. He sailed from Boston on December 15, 1884.

The voyage southward passed from the New England winter into the perpetual summer of the West Indies without incident. On January 3, 1885, the *Mary Celeste* was sailing between the island of Gonave and the long southwest finger of Haiti. The channel was about twenty-five miles wide, with no obstruction in it but a patch of coral that rose three feet above water and was plainly visible. It was marked on the chart as the Rochelois Bank. With a fair wind and a clear sky such as yachtsmen dream about, Captain Gilman ordered his helmsman to steer straight for the reef. The whole object of the voyage was to wreck the ship deliberately and thoroughly, in a place as far as possible from quick investigation by the underwriters, yet where the Captain and crew could get ashore with ease. For all these purposes the Rochelois Bank was ideal.

At 1:30 in the afternoon the *Mary Celeste*, under full sail, fetched up on the reef, where she was bound to fall apart in the first gale that blew. Gilman Parker ordered his crew to cut away the foremast "to ease her." With the stays of the foremast cut away and the foremast overboard, the mainmast could not stand long, and Captain Parker invited his men to go below and have a drink before setting off for the mainland. The Haitian coast was only twelve miles or so away, and with sail hoisted on the ship's boat they made an easy passage to a sleepy little port called Miragoane. The town, mostly hovels, lay at the foot of a mountain, and the anchorage was screened by small islands covered with mangroves. The islands had shelving beaches where a ship could be careened and scraped clean of marine growth, and vessels bound to or from Port au Prince, fifty miles to the eastward, sometimes stopped at Miragoane for the purpose.

Here Gilman Parker found an American consular agent who might have stepped out of a Central American story by O. Henry. His name was Mitchell, and any sort of shady dealing was his meat and drink. Parker told him where the wreck was, mentioned that she was well insured, and sold ship and cargo to Mitchell for $500. He and his merry men then went on to Port au Prince and took passage to the United States.

Parker and the shippers of the cargo had contrived a neat trick. True, the Captain had committed a crime called barratry in marine law, and at that time barratry involving the deliberate wrecking of a ship could be punished by death. But none of the conspirators had the least worry over that. When the crew reached the United States, Gilman quickly found berths for them in vessels outward bound, and there was no one left to talk. The underwriters of the *Mary Celeste* and her cargo soon faced claims for the full $25,000.

One thing ruined all this careful knavery—one man, really. He was Kingman Putnam, an alert marine surveyor and investigator. The part of Haiti on which Gilman Parker and his crew had landed was a long lean peninsula like a finger in the Caribbean Sea. Just across the finger from their landing place was a little port called Aux Cayes. By chance, just when the loss of the *Mary*

Celeste was reported in New York, Putnam was about to leave for an investigation into the wreck of an American vessel at Aux Cayes. The underwriters of the *Mary Celeste* asked Putnam to look into their case as well. After all, the two wrecks, one on each side of the peninsula, were barely forty miles apart.

As Putnam reported afterwards: "Several of the underwriters told me that they had just received claims from the shippers of the cargo of the *Mary Celeste*. They gave me all these documents. The steamer I took to Haiti stopped at Port au Prince. I called upon the firms who were consignees of this merchandise and obtained from them copies of the letters they had received from the Boston shippers. . . . At Miragoane I found that Mitchell had saved most of the cargo of the *Mary Celeste* in sound condition. Some packages of this cargo were still on hand. I opened one case which had been shipped as cutlery and insured for $1000. It contained dog collars worth about $50. Cases insured as boots and shoes contained shoddy rubbers worth about 25 cents each. That night I slept on board the schooner *Mary E. Douglas*. I gave the Captain some money and requested him to buy certain of these cases from Mitchell, and obtain from him a consular certificate that these packages were part of the *Mary Celeste* cargo. The Captain did this, and delivered the cases to a lawyer in Boston.

"Upon my return I went to Boston. The consequence was that Captain Parker, the master of the *Mary Celeste*, was indicted for barratry and conspiracy, and the shippers of the cargo were indicted for conspiracy. This necessitated getting the original letters written by these firms to the consignees at Port au Prince. There was no steamer going for several weeks, so we chartered the steamer *Saxon*. I was made a United States Deputy Marshal with power to subpoena men in Haiti to come to Boston. I also received from Washington an order directing Mitchell to return with me. Of course the subpoenas were of no legal value, but they enabled me to obtain from the merchants in Port au Prince all the documents I wanted. When we went to Miragoane a Haitian general boarded the *Saxon* and told me that Mitchell would take to the woods, but that he had instructions from President

Solomon to put Mitchell on board the *Saxon* with a file of soldiers, at my request. I thought that to shanghai an American consul on a vessel carrying the British flag might entail some consequences which I did not care to assume, especially as I had been signed on the *Saxon's* crew as 'Chaplain.' The general's invitation was therefore politely declined. I went ashore. Mitchell did take to the woods. We cleaned out his place."

While this was going on, the underwriters engaged a lawyer named Henry M. Rogers to sniff out the Boston end of the conspiracy. Years later Rogers told about it in the Boston Sunday *Globe*.

I kept detectives in two of the stores of the Boston merchants for more than forty days. They found that the cargo was of dried fish and ale; that the fish was spoiled and stank; the ale was the rinsings of casks and some ullaged ale, also worthless. Little by little I began to get the story. I found that the captain of the *Mary Celeste* had been asked whether he was not afraid some of the crew would give him away, and he had replied that he could buy any of them for a glass of rum.

The mate of the *Celeste* had been shipped only the day before she sailed. If I could get him, and get him to tell the true story, he would be my most important witness. I found that he was in a ship expected to arrive at Boston from Hamburg, and arranged to get word as soon as she was reported from Highland Light. I hustled down, but my man—he was captain of her—had already left. I asked where "Cap'n Joe" might be, and the watchman said he had gone home to East Boston. Casually, I managed to find out that he had been gone about forty minutes, and to get a description of what he wore. I, of course, had never seen the man.

I figured a sailor ashore—nearest saloon—say twenty minutes for a glass or two—then the ferry. At the North Ferry there was Cap'n Joe. I trailed him to his home in East Boston, and as soon as he was safely indoors hustled back to my office for the paper I needed. When I got back and rang his doorbell he had gone out again. I hunted up the nearest saloon, and there he was in the back room having a drink all by himself. I pretended to have taken a few myself and to know him. I bought more than one drink, he bought some, and then I said, "I want you to tell me, Joe, all you know about the *Marie* [sic] *Celeste*." He shut up then, but I began to feed him what I already knew—that the cargo was a fake, that the ship was piled up in broad daylight on a sunny morning on the only rock anywhere near, and that the captain wasn't afraid of what Joe might say because he could buy him for a glass of rum.

By this time Joe was somewhat alarmed. He took me to his home, and his wife joined me in pleading with him to make disclosure. I was really trying to protect him against any claim that he was a partner and a profiteer in the wrecking.

So Joseph E. Howe, the former mate of the *Mary Celeste,* hired for that final voyage, told Rogers what he knew. On the way south Capt. Gilman Parker had told him that the ship was to be wrecked deliberately at Turk's Island, to the north of Haiti. Joe knew that Turk's was a small exposed island in a maze of reefs and shoals. He said to Parker, "For God's sake don't pile her up there, we shall all be drowned." Then Captain Parker examined the chart and marked the reef called La Rochelois in the Gonave Channel. It was so small a reef that Joe quipped, "Do you think you can hit that?" Captain Parker was sure he could. Joe went on to describe how the *Celeste* was run on the reef, with a fair wind and broad sunlight, and how the masts were cut away and the ship abandoned. Armed with this affidavit, Rogers got court orders and set a watch for the former sailors of the *Mary Celeste,* all of whom had shipped away on other voyages. As they arrived back in Boston, one after another, Rogers had them arrested and clapped into jail, where he could be sure of finding them when he wanted them.

The trial of Captain Parker was, of course, a criminal case, and naturally the defense hammered away at one point—that the case had been built up really by the insurance companies to evade payment on their policies. For that reason the insurance lawyer Rogers stayed out of the courtroom; but he made sure that former mate Joseph Howe was there, scowling at the seamen as, one after another, they gave witness. None of them dared to lie.

Mrs. Howe testified that shortly after her husband returned

178

from Haiti, Captain Parker gave her a letter for him, which she produced in court.

East Boston, March 5, '85

Cap. J. E. Howe:

I wood advise you not to know to much a bout cargo fer the shippers have put in their bill of Invoice to the adgestors and the Protest and Log Book as they stand is all that I want. You will be cald over to the Insurance. Look out you do not get in the Roung track by knowing to much.

G. C. Parker

Parker was first tried on the charge of conspiracy to defraud. The more serious charge of barratry was to follow. He was plainly guilty of both, and by the human quirks of the jury system that was what saved him. Three of the jurors in the conspiracy trial held out for a verdict of Not Guilty, knowing that conviction on this charge would almost certainly bring a conviction on the barratry charge, where the penalty could be death. After forty-eight hours these men remained obdurate, and the judge was obliged to discharge the jury. The prosecution gave notice for a new trial, but eventually Parker was allowed to go free. He had been the tool of the shippers, all of whom confessed to the charge of conspiracy. One firm had collected $5000 on the rotten fish and was forced to pay it back with interest, plus $1000 for court costs. The others were dealt with on the same scale. All went bankrupt within six months, and one man committed suicide. Capt. Gilman Parker never got another command at sea. In his latter years he made a meager living as a crossing watchman on the railway line at Winthrop Beach, near Boston, and he died a pauper there in 1891.

Of all the captains of the *Mary Celeste,* from first to last, only John Nutting Parker seemed immune to the hoodoo that went with her. All the others suffered hardship, disappointment, disgrace or death—three of them actually died while in command. One lies in a lost grave in what is called "The Marsh Field" near the shore at Economy, N.S. Another lies on Saint Helena, that lone speck in the South Atlantic where Napoleon Bonaparte came in the very year that the builder of the *Mary Celeste* was born. The bones of Ben Briggs lie somewhere on the sea floor near the Azores, in the legendary sunken land of Atlantis.

Some years after he built the famous brigantine at Spencer's Island, Joshua Dewis removed a few miles along the shore to a place called Advocate, where he bought 500 acres of land, mostly wooded, beside a sheltered cove. There he built a new home and continued building ships. At the same time he operated as a farmer, mainly raising cattle, until he was a very old man. He died in 1896 as he had lived, an honest workman and a devout Baptist, and his grave is in the Advocate cemetery.

His son Robert went to sea before the mast in a Dewis ship, became a master mariner, sailed many years about the world, retired at last to the home at Advocate, and died in his bed at a good old age. The house still stands, filled with pictures, models and mementos of the Dewis ships.

In the village called Spencer's Island the old Spicer home survives also, looking down to the beach and the now flooded spot where the *Mary Celeste* was put together, and seaward toward the round hump of Glooscap's kettle. The seventh generation of the Spicer family lives there, and for the inquiring visitor they bring out scrapbooks filled with news cuttings about the Spencer's Island ships, not least the *Mary Celeste*.

And the *Mary Celeste* herself? The wreckers left her dismasted and with a broken keel on that little patch of coral named for some bygone ship or seaman from Rochelle in France. Haitian waters are thrashed by hurricanes every summer and autumn, and the twenty-four-year-old brigantine must have gone to pieces in the first big sea. Parts of her must have washed ashore on Gonave Island or the Haitian mainland, and no doubt people there salvaged bits of strange northern wood and used them in various ways, quite ignorant of their origin. Most of her metal parts must be sunk there still by La Rochelois, caked in coral, unrecognizable now, more than two thousand miles from the Nova Scotia beach where she was born.

The Lost Gold at Kejimkujik

Wherever there is gold in the world (and in many places where it isn't) you hear tales of a lost lode; of a rich strike known to one man who was killed or perished anyhow before he could tell a word of it; of a prospector stumbling over a fortune in the desert on his way to some lifesaving waterhole, and unable to find his way back. And there are the fabulous gold outcrops known only to savages, who keep their secret lest it bring down an evil rush of white men, or the wrath of whatever gods they have. And mines lost with the native race themselves, like those of the Aztecs and Incas.

In the corner of Canada where I live there is the story of a Micmac Indian who found gold and kept it secret, but "lived high on it for years." The man himself has been dead longer than Queen Victoria, in whose reign he spent most of his life; but there are people in Nova Scotia who believe his "mine" may yet be found.

The Micmacs long ago adopted French, and later some Scotch and English names. This man's name was Jim, and because his father's name was Charles the white folk naturally called the son Jim Charles. He lived in the backwoods of western Nova Scotia by the shore of a lake called Kejimkujik. The word is pronounced "kej-im-*koo*-jik," and in medical English it means "the strictured passage," or in laymen's language "the gut is choked." The Indians called it that because their fish weirs in the outlet partly blocked the stream, and so backed up the water and caused the lake to swell. Our modern woodsmen in conversation shorten the name to "Kej" and let it go at that.

When I think of Jim Charles and his famous find I'm reminded of the shepherd in *The Winter's Tale:* "This is fairy gold, boy . . . keep it close." For you see, Jim really did find gold, and sold it quietly for years, but kept his secret close. Then he ran out of luck. Not gold. Just luck.

The discovery of gold in California in 1848 drew men from all over the world, and Nova Scotia men, seafarers by trade and adventurers by nature, were among the first. Many stayed in California. Some wandered home after a few years, with nothing to show for their work and travel but a new skill at seeking and panning for gold, a stuff that people at home had never seen except in the form of coins, and precious few at that.

The famous gold strike in Australia was made in 1851 by a local man who had learned what to look for in the California diggings. That brought in a rush of people, even though many of them had to come half around the world, and the Australian's word for himself is "digger" still. There had been rumors of gold in Nova Scotia for a long time, beginning with the first hopeful French explorers. In the year 1860 someone proved a discovery at a place called Tangier on the eastern coast. Then in 1861 someone found gold on a sea beach near Lunenburg, on the western coast. During the next thirty years it was found in various parts of the province. There were dozens of strikes, and smart promoters floated companies all over the place, most of them doomed to sink in a few years. Gold was there all right. The assays proved it. The weakness was in quantity. Not to be technical about it, the gold of Nova Scotia lies in thin spidery threads of quartz wandering through the deep mass of bedrock and creeping to the surface here and there. Where two veins meet or cross there may be a rich pocket of gold nuggets and dust, plain to be seen if the junction happens in the bed of a shallow stream.

Naturally, the alluvial gold was found first, on the coast and in the rivers. Then came the inevitable drive to find the "mother lode," which took organized mining companies down into the bedrock—and into bankruptcy. For every dollar wrung out of the Nova Scotia bedrock at least twenty more were just poured down holes that led to nothing. Yet even today there are men who say the mines never went deep enough, that the mother lode is there all right, 'way down.

But that is the dream of gold miners everywhere.

Jim Charles was born in a wigwam somewhere in the Nova Scotia forest about the year 1830, when the remnant of his people still followed their ancient habit of seasonal wandering up and down the rivers and along the coast. By 1870, when the white man's diseases had ravaged the Micmacs for more than two centuries, the tribe had dwindled to small groups, wandering still, but spending their winters on the edge of white towns and villages for the ease of begging clothes and food. The Nova Scotia Government had tried to stabilize their vagrant way of life by granting every family a piece of land and a few cattle and urging them to farm. Most of the Micmacs just stopped long enough to eat the cattle and then wandered on as before. Jim Charles was one of the few who managed their lives both ways.

He had got a grant of government land on a point in Kejimkujik, where the Mersey River entered the lake on its way toward the sea. The place had been a favorite camping ground of the Indians for centuries, and in the ancient clearing he built a small log cabin and barn. He pastured his six cattle and a horse in a wild meadow nearby, and cut enough coarse hay there to keep them alive through the winters. In the Indian custom, his squaw Lizzie did most of the work about the "farm," leaving Jim free

183

to roam the forest and the streams. The region of Kejimkujik was famous for fish and game, and visiting sportsmen found Jim the best of guides. The money they paid him kept Jim in gunpowder, shot, and tobacco, and enabled him to buy a store dress now and then for Lizzie and their adopted child, a half-breed girl named Madeleine.

Autumn brought a great migration of eels down the Nova Scotia rivers, slithering away to spawn at some far mysterious rendezvous in the sea. Whenever September came, Jim and the others in the little Indian group about Kejimkujik set up their weir in the outlet of the lake. The process was old and simple. Long before the Micmacs, in a time going back out of mind, a savage people had chosen a season of low water and rolled stones into place on the river bed, forming a wide "V" from shore to shore. Every fall, Jim and the others cut branches of spruce and fir and fixed them upright in these submerged walls, so that the tips stood out of water. This green dam forced the fish down to the point of the "V," where a great woven basket trap awaited them. Fat from a long stay in fresh water, the eels usually started for the sea in dark October nights, when the autumn rains were swelling the streams after a summer's drought. On such nights the Indians caught them in hundreds, emptying the trap at intervals with dip nets, and carrying the eels to pits dug in the earth above the shore. There by daylight the squaws killed them, stirred them in the gathered ashes of wood fires to remove the slime, and skinned them and smoked them for winter food.

So Jim Charles lived the happiest life possible for an Indian. From April till November he fished, hunted, or merely roved the forest as he pleased. Then came the comfort of the snug cabin by the shore of Kejimkujik, screened from north winds by tall pine woods; with Lizzie's bins full of potatoes, turnips and corn, with barrels of smoked eels, and always a haunch or two of venison hanging in the woodshed.

About five miles east of "Kej" the post road from Liverpool to Annapolis crossed over the Mersey River at a place called Maitland Bridge. The road passed through forest most of the way across the province, and the mail coach and its few passengers came and went twice a week.

A Maitland farmer named Munro was friendly with the Indians and knew their language. The Micmacs spoke English in a slow and jerky way, and Munro's ability to talk to them in their own tongue gave him a special place in their esteem. When Jim Charles hitched his old horse to the rattletrap wagon and drove over the loggers' tote road from "Kej" to Maitland Bridge he was always welcome to eat and rest at the Munro home. On the other hand, when the young farmer went to "Kej" for a fishing or hunting holiday he enjoyed the use of Jim's canoe and his company as guide.

While still a young man Munro died, leaving his widow with a small son named Clayton. After a time she married another Maitland farmer named Nixon, and they continued the old friendship with the Micmacs. Young Clayton Munro grew up with a knowledge of the Micmac language and the forest and streams about Kejimkujik. He studied hard at the village school. In his late teens he began working with the loggers on the river drives, and saved his money carefully. His ambition, implanted by his mother, was to go away and study for the Methodist ministry.

The best of Jim Charles's sportsmen friends was Judge Ritchie of Annapolis, who liked to fish the streams about "Kej" in spring and early summer, and to do a bit of shooting in the fall. He was interested in Lizzie's efforts at small farming, and to help her in the way of cash he arranged to market the butter she made in her little cannon-and-ramrod churn. Each week she packed it in wooden firkins, homemade like the butter itself, and Jim sent off the small tubs to Annapolis by the mail coach as it passed through Maitland Bridge. The farmers, the coachmen, and Ritchie's neighbors in Annapolis, all became used to seeing the butter tubs from "Kej," and thought no more about it.

In spring when the trout were biting well, and in fall when

bull moose would come to the mating call of Jim's birchbark horn, the Judge boarded the coach at Annapolis, drove thirty-five miles over the hills to Maitland Bridge, and thence by farm wagon another five miles to "Kej." The lake made a good base for hunters and fishermen. It was surrounded by forest, and to the west of it especially ran a wild expanse of woods and streams, pathless except for the faint portage trails of the Indians from one stream to another. Although no part of it was much more than six hundred feet above sea level, the region formed the central watershed of western Nova Scotia. From it, like crazy spokes from a wagon hub, the rivers wandered away in all directions to the sea; yet their headwaters rose so close together that in no more than a day's journey, in some places less than an hour's, an Indian could tote his canoe from one to another. Thus, taking his time—and who had more time than a Micmac?—he could range with ease over the whole of the western peninsula.

Much of the hub was a rugged wilderness of granite barrens, studded with boulders left by the last Ice Age, and with pockets of swamp. In places there were glacial deposits of gravel running on for miles as trim as railway embankments, and the Indians said they were roads made by a vanished race of giants. In other places arose oval hills and ridges of the kind called drumlins by geologists, each composed of gravel, clay and loam pushed into great heaps by moving ice and shaped by water torrents that flowed along the glacier's sides. Such hills were fertile, and covered now with tall stands of forest. Streams of the present age wandered about the rough landscape, linking hundreds of small lakes like beads of wampum, in a complicated pattern that only the Indians understood. Although white timber cruisers had made working sketches of the areas of good forest, the region as a whole remained unmapped until well into the twentieth century.

The gold discoveries of 1860 and 1861 in Nova Scotia were on the coast or near the mouths of rivers flowing to the Atlantic face of the peninsula. Men back from California soon guessed that the source of the stuff was up the rivers, in the forest. This gossip reached everywhere, even to the Micmac shacks at Kejimkujik. The notion of wealth to be found at random in the woods had a great fascination for the Indians. Here at last was something that might put them on the level of the white man, without special knowledge or equipment, just a keen eye and a bit of luck. They had a word for money, *sooleawa*, which they had seen in the form of silver. When white prospectors told them about the new valuable stuff to be sought in the beds of streams they showed a gold coin for example. Thus, the Micmacs came to know gold as *wisosooleawa*, which means literally "brown silver."

One spring in the early 1870s Judge Ritchie came to "Kej" for a fishing trip and found his usually stolid guide twitching with excitement. Jim declared that he had found the "brown silver" that all the white men were talking about. The Judge thought of copper and iron pyrites, which exist in freak formations in Nova Scotia, sometimes in small cubes that can be dug out of a boulder with a hunting knife. Gently he explained to Jim about "fools' gold." For answer the Indian opened a small leather pouch and showed him a handful of nuggets and dust. He had found these, he said, while paddling his canoe along a stream. The water was low, the sun high, and there was this shining stuff on the bottom. He had stopped the canoe and scooped up some of the *wisosooleawa* with his free hand. He added that there was a lot more where this came from.

Ritchie was still doubtful but he cautioned Jim to keep mum about his find. When he returned home to Annapolis he took Jim's pouch of "brown silver" and sent it off to the United States for an assay. On his next trip to "Kej" he had the assay report. He said, "Jim, it's gold all right. Now remember, you must keep your find secret. Don't tell a soul. Fetch the stuff out a little at a time and send it to me at Annapolis. I'll arrange to have it sold in the States, so nobody hereabouts will suspect, and I'll see that you get the money." When Jim asked, "How I send it?" the Judge pondered a bit. Then he said, "In Lizzie's butter firkins. Wrap up the gold and hide it in the butter."

And so Jim Charles began to work his find. The gold went to Annapolis by mail coach in the little butter tubs, and Ritchie arranged the sale of it through a bank in the States. Whenever he came to "Kej" he brought some of the cash proceeds. The greater part remained on deposit, in the name of Jim Charles, in the bank at Annapolis. This went on for some years. It might have gone on for many more. The Judge's arrangement was quite secure. Unfortunately, Jim's mind was not. More and more the Indian hankered to spend that wonderful heap of cash awaiting him at the bank. At last he traveled by the mail coach to Annapolis, drew some money from the bank, spent it in local shops, and returned home with his purchases.

After several trips like this he was no longer satisfied with the stores of Annapolis, a sleepy little farming town on the railway line from Yarmouth to Halifax, the capital of the province. His next venture was to get on "the steam cars" at Annapolis and travel to Halifax, which by Nova Scotia standards in the 1870s was a big and bustling city. There he found shops selling wonderful things, from the finest English rifles and shotguns to saddlery and carriages. When he arrived back at "Kej" he came all the way by road, in an elegant carriage, behind a span of matched chestnut horses, and the carriage was loaded with fancy clothes for himself, for Lizzie and Madeleine.

As time went by he got a silver-mounted harness for the horses. He developed a love of fine watches, and carried as many as four at a time, with their chains glittering from pocket to pocket. When he drove with Lizzie into the village of Caledonia, or the more distant towns of Liverpool and Annapolis, they made a remarkable show. Lizzie still wore the cap of dark-blue cloth, shaped like a cowl and covered with sewn beads, which long had been the headgear of Micmac women on festive occasions; but she draped fine ladies' gowns about her skinny person, squeezed her feet into uncomfortable high-buttoned boots, and stumped painfully from carriage to store with a silk parasol aloft to shield her wrinkled brown skin from the sun.

By this time everyone knew that Jim Charles had found gold somewhere about "Kej," and furtive strangers had appeared in the district, watching every move he made. Jim was aware of them, of course, and he rather enjoyed leading them on false trails through the tangled woods about the lake. None of them ever managed to follow him to his "mine." Nobody knew how he got the gold or where he sold it. But there was bound to be trouble, and it came.

Beside the tote road through the forest from Maitland Bridge to "Kej" stood the cabin of a Micmac couple whose name was Gload, an Indian rendering of the French name Claude. They were quiet people but they had an unquiet daughter in her teens, and lately she had found a lover. He was a white man named Hamilton, a deserter from a ship at Liverpool, forty-five miles away. Hamilton struck up an acquaintance with the Gload girl soon after he made his way inland to the "Kej" district, and before long he was living with her in the Gload cabin, not far from the lake. He soon heard about Jim Charles and his gold, and like others he tried to follow Jim into the wilderness, only to get lost and suffer a hard and hungry time before he found his way out again.

One day, hot with rum, Hamilton thrust his way into Jim's cabin and demanded to know where the gold was. When Jim kept silent the deserter turned from words to blows, and when poor Lizzie tried to intervene he knocked her to the floor. The intruder was young and strong. Jim was forty-five. So he caught up one of his fine new guns. He had no thought of shooting. He had no wish to kill the man. Instead he swung the gun by the barrel and smote Hamilton's head with the butt. The deserter went down to the floor with a thump. In a few moments he was dead, and Jim Charles had something else to worry about, something burned on every Indian's mind from away back, the penalty for killing a white man.

The nearest magistrate was a man named Harlow, who kept a

store in Caledonia, twenty miles away. Harlow's customers were astounded to see Jim Charles dash up to the store in his carriage, with his horses in a lather and himself with a bruised face and wild eyes. He leaped down, ran into the store, and fell on his knees before the merchant crying, "Mister Harlow! Save me! Save me! I killed Hamilton!"

There were no police in country districts in those days, and the law wore an easy face. The village elders appointed annually a local man to act as "constable." He got no pay except for serving a warrant, in which case he was entitled to collect twenty-five cents. There was also a local magistrate who seldom knew much law but was appointed for his common sense. Harlow used his now.

He called together a coroner's jury, and they traveled in a little procession of buggies and riding wagons to Kejimkujik. There they examined Hamilton's body and heard the testimony of Lizzie and Madeleine. When all was said and done, the verdict was "death by misadventure." Nearly everybody in the district agreed with it, and said that Hamilton had got what was coming to him. But there were some who declared Jim Charles a murderer and said he should be hanged.

Not knowing how far a coroner's verdict could protect him, Jim decided not to take a chance. Instead he took to the woods with a light bark canoe, his familiar traveling equipment, and a gun and ammunition. Far up the Shelburne River he turned off to a small lake lying just to the south of it. A wandering Acadian woodsman in the early days had called it Couffin, a French word for a basket made of rushes or wood splints, such as the Indians used. Perhaps he considered the lake's shape to be that of a *couffin*. Perhaps he found a basket there, abandoned by some passing Micmac party. At all events, the French woodsmen came to know it by that name, and the Micmacs themselves imitated the word and used it thenceforth. On their lips it came out "Koofang," and because some English-speaking surveyor misunderstood the sound it appears on modern maps as "Two Fan Lake."

"Koofang" (or, properly, Couffin) Lake flowed into the Shelburne River by a meandering brook. On the semibarren slope behind the lake stood many granite boulders, some as big as houses. One of these had a cave under it, where Jim had sheltered sometimes in his wanderings, and from its top there was a good view of the Shelburne River. A man could hide and watch there, in case a party came up the river in search of him, and if they did he had two handy ways of escape. He could cross over the Shelburne, carry his canoe and gear along an old Indian portage, and paddle away down the Sissiboo, a river flowing northward to the Bay of Fundy. Or he could go a few miles up the Shelburne to its source, and portage from there to the Tusket River, which flowed to the southwest.

Jim remained in hiding at "Koofang" for three years, a fugitive from his own fears, for no one went in search of him. Sometimes Lizzie and the girl Madeleine took their canoe and traveled in secret to his hideout with supplies. No one else knew where he was. Most of the Micmacs were vagrant by instinct, the heritage of a woodland race, and it was no new thing for a man to disappear just like that. Jim's white friends at Maitland Bridge questioned Lizzie but got no news of him. He had gone, she said. Just gone.

Probably during those three hidden years Jim made secret journeys to his home at Kejimkujik, but they must have been few and far between. He could trust nobody at "Kej," not even the other Indians. The Gload girl hated the man who killed her lover. And the Indians envied his luck and his gold, and grumbled that he kept it to himself, a crime in Micmac society, where the successful hunter always shared his meat with the unlucky.

At last, however, Jim realized that the affair had blown over, and he came back to stay openly in his home on the "Kej" shore. He was gaunt from his long exile in the wilderness, especially the winters in the cave. His health was never good again, and he had in his bones the rheumatism which was to make him an utter cripple in old age. Clayton Munro had gone away to study for the church. His mother and stepfather tried to persuade Jim Charles to show some reliable white man where the gold

191

was, so that a claim could be staked and registered in Jim's name with the Department of Mines. They warned him that other bad characters were bound to turn up, ready to go to any length to get what was really his. But Jim only said what he always said when his friends mentioned the subject: "Bad luck for Injun tell where is gold." During the years of Jim's disappearance Judge Ritchie ceased his visits to "Kej," and he died soon afterwards, so that wise counsel was lost.

Then Lizzie died. She was frail and probably afflicted with tuberculosis, the curse of the Micmacs. Their adopted daughter Madeleine was now a stolid young woman in her twenties. In the primitive Indian fashion, without ceremony, probably without thinking much about it except that the squaw's duties were now hers alone, she took Lizzie's place in Jim's bed. Within a year she had a child. Some of the white folk shook their heads over this, forgetting that Indians were no more subject to the moral niceties of white folk than the birds of the air or the moose in the woods. For a time all went well with Jim, and Madeleine clearly enjoyed driving about with him in the carriage and wearing Lizzie's finery, even to the parasol.

The men watching Jim's movements in the forest now included experienced woodsmen, white and red, and he could not shake them off with his old tricks anymore. For several years he dared not venture to his "mine." He accepted the situation stolidly, thinking that it would pass, like the Hamilton affair. Meanwhile there remained a fair sum in the bank at Annapolis.

Apart from the gold hunters there were many men who came to "Kej" in search of fish and game. Some were glad to hire Jim Charles as their guide. Others had fished and hunted for years in the "Kej" country and no longer needed a guide. Three of the latter kind arrived at Kejimkujik by wagon from the railway line at Annapolis in the summer of 1884. They were townsmen from Yarmouth at the west end of the province. Jim Charles had seen them before and knew their names: Ruggles, Burrell and Stoddard. They unloaded the wagon at Jake's Landing, where the loggers' tote road from Maitland Bridge emerged on the river just before it entered the lake. They had brought a small birch-bark canoe—too small, really, for three men with all their gear and supplies, but they got in boldly and paddled around the river bend into the lake, passing close to Jim Charles's Point.

Kejimkujik Lake was five miles long and two to three miles wide, but it looked much smaller. The northern half of it was divided by a long finger of woodland called Indian Point. In the southern half lay several islands, large and small, covered with green masses of tall trees. On windy days the Indians knew how to get across the lake by working their canoes from the shelter of one island to another. "Kej" could be dangerous in sudden squalls, and the three townsmen were asking for trouble when they set out across the lake in an overloaded and cranky canoe. They were deceived by the calmness of the day. Not a breath of air was stirring as they passed Jim Charles's Point and headed for Hog Island on the way to the longer Indian Point.

About halfway to Hog Island the canoe lurched, probably in a sudden vagrant gust of wind. Over it went, pitching the three men into the water. A birchbark canoe had very little buoyancy in its materials, and when the three men tried to cling to its bottom the thing sank too far under their weight to be of any help. They yelled, and their cries were heard as far away as the home of David Lewis, a white man who lived with his Indian wife on the tote road above Jake's Landing. Lewis, of course, was too far away to do anything, even if he had known what the yelling was about. Jim Charles had seen the men go by the point where he lived, but he thought no more of them and went about his own concerns. Before anyone could reach the scene the three sportsmen had vanished, and all that remained afloat was the soggy canoe, bottom up, the paddles, and some odds and ends of gear.

Jim Charles hitched up his carriage and horses and took word of this backwoods tragedy to Maitland Bridge, and a party of farmers and loggers came out to the lake and made a futile search about the shores. The three sportsmen, burdened by heavy clothing and knee-length boots, had sunk to the bottom, there to

193

stay until their bodies bloated enough to rise to the surface. This took many days. The last corpse to appear was that of Burrell. As the bodies drifted ashore they were placed in pine coffins packed with moss, and sent by wagon to the railway at Annapolis.

Something else happened in that year 1884. At South Brookfield, fifteen miles along the highway from Maitland Bridge toward Liverpool, a farmhand digging a hole for a fence post came upon bedrock in which two thin quartz seams met and formed a pocket. There he found a quantity of free gold in the form of nuggets and dust. The news flew about the countryside. When it reached Liverpool and Annapolis the magic word "gold" went on to the telegraph wires and flew about the world. Soon prospectors arrived in threes and fours, then in dozens, then in hundreds. An army of eager men searched every acre of the farmland and forest about the villages of South and North Brookfield, and found traces of gold in the whole district which centered about Caledonia. Adventurers hurried to this new bonanza from places as far apart as New Mexico and Newfoundland. Some were experienced miners and prospectors from the American West, the rest a mixture of greenhorns, drifters, and sharpers on the make.

As the trading posts of the world's newest gold field, the quiet little farming villages changed suddenly to mining boom towns of the kind to be seen in the American West, with pineboard hotels bearing names like The Golden Home, and crude boozing shanties with no names at all. Men swaggered or staggered from hotel to hotel and bar to bar, and those from the West wore cartridge belts and revolvers as naturally as they wore their clothes. A man arrived from Annapolis with a printing press in a wagon, and set up a weekly newspaper called *The Caledonia Gold Hunter*.

The whole affair was fantastic in the Nova Scotia countryside, yet it lasted fifteen years. By that time the real miners had come to a sober fact: Except for occasional rich pockets, the new gold field was not worth the cost of mining. Then in 1898 came the siren call of the Klondike, far away in the northwest corner of the continent. Away went the busy mine promoters and adventurers. The Caledonia gold rush petered out. After a few more years nothing remained to mark it but a few rotten wooden minehead buildings and heaps of crushed rock tailings hidden in the bush. The busy barkeepers had vanished with their customers. The hotels had closed or changed their names and catered to travelers on the post road. By 1918 only the newspaper survived. Its proprietor, George Banks, added *& Farmer's Advocate* to the original name and went on printing news of the farming villages until shortly before his death in the 1930s.

In the first hullabaloo over the gold discoveries in 1884, Jim Charles and his mysterious "mine" were forgotten, but in the following year a stranger stepped into his cabin with an ominous air. He said his name was Hamilton, and he was a kinsman of the man Jim had "murdered" years ago. The Indian was now about fifty-five. He gave the newcomer the same stoic gaze that he had turned on every importunate goldseeker in the past.

"What you want?" he said.

"This gold you found. Where is it?"

"I got no gold."

"Either you tell me where it is or I'll have you hanged for murder."

"Mister Harlow say no murder."

"Ah, that damned magistrate got you clear of killing Jim Hamilton, didn't he? But I'm talking about Ruggles and Burrell and Stoddard." He pointed to the lake. "You shot those men when they were off this point in a canoe, and you swore to everyone they just drowned."

"I no shoot anybody."

"I'll find someone to swear you did, Mister Jim Charles, and I'll start with the Gload girl and the other Indians that don't like you."

And away he went toward the Gload shack on the road to Maitland Bridge.

Jim hurried to his nearest friend, the woodsman David Lewis, and told him of this encounter with a new "Hamilton." Dave Lewis was a burly man, the victor in many a fistfight among the loggers and river drivers, and he feared no one. "The fellow's lying," he said. "He made that up from a yarn with the Gload girl, as like as not. You saw those three bodies after they floated ashore, so did I, and so did a lot of other men. Not one of them had a wound of any kind. So pay no mind to this fellow. If he really bothers you, send Madeleine for me."

Jim felt assured, but there was another matter urgent in his mind. He had run out of money. He was anxious now to return to his "gold mine" after the lapse of years; but with this new rush of strangers searching the countryside, many of them armed and dangerous, he was afraid to venture there. Lewis said, "I'll go with you, if you like. What's more, I'll stake out a claim for you, the way the miners do, and you can get a magistrate to fill out a paper and send it to the Mines Department. Then all the gold in that place will be yours by law. After that's done you'd better sell it to one of the mine promoters at Caledonia. Show him the gold and hold out for a good fat sum of money, so you needn't do another hand's turn of work for the rest of your life."

And so at last Jim Charles agreed to do what his white friends at Maitland Bridge had urged on him for years. Dave Lewis went to Jim's cabin at "Kej," ostensibly on a hunting trip. With blankets, food and guns they set out in Jim's canoe, Lewis paddling in the bow and Jim at the steersman's place in the stern. They passed through the scatter of wooded islands and landed on the southwest shore of the lake. Lewis threw the canoe on his big shoulders, bottom up, with his head inside. Jim loaded himself with the rest of the stuff and led the way through the woods. It was a narrow portage trail that climbed two or three miles to a small sheet of water, Mountain Lake, so called because a humorous timber cruiser had found the way there steep and rough.

They passed over this water in the canoe, and carried overland again to a lake which the Indians called Pescawess. They paddled over Pescawess and up a stream to another lake called Pescawah. From Pescawah they carried again, but this time a trudge of only a few minutes brought them to a lake called Pebelogich, meaning "It leads in a row," or as white men would say, "It links up with another chain." It was well named, for Pebelogich led them down its outfall to a large stream flowing out of the remote backwoods and known to woodsmen as Shelburne River.

They followed up the Shelburne, passing through various lakes surrounded by silent woods, camping here and there at places where there were the charred knots of old campfires, made by Jim on his journeys years before. In places there were stony rapids where they had to carry. The stream dwindled rapidly as they reached the semibarren country where granite outcrops and boulders stood like houses in the scrubby trees. Here was the hub of the wilderness. At last they reached a small lake studded with rocks and islands. Years later, when all this back country was mapped, the timber cruisers called it Buckshot Lake. It was the source of Shelburne River.

A short distance from Buckshot through the woods to the west lay another shallow lake, the source of the Tusket River. By the peculiarity of the watershed, the Tusket flowed away in the opposite direction to the Shelburne, and reached the sea near the western end of Nova Scotia. When Jim Charles beached the canoe gently on the shore of Buckshot and pointed to the faint trace of another portage, obviously untraveled for years, Dave Lewis knew at last why Jim's secret had been so safe from the goldseekers at Kejimkujik. His fabulous find was nowhere near "Kej." It was not even on a tributary of the Mersey River, of which "Kej" was a part.

Again Dave carried the canoe and Jim led the way through patches of scrub woods and rocky barrens, and in less than an hour's tramp they reached the headwater of the Tusket. They paddled down the lake and passed through a series of small rapids and long sluggish stillwaters that wriggled in the landscape like a lazy snake. After fifteen miles or so Jim said, "Soon now!"

When you travel in the interior of a peninsula you can only go so far, and then you begin to approach the coast again. By rough calculation Lewis guessed that they had entered the backwoods of Yarmouth County, and before many more miles they would come to one of its outlying settlements. And now he heard an odd sound from downstream, faintly at first, increasing as they approached. It was a mechanical *thump-thump-thump-thump* like the heartbeat of a giant. Jim was as puzzled as Lewis. At last they swept around a bend of the river and saw on the bank a cluster of wooden buildings, the biggest of which was spouting smoke and steam. A number of men were busy in the edge of the woods, and there was a flashing of axes. Jim was dumbfounded. Dave was not. He had seen mining operations in the Caledonia district and recognized the set-up. This was a small gold mine. The sounds came from a stamp mill crushing the ore. The busy men on the surface were cutting fuel for the boiler.

Poor Jim had kept his secret too long, for during those years when he stayed away from his gold someone else had found it. In the year 1881 two brothers named Reeves, prospecting up the Tusket River, noticed the same junction of quartz seams in the streambed that Jim had seen years before. They had panned out the gold remaining in that rich pocket, and now in 1885 they had raised enough capital to buy a stamp mill and start mining the seams.

In the summer of 1944 a spry old gentleman, the Reverend Clayton Munro, came out of long retirement in Bermuda to have a last look at the scenes of his youth in Nova Scotia. He had earned the money for his education by working as a logger on the upper waters of the Mersey River, and he recalled camping with a gang of river drivers in the pines below South Brookfield church about the year 1880, when he was sixteen. On a Sunday morning he had slipped into the church, just as he was, in torn shirt and trousers, to attend the morning service. He determined then to become a minister, as his mother hoped; and so he did. After some years of study he began as a Methodist probationer, and eventually he served as pastor in Annapolis, Chester, Guysborough, Lockeport and other country towns in Nova Scotia. In 1925, Pine Hill Divinity College at Halifax awarded him an honorary degree to mark his long and faithful service. A few years later he retired to Bermuda with his wife and daughter.

He was eighty when he made his last pilgrimage to Nova Scotia, and on his way to Maitland Bridge and "Kej" he stopped in Liverpool, at the mouth of the Mersey River, to see me. We had never met, indeed I did not know of his existence, but he had read some of my tales of Nova Scotia and wanted to meet the author. We chatted about the Mersey Valley and its legends, and after a time he said, "Have you ever heard of Jim Charles and his phantom gold mine?"

I said, "Who hasn't? But of course the story ends nowhere. The 'mine' was never found."

Munro smiled. "Oh yes, it was." And he then told me the whole affair as I have set it forth here, including that last revealing journey which David Lewis had described to him when the young minister was on a visit home in the late 1880s. If anyone else heard of that *denouement* they dismissed it as another of Jim's tricks to throw people off the track. Munro recognized the truth in it, and the Department of Mines confirmed the account of the Reeves discovery on the Tusket River.

Clayton Munro died in Bermuda in 1950, and he was buried in the Wesleyan Methodist cemetery at Hamilton—a long, long way from his native "Kej."

I had picked up the Jim Charles story—so far as it went—in the course of my own rambles about the Mersey River country, and after my interview with Clayton Munro I hunted up the rest, getting a bit here and a bit there, and checking one against another.

After that one brief glitter of prosperity in his life, poor Jim
had nothing but hard luck. While still a young woman, Madeleine
died, probably of tuberculosis, like Lizzie before her, and she
lies in the long-abandoned Indian burial ground on the eastern
shore of Kejimkujik, just across the little bay from what is still
called Jim Charles's Point. Their son wandered away to the States
and never came back. In old age Jim became a rheumatic cripple,
badly stooped, hobbling a few steps painfully with the aid of two
sticks. He was crazy in the head as well. An Indian family named
Francis took pity on him and brought him down the river to live
with them outside the village of Milton, and there at Two Mile
Hill he died about the year 1905.

The Indians at Two Mile Hill were nominally Catholics, like
most of the Micmacs, and they buried their dead in the churchyard of Saint Gregory's, the little Catholic church at Liverpool,
five miles down the river. In those days the Catholic congregation
at Liverpool was too small to support a resident priest, and once
a month there was a service in Saint Gregory's by the priest from
West Caledonia, thirty or forty miles away through the forest.
For special affairs, like weddings and funerals, the priest would
come by horse and buggy through the woods, and the call to him
had to go by the mail coach, for there was no telephone service.
The denizens of Two Mile Hill seldom attended the church except to bury their dead, usually without benefit of clergy, and in
a grave dug just deep enough to hold the corpse.

Claude Hartlen ran a little shingle mill at the riverside in
Milton; and as a service to the villagers (there was no undertaker nearer than Liverpool) he made pine coffins to order and
had a simple black-painted hearse drawn by a single horse. Two
young Indian men, John and Andrew Francis, came to Hartlen
and asked him to bring a coffin to Two Mile Hill for "old Jim
Charles," and then take the coffin to Liverpool for burial. The
Indians seldom had any money, and what they got they spent
for rum, so Hartlen knew he would never get paid for the job.
He was a good-natured man, however, and he carried it out. The
body was in a filthy state, and after helping the Indians to place

200

it in the coffin, Hartlen found several lice on his sleeves. Before starting for Liverpool he said, "Have you notified the priest?"

The Indians looked at each other. Andrew said, "Yes." Hartlen knew they had not. "What about the grave?" he said. "We dug it ourselves, me and John," Andrew said. "And if the priest isn't there, what then?" said Hartlen. "Then we chuck the old bugger in anyway," said Andrew. And that was exactly what happened.

The Indian graves in Saint Gregory's churchyard were never marked by stick or stone, and most of them disappeared under a growth of alder bushes and long grass as the years went by. In modern times, with a resident priest, the churchyard was cleared of this wild growth, and somewhere under the trim turf lie the bones of old Jim Charles.

His cabin and little barn on the point in Kejimkujik tumbled down in a few years. Sportsmen and log drivers liked to camp on "Jim Charles's Point," and about the year 1907 some sportsmen from Annapolis formed what they called "The Kedgemakooge Rod and Gun Club" and built a wooden lodge near the site of Jim's cabin. It was a popular resort for many years, and some American visitors had cottages built on the point and thereafter spent the whole summer by the lake with their families. Jim Charles was a favorite subject when the guides gathered about their campfires on the point, and for the titillation of the lodge and cottage people, especially the young ladies, they would point to a small grassy mound and say it was "old Jim's grave," and that his ghost had been seen coming out of it "looking for his gold." To carry the gag farther, someone made a wooden "tombstone," carved "Jim Charles" on it, and stuck it on the mound. Many visitors to "Kej" believed the tale and carried away photos of the "grave."

The spot near "Koofang" Lake where Jim Charles hid for three years is still known to woodsmen as "Jim Charles's Rock" or "Jim Charles's Cave." As for his gold, some folk still believe it remains hidden in the forest about "Kej."

The real site of Jim's discovery, the Reeves mine on the Tusket, yielded high-grade ore for three years, but the gold content dwindled as the miners followed the veins. The mine continued operating in a desultory fashion until about 1928, and that was the end of it. By that time Jim's bones had lain in Saint Gregory's churchyard more than twenty years.

Sadie Davenport

Judge Archibald of the Supreme Court of Nova Scotia called it the strangest case in his experience; and the famous American cartoonist Ripley, in his widely syndicated newspaper feature "Believe It or Not," played it up as "the modern case of Enoch Arden." But Sadie Davenport was dead when that appeared, and Harry Croker had dropped back into the obscurity from which he came. He was not much of a reader, and as he would have said himself, he wouldn't have known Enoch Arden if he fell over him—or Ripley, for that matter. But he knew Sadie Davenport all right. A rum go it was, too. A very rum go, indeed.

Harry was born in London in 1876. His parents were poor Cockneys living in the Kennington section, and the father died when Harry was a child. When he was fourteen his mother married again. The new husband did not want a big boy on his hands, and so Harry was entered aboard a training ship for the merchant marine. She was the old wooden-hulled *Warspite*, which lay at permanent moorings in the Thames off Woolwich.

After two years' training, Harry shipped aboard the Union Liner *Athenian,* but after one or two voyages he decided to join the Royal Navy instead. This meant two more years' training in H.M.S. *Boscawen,* at Portland, a ship-school for youths under eighteen. When Harry reached that age he was posted to H.M.S. *Blenheim,* of the Channel Squadron. Then he went to H.M.S. *Hotspur* and sailed in her to Bermuda, where she was part of the North American and West Indies Squadron. In this ship he spent a year and a half cruising among the West Indian islands. On one of his shore rambles in Bermuda he had his picture taken in uniform by a Hamilton photographer, and kept two copies of it in his ditty box.

He was getting fed up with hot weather by the spring of 1899, when he had a chance to transfer to a small cruiser, H.M.S. *Proserpine,* which was bound northward for a summer's cruise in Canadian waters. He was twenty-three, with a good-conduct badge and the rating of leading signalman, which paid him two shillings and one penny a day. In June of that year the *Proserpine* entered the port of Halifax, N.S., and Leading Signalman Croker set foot in Canada for the first time. Halifax had been the North American base of the Royal Navy for a hundred and fifty years, and it was a busy merchant port as well, with all kinds of fun and games for Jack Tar.

On his first evening ashore, Harry Croker and a chum followed the other liberty men up the steep streets to the old bawdy quarter which centered about Brunswick, Albemarle and Grafton Streets on the slope of Citadel Hill. Albemarle especially was a notorious resort of soldiers, sailors and prostitutes. Harry and his shipmates came to know it facetiously as "All-be-damned" Street. (A generation later the city, anxious to abolish all its old associations, changed the name to Market Street, a dubious choice.)

In a barroom on Albemarle Street, probably the popular "Knip's," Harry met a handsome young whore who called herself Sadie Davenport. He never did get to know her real name. A davenport was a popular piece of parlor furniture in the 1890s, a large upholstered couch designed for easy conversion to a bed, and Sadie's choice was obvious. Her name was her business card.

Sadie was able to get a good price in her business, more than a signalman in the Royal Navy of those days could afford, and she had a thrifty habit of saving money. She had been born and brought up on a frugal backwoods farm in New Brunswick. The gay life of a garrison town and naval base had attracted her, and so far all had been fun and profit; but she was now twenty-seven, a serious age for a woman who knows that a pretty face and figure cannot last forever, and she had an urge to marry and settle down. Harry Croker was a healthy chap, cheerful and easygoing, and when she invited him to her lodging there was no mention of money. As Harry said afterwards, it was love at first sight.

In the course of the summer's cruise, H.M.S. *Proserpine* returned to Halifax three times and stayed about a week each time. On the second visit Harry went straight up to Sadie's lodging and, having a night's leave from the ship, spent it all with her. It was a night in late July, warm without the wilting atmosphere of the West Indies in summer, and Halifax in those days was a small city with pastures and farmhouses within a mile of the post office, and the prevailing westerly airs brought a scent of wild forest beyond. Harry was charmed with the place and especially with the good-looking young woman who had chosen him for a lover. When she mentioned casually that she had quite a lot of money in the bank, her charm increased for the young man who had been on his own, and poorly paid, from the age of fourteen. At some time in the night she suggested getting married, and the happy-go-lucky sailor agreed without a doubtful thought.

As soon as morning came, Sadie hustled away to notary J. H. Barnstead for a marriage license. Then, with two female friends for witnesses, she led Harry to a Church of England parson, the Reverend E. P. Crawford. She was determined to have everything according to the mode of nice young women in the last years of Queen Victoria, and so the wedding had to be in church. Mr. Crawford was dean of a little wooden church, Saint Luke's, which was dignified with the name of "cathedral" until it was destroyed by fire in 1904. Mr. Crawford obligingly performed the wedding rite before the altar rail in Saint Luke's, and dutifully wrote out a marriage certificate and had it recorded.

The bridegroom was due to report for duty that night aboard his ship, which lay at anchor off the dockyard, but of course he did not. When he did report the next day he was reprimanded for absence without leave, and away went his good-conduct badge. He was refused shore leave for the next four days, and then the *Proserpine* went off to sea for another cruise. She returned to Halifax once more and stayed a week, in which Harry spent every possible moment with his bride. Then the *Proserpine* carried him off to the West Indies for the winter.

So Sadie had got herself a husband, but a husband in bondage to the Royal Navy, which could send him anywhere in the world for any length of time. In reply to her questions, he had told her that there was only one way to get his discharge from Her Majesty's service, a process called "buying out." In his case it would require a sum of £12, which was roughly four months' pay. A man who liked his beer and fun ashore could never save a sum like that. But Sadie had. In fact Sadie had "heaps of money," as Harry put it afterwards. During the long months of his absence in the West Indies she undoubtedly added more in the way of her trade, but she must have looked forward with some impatience to her bridegroom's return, for her plans were firmly made, and the return took much longer than she had expected. H.M.S. *Proserpine* did not anchor in Halifax harbor again until September 1900, more than a year after Harry last had his bride in his arms.

Once he was back, the happy pair moved quickly. Sadie paid the £12 to buy him out of the service, and on September 25 he stepped ashore a civilian, in a smart civilian suit that Sadie had bought for him. When he entered her lodging this time he found another person with her, a little girl aged four, named Lorna Doone. Sadie smoothly explained the mischance that had brought forth this hitherto unmentioned daughter, and Harry cheerfully accepted her as part of his new family. He liked the child and was always kind to her in the years they were to be together, especially as he and Sadie produced no children of their own.

The next thing was the matter of a home. Sadie wanted to settle down as a respectable wife and mother. That would be impossible in Halifax, where she was well known to rakish young officers of the garrison and other bounders of the town. Harry himself, like a true Cockney, preferred life in London to any other in the world and made no bones about saying so. Thus the matter resolved itself neatly. With Sadie's money they bought passage to Liverpool, entrained for London, and stayed for a time with Harry's mother and stepfather. Then they took lodgings in the same quarter of South London, the district of Brixton. Harry had no trouble in getting a job as a mail porter with the Post Office, which paid him £2/7/6d per week. England was full of the excitement and bustle of the Boer War. As a veteran of several years' service in the Navy he joined the Fleet Reserve, which merely meant that he got paid for a week's drill every year at Chatham. The war was an affair of landsmen at the bottom of the world, and the Navy had little or nothing to do with it.

The Crokers lived in Brixton for two years and then moved to a block of new working-class flats in nearby Lambeth. Here they passed another two years. Harry was content, but Sadie was not. Marriage on less than fifty shillings a week lost its charm, and she missed the old gay life across the sea. She had furnished the flat with her own money, and any luxuries for herself and Lorna had to come from the same source. Her "heaps of money" were dwindling, while Harry remained unambitious. He was no longer the lively young sailor but a townsman satisfied with pub and pipe. After four years in England, Sadie determined to break off their marriage and leave him. For his own part, love had gone out of the window long ago. He knew what she had been before he married her, and as a wife she had proved a bit of a shrew. Quite amiably he agreed to the parting. Their furniture and other belongings had been bought with Sadie's money, and as he put it afterwards, "she sold the whole lot—body, stock and barrel." When she and Lorna took train for Liverpool, the amiable husband went to Waterloo Station to see them off.

In 1908 Harry Croker went through the form of marriage with another woman, a Cockney like himself, and about that time or soon afterwards he lost or gave up his job with the Post Office and went back to the sea. In 1909 he shipped as a merchant seaman on a voyage from London to Australia and back. At that time the Board of Trade did not require every British seaman to have the now familiar little blue book, listing every signing-on and discharge, with mention of ability and conduct, signed by the master. So this part of his life remains vague. Apparently he remained in the merchant service, sailing out of London, until November 1914, when as a member of the Fleet Reserve he was called up for active service in the First World War.

The Navy did not hold him long. A hernia operation got him discharged as medically unfit in 1915, with a token pension of sixpence a day for twelve months. Civilian jobs of all kinds were available and well paid during the war, and Croker seems to have spent most of the next three years ashore. In the meantime every British merchant seaman was required to have the little blue book of the Board of Trade, with every signing-on and every discharge recorded, and with details of his rank and service. Also, tucked inside the Board of Trade book, he carried an identification booklet in case he was questioned ashore by police looking for deserters and conscription dodgers. This booklet contained a photograph of the seaman, together with written details of his age, height, general appearance, and any identifying marks or scars.

In May 1918, during the last six months of the war, Harry Croker made a short voyage around the coast in S/S *Tuscarora* from Sunderland to Plymouth. He signed on as an able seaman and was issued the customary Board of Trade book and identification booklet. The latter mentioned that he had a dragon tattooed on one arm, and on his chest two large snakes "tied in a knot" and just above them a butterfly. In this booklet also Harry tucked one of the photographs of himself in naval uniform, taken in Bermuda long ago. Another copy of this photograph was in the hands of Sadie Davenport Croker, and she kept it to her death.

The war ended in November 1918, and for most of the next seven years Harry sailed out of London in British merchant ships, voyaging to Australia, the United States, South America, Japan, the Persian Gulf and India. In the autumn of 1922 he set foot on Canadian soil again for a time, in Montreal, where his ship loaded cargo for Britain. The final entry in his Board of Trade book showed his discharge from S/S *Arabistan* in London in August 1925.

What he did for a living after that remains unknown. He was then forty-nine and probably tired of knocking about the sea. After his bigamous marriage in London in 1908, he had made his home in the Stepney slum, near the docks.

Let us now return to Halifax with Sadie and her eight-year-old daughter Lorna Doone in the year 1904. Sadie was now thirty-two, still a handsome figure of a woman, and she had forgotten none of her art in the figure trade. She resumed it at once, changing her lodging from time to time as whores must when the landlord becomes too grasping or the police too intrusive. In 1908, when Lorna reached the age of twelve and became an embarrassment in Sadie's trade, she put the girl in the (Roman Catholic) Home of the Good Shepherd on Spring Garden Road.

Sadie was busy and prosperous. She bought a suburban residence on Kline Street, in what then were largely open fields in the west outskirts of Halifax. What was more important, she became owner and madame of a brothel on Water Street, close by the docks. (A lawyer who inspected the house long afterward, when it had become a respectable tenement house for dock workers and their families, observed that it still had a brass railing up the middle of the stairs. An old "sporting girl," once on the brothel staff, told him that it was to separate the customers going upstairs from those coming down. She added that after a busy weekend she had helped the madame count money literally by the bucketful.)

Sadie's ownership of this "sporting house" shows that about 1908 she was able to promote herself well above the old casual street and barroom trade. But in 1912, when she was forty, something changed the tenor of her life. What it was we do not know. Her looks and physical abilities must have wilted sadly by that time. Whatever the cause, she did two remarkable things in 1912.

First, she made a will, leaving all her money and possessions to the Salvation Army, with no mention of Lorna Doone or Harry Croker. Second, she removed from Halifax and went to live with her mother on the small home farm near Andover, New Brunswick. She sold the suburban residence on Kline Street but kept her ownership of the sporting house on Water Street. From this time, too, she abandoned the name Sadie for its more dignified form Sarah, and called herself Mrs. Sarah Croker, explaining that her husband had been drowned at sea.

Her mother did not have the prodigal daughter under her roof very long. Sarah had determined on a home of her own in the neighborhood. She bought a site and in the summer of 1912 hired a middle-aged farmer named Blanchard Giberson to dig a cellar and help in the building of the house. As soon as it was finished she bought furniture and moved in. She remained on visiting terms with her mother and with a Mrs. Melissa Greene who lived across the road. Also, she took care to keep the acquaintance of Blanchard Giberson, who was a bachelor. An old urge had come back to her, the longing to be a respectable housewife, with a husband not only visible but recognized as hers by benefit of clergy.

Giberson's farm contained 125 acres, partly tilled but mostly woodland. Like most farmers in that region his main crop was the potato, and there were good years and lean years according to the market price in Woodstock and Fredericton. In winter he cut and hauled logs from his timberland, selling them to local sawmills. The name Giberson (pronounced *Guy*-bers'n) was borne by many people in that part of New Brunswick, descendants of Loyalists who came there after the American Revolution. Many were highly intelligent and people of mark in the world. Blanchard Giberson, however, was a man of no ambition, with little education, knowing and caring nothing about the world outside of Andover.

All through 1913 Sarah Croker made a point of seeing Giberson frequently, getting him to do odd jobs for her, and paying him well. She never told him much about herself, except that she was a widow with quite a comfortable income. As with the bygone Harry Croker, the knowledge of Sarah's money added a good deal to her charms, and when he was faced with the prospect of marriage to her, Blanchard Giberson did not back away. He made up his mind, or Sarah made it up for him, in the cold and snowy month of January 1914. They set off together with horse and sleigh for the village of Bath, twelve miles away, but found nobody there authorized to issue a marriage license. Finally they got a license at Florenceville and returned homeward as far as Bath. There in a small hotel kept by a distant relative of Blanchard named Turney Giberson they were married by another, an itinerant Primitive Baptist preacher, the Reverend T. Addington Giberson. In due course the marriage was entered in the provincial records.

The newlyweds spent that night at the Giberson Hotel and went on the next day to the bridegroom's farm near Andover. There they lived until 1917, when the wartime rise in farm values enabled Blanchard to lease his property for a good rental. He and Sarah then removed to her own house. In 1919, just after the war, when the lease on Blanchard's farm expired, he moved back to it. Sarah, however, remained in her house some distance away. She was there alone in the early summer of 1919, when she had an unexpected visitor, her daughter Lorna.

Lorna Doone had left the Home of the Good Shepherd in Halifax in 1913, when she reached the age of seventeen. The nuns got her a post as student nurse at the Children's Hospital and she completed eight months' training, but she did not like nursing and she got a job as clerk in Kinley's drugstore on Barrington Street, which suited her much better. It was in the city's main shopping district, the scene of a lively bustle all through the First World War, when Halifax was thronged with soldiers and sailors. In 1919, when the postwar depression fell on Halifax like a wet blanket, Lorna met and married a young merchant seaman. His home was in a small fishing village many miles away along the coast; he was tired of long voyages, and now as a married man he was going home for good.

First, however, Lorna suggested a honeymoon trip to visit her mother in New Brunswick. She had kept in touch with Sarah Croker in a fitful way through the years, exchanging postcards now and then. Sarah had always regarded the child as a nuisance, and in 1908 she was thankful to get her off her hands. Lorna Doone was well aware of her mother's profession, of course, and she kept it a distasteful secret during her years at the Home. Apparently, she did not suspect the truth about her own birth. She considered herself Harry Croker's daughter, and in later years she invented fanciful stories about him, saying he came of a good English family and had brothers at Oxford University. She believed Sarah's story that Croker had perished on naval service during the war, and that she had married again and was living quietly on a farm at Andover.

When Lorna and her husband arrived there without warning, Sarah Croker Giberson was more surprised than pleased. She refused to let Lorna's bridegroom enter her house. She did not say why. Probably as the former madame of a busy waterfront brothel, she had no wish to meet a former merchant seaman from—of all places—Halifax. She made it clear that Lorna herself could only stay for a short call. Her neighbor Mrs. Melissa Greene was there at the time, and she was there through the stiff little conversation, including Lorna's "Goodby, Mother" at the door. The somewhat crestfallen newlyweds departed at once for Nova Scotia and Mrs. Greene went back across the road to resume her household chores, leaving Sarah in her chosen solitude.

Sarah's second marriage was going the way of her first. She was bored by stolid Blanchard Giberson and the whole dull round of life in Andover. Sometimes she stayed with him on his farm, but often she went to her own house and stayed alone for weeks. For his part, Giberson was just as tired of Sarah and her moody ways. Until middle age he had been a bachelor by choice, and he had been lured into marriage by the prospect of Sarah's money and an easy life. Yet all he ever knew about Sarah's money, as he said afterwards, was that every three months he had to drive her to town, were she disappeared into the bank for a time and came forth mum as an oyster.

In 1924 Sarah once more came to a decision. Her mother had died years ago. She had no kin ties in Andover, and she told Melissa Greene that she had lived most of her life in cities and she liked the city life. She informed Blanchard Giberson that she was unwell and was going to Halifax for medical treatment. She would need money, and so she was selling her Andover house and furniture. When that was done, away she went. Blanchard Giberson never saw or heard from her again. He made no effort to find where she was or what became of her. She had drifted out of his simple life exactly as she drifted in.

Sarah was now fifty-two and truly ailing. She returned to Halifax and lived thereafter in various shabby lodginghouses, moving like a ghost about the old naughty quarters which were gay no more. In August 1927, she deposited $1100 in the Halifax office of the Canada Permanent Mortgage Company and opened a checking account. She came in there from time to time, and the tellers remembered her as a shaky and nervous woman with white hair, and shabbily dressed. She still exchanged notes and postcards with daughter Lorna, but she had no communication with Blanchard Giberson or any of her old neighbors in New Brunswick.

The house she owned on Water Street had become a poor but honest tenement house after 1918, when the Great War ended. Times were hard in Halifax, especially in the shipping trade, and the Canadian Government had reduced the army garrison and the naval establishment to a shadow. The motorcars of the post-war era transferred the brothel trade to roadhouses outside the city, where there were no police to be troublesome. The days of the old-fashioned sporting houses on Brunswick, Albemarle, Grafton and Water Streets were gone forever.

Early in June 1936, an elderly woman, poorly clothed and obviously ill, came into the office of the Salvation Army in Halifax. She approached the desk of the man in charge, Major Mundy, and threw on it a manila envelope. "Here!" she cried. "Take this. It's all yours. They're after me!" With that she darted out into the street and vanished. Mundy opened the envelope and found a pair of bank passbooks showing total deposits amounting to about $800, a deed to a property on Water Street, a sheet of letter paper with the heading of a trust company, on which a number had been scrawled in ink, and a will dated in 1912, signed Sarah Croker, leaving all her possessions to the Salvation Army.

The woman was obviously deranged, and Mundy waited for a couple of days expecting her to turn up again. But she did not. He consulted Halifax lawyer (later Judge) M. B. Archibald, who told him to keep the envelope and its contents until Sarah Croker could be found. They had not far to look. The evening newspapers had a brief paragraph about a suicide. An elderly woman had jumped into the harbor from the breakwater at Black Rock, near Point Pleasant Park. Her body was recovered, and the police found in her clothing a piece of paper with the address of a cheap lodging house on Barrington Street. The newspapers gave a description of the woman and her clothes, and Mundy phoned Archibald saying, "That's the woman!"

He and the lawyer went with the police to the lodginghouse and found that a Mrs. Sarah Croker had been staying there for some time. On the previous day she had gone out, leaving her baggage in her room but paying her bill, and she had not come back. The men searched through her stuff. There was nothing of any monetary value. Some clothing, a Bible, two or three photographs, and a letter addressed to Mrs. Sarah Croker. The letter had some inconsequential news from somebody named Lorna, and the postmark on the envelope was that of a small village about two hundred miles along the coast. One of the photographs showed a young sailor in Royal Navy uniform, a suit of tropical whites, and the photographer's gilt stamp on the mounting showed that it had been taken in Hamilton, Bermuda. Another photograph showed the same young man in civilian clothes, with a handsome young woman and a little girl of about four. This had been taken in London, England.

Major Mundy took charge of these things, having shown the police Sarah Croker's will. He then made a long-distance call to the Salvation Army in a town not far from "Lorna's" village and asked them to make inquiries there for a daughter of Mrs. Sarah Croker. The next day he had a phone call in reply, and in a moment more Lorna herself was on the line. She had seen the description of the suicide in a Halifax paper and recognized it as that of her mother. She added quickly that she herself was poor, she could not come to the funeral, nor could she pay anything toward the expenses. Mundy said that the Salvation Army would pay the funeral expenses. He mentioned Mrs. Croker's will and the $800 in the banks. He asked the woman to come to Halifax at the Salvation Army's expense, to make positive identification of the body and attend the funeral.

And so Lorna Doone, now about forty, came by train, identified the body, and attended the last rites, which were conducted by the Salvation Army in Camp Hill Cemetery. Afterwards lawyer Archibald questioned her and found her very secretive about her mother's past. He had checked with the two banks and found that Sarah Croker did have about $800 on deposit. He also checked her title to the property on Water Street, a dilapidated house worth little in the depressed conditions of 1936. On the face of it, Sarah Croker had not left much, after the funeral expenses and Lorna's expenses were paid. However, Archibald was curious about the single number written on a sheet of trust company stationery.

He and Mundy went to the trust company's office, and showed

the manager Sarah Croker's will and the sheet of paper. By any
chance did Mrs. Croker have a safety deposit box here with
that number? She had. But no key had been found in her possessions. When Archibald made a formal request to have the box
opened, the job had to be done with an oxy-acetylene torch, a
delicate piece of work. Inside they found a bundle of government
bonds amounting to more than $20,000. Mundy, a conscientious
man, felt that he should tell Lorna Doone of this surprising de-
velopment, even though she was not mentioned in the will. When
he did so, things began to happen.

Lorna went to a lawyer, and her memory cleared up remarkably. Among other things she remembered that her father had
been lost at sea and her mother had married a man named
Blanchard Giberson in 1914. Her lawyer seized on this at once.
Sarah Croker's second marriage invalidated the will made in 1912.
The way was open for claims to the whole estate by Giberson
and Lorna. When Major Mundy was told of this he was ready to
drop the matter, but lawyer Archibald insisted that the second
marriage should be checked. He sent his partner Doyle to make
inquiries in New Brunswick, and Doyle found that a Mrs. Sarah
Croker had indeed married Blanchard Giberson in January 1914,
and that they had lived together until about 1924.

Meanwhile Lorna had got in touch with Giberson, who
promptly hired a lawyer himself. Major Mundy was unwilling to
involve the Salvation Army in a legal brawl over the dead
woman's estate; but Archibald pointed out that, whether the
1912 will remained valid or not, Sarah Croker's words and actions in Mundy's office showed that she still wished to leave
everything to the Army and nobody else. So Mundy agreed that
Archibald should try to uphold the 1912 will.

The first move was to confirm the marriage of Harry Croker.
The Halifax records showed that he had married Sadie Davenport there in 1899. The next move was to confirm the alleged
death of Croker prior to January 1914. Archibald sent young
Doyle over to England to investigate. Doyle went to the Canadian High Commissioner in London, and through the Commis-

sioner he soon had Scotland Yard and the Admiralty Records Office digging for information.

Scotland Yard came up with the fact that a man named Harry Croker had married a London woman in 1908, which was interesting but not very useful. The Admiralty records were better. Harry Croker had been serving on H.M.S. *Proserpine* when he bought himself out of the service at Halifax in 1900. In England soon afterwards he had volunteered for the Fleet Reserve. In November 1914, when the First World War was getting into stride, he was called up for active service. He spent about twelve months on duty and was then discharged as medically unfit. He was paid a pension of sixpence a day for the next twelve months. The pension records showed that Harry Croker had cashed his pension checks regularly until they ended in 1916. They also showed his last mailing address.

So Harry Croker, or someone forging his name, had been alive as late as 1916! And in any case he had joined the Navy for active duty in November 1914, ten months after his "widow" married Giberson in New Brunswick. Therefore, her second marriage was bigamous and the will written in 1912 still valid. Of course these matters would require thorough proof before the strict Court of Probate in Nova Scotia—proof that the Harry Croker of the Admiralty records was the Harry Croker who married "Sadie Davenport" at Halifax; proof that "Sadie Davenport" was Sarah Croker who signed the 1912 will, and so on right down the line. The lawyers for Lorna and Blanchard Giberson were bound to dispute the case inch by inch, and only one witness in the world would be indisputable. The man himself. Was it possible that Harry Croker was still alive? If so, where was he?

Doyle went to the last address shown on the naval pension record, but nobody there or in that neighborhood had ever heard of Harry Croker. None of them had lived there twenty-one years ago. After a lot of leg work from door to door, young Doyle was still undismayed. Rummaging the secondhand bookshops, he found a set of London directories going all the way back to 1914. There was no mention of Harry Croker in any of them. It listed householders only, and probably Croker was just renting a room in which he lived with his second "wife." However, in the 1916 volume Doyle made note of the names and addresses of the people who were householders in the immediate vicinity of Croker's last pension address. Then laboriously, volume by volume, he traced the movements or marked the disappearances of these people through the years. It took a long time, but at last he came down to the addresses of three people who, as far as he could see, had lived in Harry Croker's neighborhood in 1916.

He hastened to call on them. The first two knew nothing of the man he sought. At the third address an old lady exclaimed, "'arry Croker? Why, of course, I knew 'arry Croker! What's more, I can tell you where 'e's living now. It isn't very far from 'ere!" Doyle went to the address she gave, and the man who came to the door was unmistakably the man of Sarah Croker's photographs, despite all the years that had passed.

Doyle told him the whole story, including Sarah's death, her will, her daughter, and her second "husband." He pointed out that there was nothing in it for Croker except a chance to see justice done, and he asked the old sailor to come with him to Halifax and testify in the Court of Probate. The Salvation Army would pay his expenses there and back to London again. Croker pondered a bit. In view of his own bigamous marriage four years after Sarah deserted him, he was in a delicate position. Doyle guessed the cause of his hesitation, and said frankly that he knew about Croker's second "marriage." He added carefully that it could not influence the case of Sarah's will, and the Court of Probate was concerned with that alone. So Harry agreed to come. He was a well-preserved sixty, with something still of a sailor's spirit of adventure, and after all this time it would be interesting to see his old Halifax haunts again, including "All-be-damned" Street.

To gain the necessary time for Doyle's searches in New Brunswick and England, Archibald had entered a *caveat* in the Court of Probate at Halifax, requiring what lawyers call "proof in solemn form." With this he was able to delay final decision in the case until January 1937, despite the protests of the opposing lawyers. They suspected why he wanted the delay, but they felt a reasonable certainty, after one or two futile cablegrams to London, that (a) Croker had died before 1914 as Sarah and Lorna declared, or (b) if by some weird chance he was still alive it would be impossible to find him after more than thirty years. They concentrated their efforts on proofs of the Giberson marriage, and proofs that Lorna was Sarah's acknowledged daughter by her first marriage.

The final hearing of the case came before the Probate Court in Halifax in January 1937. There was a long legal wrangle over the admissibility of this or that evidence regarding Sarah's two marriages. Preliminary hearings had been held in June and September 1936, at which Blanchard Giberson, Melissa Greene, Turney Giberson, Lorna Doone and various other witnesses had testified. Now in the final hearing the lawyers for Blanchard and Lorna brought forth once more their proofs of the Giberson marriage in 1914, and proofs that Lorna was the acknowledged daughter of the Croker marriage. In the latter, the proofs included such things as a certificate of Lorna's entry into the Home of the Good Shepherd, signed by Sarah Croker as her mother, and the statements of Melissa Greene about Lorna's honeymoon visit in 1919.

Archibald fenced with them shrewdly on all these points, showing that Sarah continued to call herself Mrs. Croker more often than Mrs. Giberson after the 1914 marriage, that she continued to sign all her checks etc. as Sarah Croker, that finally she left Giberson altogether. Obviously, he told the Court, she did not consider the peculiar 1914 ceremony a valid marriage at all.

Then came Archibald's turn to prove his own case. He produced a certificate of the marriage of Harry Croker and Sadie Davenport in Halifax in 1899. He had experts in handwriting to attest that Sadie Davenport, Sarah Croker, and Sarah Giberson, were one and the same person. And so on. Finally he called his star witness, who had seated himself quietly in the back of the courtroom.

"Harry Croker!"

In the staid atmosphere of the Probate Court it was like a sudden eruption of fireworks in a quiet night. The old sailor took the stand. Calmly and cheerfully he told the whole story of his marriage with Sadie Davenport, including her possession of a four-year-old daughter at the time of the wedding, a child named Lorna Doone. He produced his documents, including his Board of Trade seaman's book and the identification booklet with the Bermuda photograph, a photograph that matched exactly the one found in Sarah Croker's room after her death. Archibald clinched his case with further evidence, including another photograph found in Sarah's room, showing Harry, herself and little Lorna together; and another showing Harry with his fellow porters outside a London post office. He referred to the tattoo designs mentioned in Croker's documents; and to the delight of the whole court, except the opposing lawyers and Giberson and Lorna, Harry Croker threw off coat, vest and shirt, and showed them all the dragon, the butterfly and the "snakes tied in a knot."

At the close of the hearing the court reserved judgment, but when the verdict came down it was exactly what Archibald expected. The Giberson marriage was bigamous, Sarah Croker's 1912 will was valid, and her entire estate belonged to the Salvation Army.

Soon after the case closed, the world-famous newspaper feature called "Believe It or Not," by American cartoonist Ripley, described the Croker affair and called Harry the modern Enoch Arden. By that time Harry had vanished back into the obscurity of a London slum, never to be seen again.

Sarah Croker had died at the age of sixty-four, and the Salvation Army placed on her grave a black marble headstone inscribed simply with her correct married name and the dates of her birth and death.

Why did she quit her trade and make that will in 1912?

The answer is obvious. She had seen too much life in the mean streets; and she had noted that, of all the religious bodies, only the Salvation Army ventured to pick up the paupers, the drunks, the broken-down prostitutes and other human debris.

"Sadie Davenport" had a conscience after all.